MW01223443

Divas in Cahoots

a comedy of murder

Jon McDonald

To Karen,
I hope you enjoy reading this
as much as I enjoyed writing it.

Jon McDonald

Divas in Cahoots

a comedy of murder

Copyright © 2013 by Jon McDonald
All rights reserved.

The contents of this book constitute a work of fiction. All events, themes, persons, characters, and plots are fictional inventions of the author. Any resemblance and/or reference to actual events, as well as to any persons living, deceased, or yet to be born is purely coincidental and entirely unintentional.

No part of this book may be reproduced or transmitted in any form or by any means, graphic, electronic, or mechanical, including photocopying, recording, taping, or by any information storage retrieval system, without the permission in writing from the author and publisher.

email: jon@jonmcdonaldauthor.comWebsite:
Website: **www.jonmcdonaldauthor.com**
ISBN-13: 978-1490996974
ISBN: 1490996974

To Shirley - the grandest of all Divas

Introduction

Welcome once again to the cozy coffee circle at Portabellos Market where the Divas of Santa Fe gather to dish and scrounge for the latest breaking news. *Divas Never Flinch* first introduced us to Sonora, Connye, and a cast of colorful characters who are back once again, along with a whole new troop of eccentrics to mix it all up. Peace and calm cannot long last within this group. A whole series of new adventures await these devilish ladies. Hope you enjoy the ride.

Extra, Extra, Read All About It

HEIRESS BELLA HARRINGTON – CRENSHAW FOUND MURDERED

That was the scandalous newspaper headline that blasted the shocked citizens of Santa Fe, New Mexico on that fateful autumn morning. Mrs. Harrington-Crenshaw was a leading figure in the Santa Fe social scene, imported from the East coast with her family's old banking money and Washington political connections from her late father. She had never married, but had adopted the title of "Mrs." as a tribute to her wealth and stature. It was also widely recognized she thought a great deal of herself.

The police reported that a panic button had been activated by Mrs. H-C at her bedside, but when the police arrived, they found the house secure with no break-ins or any signs of forced entry, so it was likely Mrs. H-C knew the murderer or murderers and had let them in herself. But the question remained, had the murderer then set the alarm and locked the door when they left? The alarm company confirmed that the alarm had, indeed, been reset *after* the panic button had been activated, so it was pretty certain the murderer had the alarm code.

The alarm company security patrol was already investigating the scene when the police arrived, and the police authorized entry. Mrs. H-C was found garroted in the kitchen with the type of wire used to hang pictures. She was holding a chef's knife in her hand. There were a few drops of blood on the counter and the floor, but after careful examination it was found that she had no visible wounds so the blood was presumed to have been that of the assailant. The DNA from that could be decisive in identifying the killer.

Robbery was ruled out as a motive as there was nothing missing, the housekeeper later confirmed – even though there was very expensive jewelry strewn about her dressing table – the safe in the library was wide open and filled with cash, more jewels, and private papers - and her priceless Picassos, Van Gogh's, Seurat's, and a stunning collection of impressionist paintings were unalarmed and untouched. There were no fingerprints, no footprints, nor any clues inside the house as to who the murderer might be. And as she lived far away from any neighbors, the police had been unable to find any eye witnesses. And as neither of the domestics lived in, they were not there to witness anything. That evening the house keeper was at home with her family, and the chauffer had been at a party with dozens of witnesses - so they were not suspects.

The police were completely baffled, Captain Chavez reported, but he assured the public that all the available investigative resources of the police department were working full time to solve this horrible crime.

◻   ◻   ◻

The morning coffee and gossip circle on the patio of Portabellos Market was in shock. Well, at least as much shock as was possible with these very vocal and strongly opinionated ladies. No one here was known for her reticence. However, this morning there was not a single lady present who did not suspect that at least one other of the group might have had a hand in the murder - even if indirectly. Bella Harrington-Crenshaw had been a thorn in everyone's side at one time or another. There was no love lost for her amongst the ladies of this group.

"Who do you suppose could have done it? They say it wasn't a burglary," Roberta, the pie lady, asked in wonderment. "It must have been someone she knew. They say the alarm came from her bedroom. Could it have been a secret admirer? A crime of passion?"

Connye let out a hoot of laughter. "Don't think there have been any dogs hunting in *that* neck of the woods since she arrived in Santa Fe."

"Well, I heard the body was to be embalmed and entombed in a shrine at Lourdes," Honey snidely remarked as she sipped at her tall latte with extra foam.

"Now, Honey, I think that's overreaching a bit, don't you? After all, we must show some respect for the recently departed, don't we all agree?" Sonora, one of the circle's recognized leaders, tried injecting a tonic of reason into the conversation.

Connye shifted her considerable heft in the delicate patio chair and asked, "Respect? I am one who has always been of the opinion that one has to *earn* respect. And I would like to ask everyone here if they think she was owed one iota of earned respect?" No one could speak up in her favor. "Yes, just as I thought," Connye trumpeted. "Tragic as her untimely death might be, I don't think there is one of us who can truly say we will miss her all that much."

Sweet Roberta hesitatingly raised her hand. "Well, I know she was not very nice sometimes, but I do think we need to forgive her at least a little."

Sonora continued, "Yes, my dear, you might be right. But when you reflect back to when she first arrived here there was so much excitement and anticipation. She held such potential and promise – but ended up disappointing us all so deeply."

"Well, all I have to say is that she was one of my better clients," Olivia, the Helena Landau Cosmetics lady, spoke up.

"And that is because she so desperately needed *all* the cosmetic enhancement she could pile on," Connye added. "What was she, a hundred and twenty?"

"Now, now…." Roberta tutted, patting Connye's hand.

Sonora tried, once again, to bring the rhetoric down a notch, "Well, let's just remember her and move on. There's no point in dwelling on the past. Let's all resolve to make a fresh start, shall we?"

"That's the problem with Santa Fe, far too many wannabe's flocking to our splendid weather, charming arts scene, and scintillating social circle. We really must impose some sort of a moratorium on unchecked migration from the spoils of industrial America," Honey added, as she closed her purse and prepared to leave. She had a house showing in half an hour.

Sonora countered, "Yes, but you must remember almost all of us, except for you darling Olivia, have migrated from somewhere else just as Mrs. H-C did. And you Honey, as a real estate agent, would be sorely affected if all the Santa Fe newbies suddenly dried up."

Sonora rose – shopping time – a little birthday event for her dear friend, Lionel, turning a luxurious 78 today. "Well – I'll see you all for dinner this evening. And remember it's a birthday *surprise* party so no loose lips. And I have been informed by an inside source that birthday presents are *not* required, but if one *must,* then there is a preference for Turkish Delight. I believe they carry it on isle four in the candy section. Oh, and only the imported goodies, no domestic imitations, if you please - as someone unnamed so graciously informed me only this morning. Toodle-loo." Sonora waved and disappeared into the market.

◘   ◘   ◘

Sonora's cooking abilities were limited to toast, coffee, and plunging pouches into boiling water. So it was to be her darling housekeeper, Henrietta, who actually *prepared* the food for the party. A buffet seemed more appropriate for the occasion than a sit down dinner - much more casual. This also allowed Henrietta to prepare dishes in advance. Because of Lionel's addictive fondness for Turkish Delight, Sonora planned a menu of Turkish delicacies, most of which could be served at room temperature – wonderful eggplant smothered in a rich, cinnamony tomato sauce, succulent kabobs, and nutty pilaf salads were to be just some of the treats. Besides Sonora's beloved Champaign, there would be various wines, and in tune with the Turkish theme – Raki.

Lionel loved surprise birthday parties, especially when he was the guest of honor. Of course, Sonora *knew* that *he* knew. And *he* pretended not to *know,* as she also pretended that he did *not* know that she *knew.* Little games were what kept interest alive in this rather small, and inbred community. She also had a little surprise for Lionel that would please the other guests as well. Now, this was about something she *knew* and he could not *know*.

Sonora, as was befitting the occasion, dressed in Harem pants and a very tasteful gold embroidered jacket that would put to shame even the most exalted Sultan. On top of this charming ensemble she wore her diamond, emerald, and ruby necklace.

First to arrive were Olivia and Honey. Olivia Valdez, was the only local in the group. Everyone else and been part of the Santa Fe migration from other less desirable parts of America. Spicy and motivated, she ran her own very successful cosmetics business. Most in the group were her clients. As requested, both bore boxes of Turkish Delight for the birthday boy.

"Darlings." Sonora greeted. "So glad you came early. We wouldn't want to spoil Lionel's surprise by everyone showing up at once, would we?"

"So nice of you to host this event, considering the recent sad occasion," Honey sneered, referring to the Bella.

"Now Honey, a little charity, please. Let's make this a sparkling celebration. Seventy-eight years old. Just imagine. I hope I shall be long gone by the time I reach that age."

"Surely not," Olivia soothed. "With your skin you will look radiant well into your nineties."

"Too kind."

Roberta, Sonora's partner in the pie shop, waddled in bearing a splendid bouquet of peonies. Roberta was as darling as a teddy bear and not much larger. Small, round, and twinkling, she danced over to Sonora. "These are for you," she cheered.

"Why, thank you darling. But it's not *my* birthday."

"I know, but you're the hostess, and ever so deserving just the same."

The boys had just arrived. Lincoln and Carlos are a couple, who own the Quacking Aspen Inn, a small, charming boutique hotel. They sidled over, each one kissing one of Sonora's cheeks at the same time. Sonora sputtered and pushed them playfully away - too much naked sentiment for her.

Lincoln, still trim at 50-something, showed Sonora a lovely African violet. "For the birthday child. I know how he loves them and I was assured this was a new color. Where should I put it?"

"Over there with the other presents," she pointed to the coffee table. "So glad you could make it. Is your business still good?"

"Thriving," Carlos, the younger, responded. "Booked solid for months."

Linda Etter, Sonora's friend from their New York City days came in, followed by the Getgoodes – Brenda and the Major, and the Gladscows - Ruth and Howard – two couples with more money than wit. And more sense than charm. But loyal and constant, they were always supportive of our odd collection of divas.

Last to arrive, and only minutes before the birthday guest was due, Connye entered with the darling Kaiser sisters - Kate and Helen, both near 80, they had been billed the Grandma Moses' of the southwest for their fine landscape paintings.

"I hope we're not late. Took some time to get the sisters moving," Connye spoke aside to Sonora.

"Not at all. Just fine."

Connye scanned the guests then asked, "No Oz today?"

"No, he's in New York on personal business for a few days."

Olivia spoke up, "Are we to hide? Isn't Lionel due soon?"

"Not necessary. I'm sure he will know when he sees all of your parked cars in front of the house."

"Didn't think of that. What dummies we are," Brenda said half to herself.

Lionel suddenly appeared at the entrance. Feigning surprise, he flailed his arms up in the air and pronounced, "Well, what is all of *this*?"

Caught off guard, cries of "surprise" intermittently flowed through the group.

Turning to Sonora Lionel said, "I thought we were going out to supper - just the two of us."

Sonora laughed. "Well I had to tell you *something* to get you over here. I hope it was a real surprise."

"Of course, my dear." Then leaning in towards her he said softly, "And now, I have a little surprise for *you*."

He retreated back outside and returned leading the one and only Quinto – Sonora's on and off romance of years past and now a major motion picture star.

Lionel announced, "Look who I found lurking in a limousine outside your door."

"Hi, all you lovelies," Quinto greeted.

Everyone in the room gasped, including Sonora.   The guests rushed forward to greet the *real* surprise guest.   Sonora shot Lionel one of her quick secret smiles.   He nodded.

Quinto, after greeting the other guests, walked over to Sonora, who had stood aside not wanting to be part of the crush.

"Hello there, lady," he whispered, taking her in his arms and dipping her backwards as he landed her a welcoming kiss.

"Hey, whose birthday is this anyway?" Lionel joked.

Sonora, disengaging from Quinto, clapped her hands loudly.   Immediately a staccato drumming sounded from outside the patio entrance.   A male and female belly dancer came gyrating inside, hand cymbals flashing.   The male danced over to the guest of honor and made Lionel's day by making it perfectly clear that the dancer was Lionel's main birthday present.   The female danced over to the Major Getgoode who flushed a hot fuchsia red and sought refuge behind his wife, the formidable Brenda.

All in all the party was a great success.   True surprises popped up where least expected.   And expected surprises were all part of the delightful game of "guess who knows what."

The Bellas Arrive

one year earlier

Honey had a new client - Bella Harrington-Crenshaw. What a catch! Fresh from the east coast and in the market for an exclusive property in the three to four million dollar range. The commission from *that* sale would certainly help with college tuition for her twins – the boy, Aaron, and the girl, Rachel, now seventeen and earnestly applying to a number of colleges and universities.

Honey was a perky and somewhat eccentric, but very successful, real estate agent. She was lead agent for Chamisa Springs – a gated and very exclusive community where she and the two, still scintillating widows, Sonora Livingston-Bundt and Connye Andreatos, part of the coffee circle, lived in luxury and serenity. These latter two were generally recognized as the queens of the Santa Fe social scene, but they were often locked in fierce competition with each other as neither particularly liked to *share* that title with the other. Each preferred to reserve that title exclusively for themselves.

Today Honey was preparing for her first showing with Bella. She had three very exclusive properties scheduled for viewing this morning. She was running a little late and was rushing getting dressed. Somehow, she had never managed to progress exclusively into adult attire, and this morning was wearing a short tartan plaid skirt with saddle shoes, knee socks, and a pink blouse with embroidered poodles. And with two seventeen-year-olds, you can imagine what her *real* age must have been.

Honey scurried to her BMW and tore off to meet Bella at her hotel. Bella was pacing outside the entrance, obviously not in a good mood. She had not yet learned the mañana ways of laid back Santa Fe. Her inner clock was still ticking on east coast time, with New York City expectations.

"I am so-o-o very sorry, have you been waiting long?" Honey called out as she sped up to the curb, reaching over and opening the passenger door for Bella.

"If you *expect* to remain my agent I expect *you* to be on time. Is that understood?" Bella commanded as she shuffled into the passenger seat. "So, what have you got for me this morning?"

"And a cheery good morning to you," Honey greeted, as she charged off to the first appointment.

Now Bella was not what you would call a handsome woman. She was a stalwart sixty something, heavyset, and with what could politely be called a strong face – and not so politely - horsy. She had bosoms like the Pacific continental shelf, and her hair was, unfortunately, baby fine, and tinted a bizarre persimmon orange. It held no shape and, piled on top of her head, slipped to one side like a tam-o-shanter on windy day. She squinted from behind heavy gold framed, thick glasses, and one could see she would be required to shave her upper lip at least once a day if not more frequently if she had an evening engagement.

She had, also, not yet caught on to the fact that Santa Feans dressed casually for daily wear. There was nothing light-weight or wash-and-wear about her. She was wearing a stylish, though very uncomfortable looking, black dress with massive swags of gold jewelry and chains – all of it real gold, by the way - festooned across her bosom like Christmas at Rockefeller Center.

Honey was too much of a professional to take Bella's admonition with any pique, and breezily jumped right into describing the first house on the morning's list. She made every listing sound like the perfect dream house, and waxed eloquently about the first house's many fine features as they drove into the foothills to view the property.

The first showing was of an estate on top of a secluded hill with a fine sunset view of Santa Fe stretched out below and the Jemez Mountains across the valley. The house was surrounded by Piñons, Junipers and low level Ponderosa Pines. The house had many patios, a swimming pool and spa, and a gourmet kitchen designed by Martha Stewart.

Bella walked silently around property like a vegetarian visiting a slaughter house. Honey was extolling the many features and virtues of the house, but Bella did not respond with a single word - not even a grunt. Finally Honey asked directly, "Isn't this a splendid property?"

Bella gazed out of the living room windows and acidly replied, "I want something with a morning view," and proceeded to walk out the front door and back to the car. Honey scrambled to lock up the house and follow after.

"Well, I'm afraid the second property won't do for you either, then," Honey said, "So let's go directly to the third. May be just the perfect setting for you."

"Humph," was all Bella could muster in response.

"Anything you liked about the first property? The more specific you can be for me the easier it will be to find the kind of properties you might like to view," Honey added, trying to engage Bella in the process.

"I'll know what I like when I see it," Bella barked and stared out the passenger window.

This next property was likewise unsuitable. Bella found the rooms too small, the neighbors too close, and the driveway too steep. Poor Goldilocks seemed unable to find anything "just right" and Honey was ready to call in the bears.

Honey had planned a charming lunch at one of her favorite secluded restaurants for the two of them to discuss what they'd seen and what she had lined up for the afternoon, but Bella wanted to return to the hotel, and scrapped plans to view any more properties the rest of the day, giving no reason. As Bella retreated into the hotel, Honey was at a complete loss as to how to proceed with this client. She had had difficult clients before, but none quite like this gorgon.

◘   ◘   ◘

Sonora considered herself the consummate hostess. She was expecting Lionel for tea and wanted to float her latest idea for a scintillating event.

"Darling Sonatina," Lionel greeted Sonora at her door, "looking radiant as ever."

Sonora nodded demurely and ushered him in. Immediately, IT, Sonora' scruffy terrier, came charging through the house and jumped up at Lionel like an attacking kangaroo.

"Gracious, such a welcome," Lionel exclaimed as he held IT at arm's length, offering him back to his mistress. He then had to brush dog hair from his newly cleaned and pressed linen suit.

"You were hinting at a soiree on the telephone," Lionel said as he settled into a comfy chair, ready for his first cup of afternoon tea. "Something scandalous, I hope."

Sonora poured. "I'm sure you've heard that we have a new arrival in town – Bella Harrington-Crenshaw."

"I have. But the grapevine seems to be bearing rather bitter fruit. One hears stories...."

"That may be, but I feel we have a civic duty.... One must reach out. Was thinking about some sort of a reception. Nothing lavish, mind you...."

"But wouldn't that give the wrong impression? Certainly we should give her no excuse to dismiss us as amateurs."

Sonora nodded, thinking. "You have a good point. She is East coast after all – both New York *and* Washington. Can't have her thinking we live in sod huts. Why not - let's go the whole hog."

Lionel added, "Perhaps you might want to invite Connye to co-host. Let the new lady see the *two* who are really in charge. We don't want to encourage another Amanda Beor-Bink. What a disaster that was.

Sonora thought, "Host with Connye....I don't know."

"But the two of you united so forcefully in the Amanda affair. Wouldn't it be useful for Bella to see the power of the two of you united in action? Mustn't give her any opening to think she might dominate our little circle."

"Lionel, what would I do without your ever brilliant insight and comfort?"

Lionel nodded modestly, "Well, we do what we can."

◘   ◘   ◘

Reno Nevada was laid to rest at age 9 and two weeks later was resurrected as Bella Le Balle after moving to Santa Fe. One had to reinvent oneself periodically, and what better occasion than a move to a new city?

Pinky Powell began his drag career as Tupper Ware – but that incarnation only lasted a few months – too much unbreakable plastic. Then Heidi Go-Seek played the gay bars in Milwaukee for a couple of weeks, but as she was unappreciated by the rather dour German types she morphed into Sweet and Lowdown. She played quite successfully in LA for a few years until clamoring creditors forced her to reinvent herself up in Seattle as Reno Nevada. And now, pushing forty, Pinky was once again casting out into the seas of transformation hoping to land the Big One.

Bella Le Balle was to be no ordinary drag act – oh no. Bella would shine and shimmer. She would glisten and gleam. She would stun them all. Pinky had landed an engagement at The Carousel Lounge, a gay club with a mixed clientele that included many of the more soignée citizens of Santa Fe. The club served as a hub for the bohemian and eccentric, as well as the chic and tawdry. The drinks were not *too* watered down and the entertainment was mildly amusing.

But Pinky, as Bella, needed a complete new wardrobe. Not something pilfered from the thrift shops this time, but something grand – transcendental – 30's *MGM* on steroids.

Pinky picked up the phone and called Lionel Eastwood, an ex-Hollywood costumer designer, recommended by an old LA friend of them both. Pinky would cash in his meager savings and this time, go for broke.

◘   ◘   ◘

Connye was having a little afternoon siesta in her comfy chair by the indoor lap pool. A book of qi gong meditation lay open over her ample stomach when Sonora called.

"Yep?" Connye answered the phone. Sleep deprived her of her usual social graces.

"Beloved, this is Sonora."

"Uh huh."

"Did I catch you at a bad time?"

"Oh, Sonora - no. What's up?" She was still clambering up from the well of her nap.

"Dearest, if you are not too tied up I was wondering if we might wander down to the club house for coffee and a brioche. Have a little event I'd like to discuss with you. Are you free?"

A brioche was sounding particularly inviting just now. "Well yes, I'm sure I can free up my schedule. What time were you thinking?"

"Right now - if that suits you. Shall we meet in the club house lounge?"

Connye had no idea who might be in the club house this afternoon - best to freshen up just in case. "Just need to powder my nose. Give me ten minutes."

"See you shortly."

◘   ◘   ◘

Mrs. H-C had not returned any of Honey's urgent calls to set appointments for the next showings. Honey was finding it very difficult not to be furious with this lady. Fortunately she had signed a buyer's agent agreement, so the old battle-ax could not go shopping around for another agent. Honey was a *really* good agent, and earnestly struggled to find just the right property for each of her clients. She had lined up some really splendid properties that she thought would fit Bella's needs, but if she couldn't show them to her what could she do? It had been a week now since Mrs. H-C had abandoned her at the hotel and Honey was getting panicky.

Honey was visiting the main office today, as she was usually at the office annex at Chamisa Springs. Charles Appleby, senior partner of the real estate firm leaned out of his office when he saw Honey. "Can I have a word?"

"Certainly."

Charles closed the office door and she sat opposite him at his desk. "I think we have a problem," he said gravely.

"Which is?" Honey was beginning to clutch inside. Was it something she'd done?

"If I remember correctly you signed a buyer's agent agreement with that New York lady, am I right?"

"Bella…?"

"Yes."

"I certainly did." She pulled it from her brief case and handed it to him.

"Well, just this morning, I received a call from our attorney telling me that this Mrs. Harrington-Crenshaw has just signed a sales contract directly with the seller on a house *we* listed and *you* showed her."

"Which house?"

"The Ridgeview property."

"That's the first one I showed her and she seemed to hate it."

"Well, obviously not."

Honey was speechless. "How can that be?"

Charles shook his head. "I have never in my twenty-some years in this business ever come across such chutzpah. This broad just went around all the legal contracts and set her own agenda."

"And what does our attorney say?"

"He contacted her and told her of all the legal shit she was stepping into and she just hung up on him. Then an hour later he was besieged with calls from her attorneys in New York *and* Washington, and was told, in no uncertain terms, that if we so much as sneezed at her they would bring a firestorm of lawsuits against us that would tie us up in the courts for years and cost us more than our firm is worth."

"So nada? Right?"

"Absolutely right. They said money was no object to her if she decided to sue. Do you really think a little firm like ours could win against Harrington USB Bank? Sometimes you have to just walk away. But let's not make a habit of it, okay?"

"Oh, I could just strangle the bitch," Honey vented.

◘   ◘   ◘

Lionel was having a little gardening morning at home. He was misting his orchids and repotting a few Christmas cacti that had out-grown their pots.

Lionel had retired from the film industry as a costume designer, when was it? Fifteen years now? His little condo was a mini-museum of his many exploits, and he loved nothing better than to potter amongst his beloved mementos.

Lionel was slight but sprightly, and his little mustache twitched as he concentrated on whatever task he was focusing on at the moment. Lionel was just now sweeping up the spilled soil from the repotting when the phone rang.

"Lionel Eastwood," he announced.

"Is this the Lionel Eastwood of stage, screen, and drag queen regalia?" a strange voice asked over the phone.

"I beg your pardon..." Lionel asked with some indignation. He had never associated himself with any drag acts, and had no idea what this caller was referring to. "Who *is* this?"

"You don't know me, but I'm a friend of Dorothy Steinberg. She suggested I call you. Said we *must* meet."

"Dorothy! You know Dorothy? How is she? We haven't spoken in months."

"Oh yes, Miss Dorothy is *just* fine. And she sends you oodles of kisses."

"That's nice. And who are you?" he asked, still mystified by this strange and eccentric sounding caller.

"Oh yes, sorry. I'm Pinky, otherwise known more recently as Reno Nevada.   And now reborn as the delightful...the stunning...the radiant and soon to be the *ravishing* Bella Le Balle – the singing and dancing sensation of Santa Fe – all live singing, no lip-synching from this lady – and with your help, of course."

"I don't understand. What have I got to do with this?"

"Oh my dear, I am calling upon you for your professional design services. I need you to remake me into a stellar, celestial, universal star!"   He paused.   "And I am willing to pay handsomely."

◘   ◘   ◘

Connye was very fond of the Seville orange marmalade provided with the brioche at the Chamisa Springs club house. She had consumed two already - to Sonora's brief nibble at but one. While Connye carried her heft with a certain style, Sonora had retained her trim dancer's figure even after all these years. Both ladies were in their late forties to early fifties. And both had managed to have their natal records sealed so no one could *ever* find out for sure what their exact ages were.

Connye was somewhat suspicious of exactly what Sonora's intentions were this afternoon. They only ever united in common interest under the direst of circumstances - such as their need to oust that dreadful Amanda Beor-Bink, who had tried unsuccessfully to command the Santa Fe social scene all by herself, elbowing out both Connye and Sonora for a short period of time. So the fact that Sonora wanted to confer with her about some event this afternoon truly puzzled her, as there seemed to be no common threat lurking on the horizon.

"You said you had an event you wished to discuss?" Connye jumped right in.

"Yes. As I'm sure you are aware, we have a new addition to our little Santa Fe clan. One Bella Harrington-Crenshaw - Mrs. H-C as she is now fondly referred to locally."

Connye nodded. "I have heard."

"Well, I was thinking of giving a little welcoming event to introduce her to *those she must know*. And Lionel astutely observed that if the *two* of us jointly sponsored this event together, then she would see exactly what she would be up against should she be tempted to stage a takeover like that presumptuous La Bink tried to do. I'm sure you can see the wisdom in that."

"Your precious Lionel - so insightful."

"So would you be prepared to join me in this little endeavor then?"

"And where exactly would you dream of holding such an event?"

"We need someplace really magnificent...

"And intimidating..."

"Precisely."

"How about at the Governor's mansion?" Connye finally suggested after giving it some considered thought.

"Oh how could that possibly be? Certainly the governor would never allow that."

"Well, I guess it's all in who you know."

"Could you... would you?" Sonora asked, truly impressed.

"Let me get back to you on that." Connye eyed Sonora's remaining brioche. "May I?" She asked as she zipped the delicate pastry onto her plate.

◘   ◘   ◘

Lionel answered the front door.

"Aren't you just *too* cute?" Pinky cooed, "I've always had a thing for older men."

"You must be Pinky." Lionel stepped back and let Pinky breeze his way in.

Pinky danced down the hall into the living room singing, "All of me - why not take al-l-l of me. Can't you s-e-e-e I'm nothing without you...."

Pinky was hardly what you would call svelte. At six feet two, two hundred and fifty pounds, and bald, it was certainly going to be a challenge to turn Pinky Powell into an international drag diva. Of course real talent could transform almost anyone, but there was no way for Lionel to know at this point in time with what native talents Pinky might be blessed. Lionel would have to take on this project as an article of faith.

Now, it was not the money that intrigued Lionel. He was not hurting, as they say. But having successfully draped some of the most celebrated Hollywood women in the 1950s and 60s it would be a unique challenge to change this nugget of coal into a celestial diamond.

Lionel stood back and walked around Pinky with a critical eye.

Pinky nodded and twirled, with his arms stretched out wide, "Quite a lump aren't I?

"Well..." Lionel prevaricated.

"Hey - never said it would be easy."

Lionel laughed. "Well, I hope you're not going for the delicate Audrey Hepburn look."

Pinky hooted. "Oh no. Let's start with Divine and work backwards. Maybe something in the middle. Maybe a little Bette Midler – a little Cher. Down to earth - but glammy. You know.

"Might be doable. Of course, I'll need bolts and bolts of fabric, and a very convincing wig or two."

"O-o-o-o, you are so wicked."

"Not wicked – realistic."

Pinky suddenly melted. "So, can you do *anything* for me?" he wailed.

"I've got a few ideas. Give me a couple of days to work up some drawings and let's meet again."

Pinky kneeled down and showered kisses on the back of Lionel's hands.

"I hope this kneeling position does not suggest any further activities. I am somewhat more chaste in my golden years."

Pinky rose up and clamored, "Oh, oh, the very thought….how you make me blush."

"I somehow doubt that," Lionel smiled sweetly but with a twist.

"Strictly business, I assure you." Pinky struck the pose of a vastly offended diva and swept towards the front door. "Call me when you have the drawings." Then he turned before he exited. "Dorothy will be so pleased to know we met. Bye-bye. And please, please make me *stunning*."

◘   ◘   ◘

Connye knew the housekeeper at the Governor's mansion and gave her a call.

"Kitty, darling, how *have* you been? It's been simply ages since we last chatted."

"And this is….?" Kitty enquired.

"But darling, it's Connye. Has it been so long? Have you forgotten my voice?"

Kitty knew exactly who it was, but wanted to play a little hard to get as she knew Connye only *ever* called her when she wanted something.

Divas in Cahoots   Jon McDonald

"Oh yes, Connye. Why I haven't heard from you since you wanted me to put your name up for the Governor's list. What would you like this time?"

Connye was shocked, but could see she needed to play this with some diplomacy. "Kitty, precious one, I am appalled if I have been negligent in keeping in touch. I am truly sorry. But with my frequent jaunts to Georgia to be with Jefferson the time has just flown."

"Who's this Jefferson?" Kitty asked.

"Oh my, it has been a long time hasn't it? Why, Jefferson is my partner. We met in New Orleans when I was there for my Lobster Pot company board meeting."

"He's with your company?"

"No, my dear, not a business partner, a romantic partner."

"Really?"

"He just swept me off my feet, but as he lives in Augusta and has an aging father, and a thriving art appraisal business, he cannot move here; and I with *all* my demanding activities cannot move there, so we shuttle back and forth as best we can."

"Sounds exhausting."

"One can hardly imagine...."

"But of course, it must help that you have your own plane."

"Well, there's that...."

"Okay, look, got a really busy day here so what's up? You must want something."

"My dear, just a friendly chat to say hi and catch up. It's been so long." Connye had to be ver-r-r-y careful how she proceeded.

"And you want to know how I am?" Kitty asked, with some incredulity.

30

"Why yes, of course."

"Toby got hit by a truck couple of month's back. Broke from his leash and dashed right out into the traffic."

"Oh my dear…."

"But got a new puppy - Skipper. Little mutt from the shelter. Cute as a cauliflower."

"How charming."

There was a silence as Kitty had concluded her news.

Connye gently eased her way forward. "So Kitty, my friend Sonora and I were thinking about putting together a little evening to welcome a prominent new resident to Santa Fe. And I was wondering if there might be an evening free in the next month or so when the Governor would be out of state and we might be able to rent the public rooms at the residence for an evening. We would make all the arrangements. You wouldn't have to lift a finger. Would that be possible?"

"Ah ha," Kitty replied, "now we get down to it. Okay, let me just check the governor's calendar."

"Oh, you *are* an angel."

◘   ◘   ◘

Lionel had his drawings proudly spread out on the dining room table. Pinky was due at any moment. What was he doing? Lionel had no idea why he had agreed to do such an absurd project. But it had been kind of fun. He always liked a challenge, and to transform Pinky in to a glamorous star was certainly going to be a challenge, indeed.

"Look at me. What was I thinking?" Pinky stood at Lionel's front door. "How in the world are you ever going to transform all of this?" Pinky spread his arms out to indicate his size and girth. "I look like an elephant walrus."

"Come, come, come now. We'll have none of that." Lionel encouraged Pinky to come inside. "You might be surprised. Let's go take a look at the drawings."

Lionel shepherded Pinky into the dining area, presenting the drawings. "There, what do you think?"

Pinky studied the drawings in hushed awe. "Oh my..." he hardly dared speak. "You did all of this?"

"Every one," Lionel beamed proudly.

"I never thought..." He was lost in wonder. He looked up. "But it's going to cost a *fortune*."

"Not as much as you think. I have my resources."

Pinky brooded. "But these are drawings. Of course they are idealized. But all this has to fit on to *me*."

"I understand that. But it's all in the fitting and shaping. I have my little secrets. Come, let's take some measurements, and then I can start on the construction. I promise you, you will not be disappointed."

Pinky just stood there and began to bawl like a baby.

◘   ◘   ◘

Honey absolutely refused to attend the welcoming event for Bella at the Governor's mansion, however nice the spread was going to be. Connye pleaded with Honey to come, but when she reminded Connye what Mrs. H-C had done, Connye fully understood. And indeed, she wondered if it was the right thing to even be giving this event if Mrs. H-C behaved like such a vandal. But it was too late now. All had been arranged for, and all she could do at this juncture was plan what she was going to wear this evening.

Connye had a nefarious habit of searching through her hidden telescope every time she and Sonora were to attend an event together. Connye had to see what Sonora was wearing *before* she could choose her own outfit. It gave her just that little edge to know what Sonora was going to wear first. As Connye trained her telescope across the golf course this evening to Sonora's house she could see Sonora parading around in her tweed hacking jacket and matching skirt - very Balmoral. Connye wondered if Sonora had also arranged for an accompanying pack of hounds.

In any case Connye decided to up the ante and dressed in one of her more splendid evening gowns – the deep burgundy one, accompanied by her diamond and ruby necklace, earrings, and bracelet. Sonora would seem like a shabby country cousin compared to her.

At the appointed time Sonora's limo collected Lionel and Connye and off they whisked to the much anticipated evening. Now everyone could finally see exactly who this Mrs. Bella Harrington-Crenshaw really was.

Sonora and Connye decided to stand together, united, as hostesses. They wanted to present a firm front to the Mrs. H-C. There was to be no mistake as to who exactly was in charge of the Santa Fe social scene. They would be welcoming, but also firmly in charge – more united and invincible than the clan of Borgia.

The Governor's mansion was located in the foothills of north Santa Fe. It had a rural feel, nestled as it was amongst stands of Piñon and Juniper. Valet parking was necessary because of the expected crowd. None of the regulars wanted to miss this intriguing event. Everyone had heard of Mrs. H-C but few had actually met her yet.

Connye, Sonora, and her tag-along pal, Lionel, were stationed loosely near the entrance of the hall in an informal receiving line. Connye's caterer had done a splendid job, once again, and the serving tables were laden with a Mexican fiesta of food, tequila, ice cold beers, and as a nod to Sonora, who rarely imbibed anything else – Champaign. After all, one needed to maintain a certain standard.

The Gladscows and the Getgoodes, two established older couples were the first to arrive, followed by Roberta and Olivia.

"Honey not here yet?" Olivia enquired? "She's usually one of the first."

"I hate to tell tales out of school but..." Connye took Olivia aside and explained to her about Mrs. H-C's shocking behavior towards Honey and why she had refused to attend.

"Oh yes, Honey told me all about that," Olivia confided. "But then why are we even having this affair? Mrs. H-C hardly seems the type of person we want to have in our group, however rich and illustrious she might appear to be."

"We have certain standards to uphold," Connye responded, "Let us never be accused of judging without proof. And besides, we had already scheduled the event. Wasn't about to pay a cancellation fee to the caterer."

Many more guests were pouring in and beginning to mingle and sample the taste treats, but still no Mrs. Harrington-Crenshaw.

Linda, Sonora's old friend from her New York days came forward in a warm greeting. "Sonora, Sonora, Sonora, how ya been, sweetie? How's Pie?"

Sonora and Roberta had opened a pie shop together – Pie in the Sky - with Sonora as the investor and silent partner. Sonora answered, "Splendid. Can you believe, we've been offered a *huge* sum to franchise the business? Way more than I ever put into the business. What is going to happen to all my intended tax write-offs? Can't seem to lose money no matter how hard I try."

Linda who was constantly struggling to make ends meet was not feeling any pain for Sonora this evening. "So sorry, life can be such a bitch. But somehow I think you'll get through it all."

"Most likely. But one suffers so." The two of them often joked like this.

"Off to sample the spoils of your labor. Tasty looking treats. See ya." Linda scooted off.

Suddenly there was a scurry of activity at the entrance. Connye and Sonora turned to see two Borzois – one white and one black – straining at their leashes, (both rented by the way, but who would know?) followed by the cool and composed Bella Harrington-Crenshaw.

"Good evening ladies," she announced as she came up to Connye and Sonora. "How gracious of you to invite me to this charming gathering in my honor. I have been greeted with such warm and inviting hospitality since I've arrived in Santa Fe. You put my New York City friends to shame. Hope you don't mind my darling puppies. Completely house trained and will not be a nuisance at all."

"Charmed to have all of you," Sonora greeted. "I am Sonora Livingston-Bundt and this is Connye Andreatos, your hosts."

Bella looked around the room. "Well, you ladies certainly know how to host a splendid gathering. I can see I will have to call upon all of my most creative resources if I ever hope to compete with the two of you. But then, in this warm and friendly city who would be thinking of competition? I just want to be part of a compatible circle of friends. I hope you will accept me, and I will do all that I can to fit right in."

Connye and Sonora exchanged glances. This was most puzzling. Could this be the same terrifying Bella Harrington-Crenshaw of Honey's report?

"Please, introduce me to some of your delightful friends. I want so much to be acquainted with all of them." Bella breezed a gracious smile.

A security guard stepped up to Bella. "Excuse me ma'am, but I'm afraid dogs are not allowed in the Governor's mansion.

May I take them for you? I will make sure they are comfortable outside."

Bella looked startled for just a moment. "Of course, how kind of you. And if you could give them just a little water, I would be so grateful."

"Of course." The guard led the dogs away.

Sonora caught just a brief glimpse of daggers in Bella's gaze before she recovered and turned back to her hosts.

"Oh my - breaking decorum. How silly of me. So sorry to cause such a disturbance." Bella came between Sonora and Connye and taking both their arms asked, "Now then, shall we meet the other guests?"

◻   ◻   ◻

Everyone in the coffee circle made a concerted effort to be on the patio at Portabellos the next morning. So many rumors. So many questions. So much to discuss. There was a scramble for tables as they gathered to dissect last night's gala evening at the governor's mansion.

"Ugly as a gunny sack, but ever so charming," Ruth Gladscow, president of the opera board began. "I wonder if she's an opera fan." She was already drafting a solicitation letter in her mind.

The ever sweet Roberta added, "I went outside to see the dogs after they were removed. Felt so sorry for them. But they were fine."

"I have to say I am *totally* confused," Connye spoke up. "On the one hand Honey has related the horror story of what Bella did to her over that real estate business, and then there was last night. She was charming, gracious, and seemed genuinely interested in getting to know all of us. How can this be? Have we got a Jekyll and Hyde in our midst?"

Honey had been silent up until now. She suddenly became very animated and launched into, "Well, she's all Hyde as far as I'm concerned. She never showed *me* one gracious moment - but was ruthless and manipulating to both me *and* my firm. Screwed us out of two commissions. *And* threatened financial annihilation if we so much as lifted a finger to thwart her. As far as I'm concerned you can have and keep your Bella Harrington-Crenshaw. I cannot see how she could ever become a welcome addition to our circle."

"Well, that seems clear enough, Honey. I certainly understand your position, my dear, but one incident may not be reflective of the entire person. I for one would wish to give her the benefit of the doubt for now," Sonora added.

Olivia kicked in, "Yes, I thought her thoroughly charming. She was ever so attentive, and quite interested in seeing my line of cosmetics. I have an appointment to show her my samples tomorrow morning."

Honey scowled at Olivia, "Well, make sure you cash her check *before* you hand over any products, that's all I can say."

"Oh poo, you. Who knows what reason she had for doing what she did. She might have had a very legitimate reason," Olivia countered. "No one else has related anything disagreeable about her."

Sonora was pondering all of this. "Most mystifying. I guess we are just going to have to wait and see. It's like a quiz show. Will the real Bella Harrington-Crenshaw please step forward?"

"Oh Lord, heaven help us all," Honey added with some finality.

Ever So Delicate a Matter

"Senator Spangler, what a surprise. Whatever brings you to our lovely Santa Fe?" Bella greeted on the phone.

"Just being a tourist, like so many."

"Yes, any excuse to flee your brutal Minnesota summers. I once spent six years of summer in just one week in Minneapolis. How do you put up with that humidity?"

The Senator laughed. "You are fortunate to be at seven thousand feet and in the mountains - dry and relatively cool."

There was a pause. Bella had a sense that Chetworth Spangler had something else on his mind other than a polite hello and how are you.

"Is Deloris with you?" Bella asked trying to drive the conversation forward.

"No. Deloris and I are no longer together."

"Oh, I *am* sorry to hear that. Is that going to be a problem when you need to seek re-election? "

"Not sure there's going to *be* a re-election."

"I see."   There was another pause.   "What's going on Chet? I sense there's something more you want to tell or ask me."

"Can we meet? I need to talk to you privately."

"Of course. Want to come to dinner? My Rene does a lovely Halibut."

"No, can't meet at your place. It might compromise you. Needs to be at an out of the way public place that can no way connect me with you. It's for your own protection."

"My my, very mysterious." She thought for a moment. "There's a little restaurant at the edge of downtown and out of the way - Chilini's. Seven-thirty?"

"I'll find it. See you there."

◻   ◻   ◻

Sonora needed to confer with Roberta today about the offer presented to them by the franchise company. Pie in the Sky had started out so small, but had grown into a rather substantial business. It now comprised a much enlarged shop, a new kitchen in Santa Fe, two new shops in Albuquerque, and a robust and growing mail order business. And while Roberta was an expert at making her pies, she had left all the business decisions to Sonora, who, after all, had been the major - well actually, the only investor - and who continued to oversee the financial side of things.

Lionel accompanied Sonora this morning as they were headed out to lunch, after her meeting with Roberta, to a new restaurant that had created some buzz in the circle. Also he was itching to tell Sonora his little secret about the *other* Bella. He had not told her anything up till now, as he had been unsure if he was actually going to proceed with this amusing project.

The little bell tinkled on the front door of the shop as they entered.   Ruth Gladscow was custom ordering a couple of quiches from Roberta for an intimate dinner party when they walked in.

"Oh splendid," Ruth gushed at seeing Sonora, "I have some wonderful news that just *cannot* wait till coffee at Portabellos."

"Can't wait to hear," Sonora replied.

"Come let me buy us all a round of coffee then we can sit and chat." She proceeded to order for them all and they gathered at a corner table.

Roberta served the coffee and sat down in eager anticipation. "Now then, tell all."

Ruth leaned in. "I was most pleased to meet Mrs. H-C at your charming reception the other evening, Sonora. We chatted casually about the opera, and I was telling her that the board was in the process of fundraising for the construction for a new costume shop with additional storage, as we are so cramped, as you know."

"I do."

"Well imagine my shock and surprise when I got a call from her earlier this very morning offering to fund the *entire* project herself. It is *so* exciting."

"Good heavens, that is a substantial amount," Sonora gasped.

"See, I told you she was a sweetie," Roberta chimed in.

"But you've already raised most of it, haven't you?" Lionel asked, "Surely her portion can't be all that much?"

"No, that's what's so spectacular, she insists on paying the *full* amount for the addition herself. She urged us to use what we've already raised towards our next project - the dining pavilion."

Sonora, however, added, "But it has always been my contention that there should not be just *one* major donor as it becomes more a *part* of the community when the *whole* community pitches in, don't you agree?"

Ruth thought about that before answering. "In this economy that is not always so easy or successful."

"Well, she's certainly planning to make *her* mark on the community, isn't she?" Sonora replied. "Did she suggest a name for this new addition?"

"Well, not directly, but in consideration of her generous contribution I was thinking we should name it the Harrington-Crenshaw wing. Only fitting don't you think? After all, we did name the fountain in the reception court after *you* when you so generously gave us that. And not to be mean, or anything, but Bella's gift vastly out-ranks your ever more modest gift."

Sonora was not at all pleased to hear that. "Oh really? So you believe size really matters?"

"I've always thought so," Lionel added archly.

Sonora swatted Lionel's shoulder. "Hush." She turned back to Ruth and composed herself to say, "Well, I am sincerely pleased to hear this good news. And I am gratified to hear that *some* of all that money the banks stole from us in the great recession will be going to some good use now."

Roberta was a little shocked, "Oh Sonora, really, that's a little mean, don't you think?"

"Well, if the shoe fits...."

Ruth continued, "But that's not all. She is going to host a reception on the opera stage for the announcement of the gift, and she is going to pay for all of that as well."

"Goodie. Then perhaps we should erect a statue of her as an enduring memorial, or perhaps rename the city after her," Sonora dished. She stood up, "And I believe it is time for us to go, Lionel."

"But we haven't discussed the franchise agreement yet," Roberta protested.

"That can wait. I'm in no mood to deal with that just now. Come Lionel, I'm in need of some fresh air and culinary refreshment." She grabbed Lionel by the hand and swept him out of the shop.

Oh dear," Ruth commented to Roberta, "I don't believe Sonora was too pleased to hear *that* bit of news."

"Yes, she can sometime be a little testy. But she is such a dear - usually."

◘   ◘   ◘

Lionel stood back to appraise, as Pinky struggled to fit into his first new gown. He could only get the zipper up half way.

"Pinky, have you been putting on weight?" Lionel scolded.

Pinky looked a little sheepish, "Maybe a little. I've been snacking. It's the stress, you see."

Lionel was peevish, "Do you want to do this or not? After all, there is only so much I can do with the figure with which I am presented. I cannot work miracles - only semi-miracles. And you have to do your part, Pinky."

"Yes, I know. So sorry. I'll do better, I promise."

Lionel went over and heaved on the zipper. "Suck it in, buddy," Lionel instructed. The zipper finally yielded and Lionel stood back once again to scrutinize the disaster. "No, no, no. This is not going to work at all. You look like a watermelon pretending to be an apricot."

"Oh Lionel, please don't give up on me."

Lionel gave a great sigh, then contemplated the alternatives. "Got to scrap it all. Need to go in a new direction. There's no way you're going to achieve glam. There's only one solution – high camp."

"What are you, the director of my show now?" Pinky resisted.

"I'd better be, if you don't want to make a complete ass of yourself."

"But my vision – my art! And besides you've already spent *all* that money."

"Can't be helped. Think I might be able to salvage some of the material. But Pinky, you've got to start thinking muumuus and Ethel Merman. You are *never* going to channel Cher."

"But what about my act? I've been working up a really sexy, new routine."

"Scrap it. Dig deep into your Sophie Tucker, Mae West, or Bette. At best you might carry off a Tallulah or a Streisand – but a Monroe or a Russell – forget it."

Pinky thought for a moment, then belted out, "You'll be swell. You'll be great. Gonna have the whole world on a plate... That what ya mean?"

"You got it baby. Now let me rip down some drapes, we got some *big* dresses to assemble."

◻   ◻   ◻

Chilini's was an intimate little northern Italian restaurant that was fairly quiet on a Tuesday evening. Chetworth had selected a secluded corner table at the back of the restaurant out of site of the front windows. He had been early so he could select the table, hoping Bella would not arrive before him. Chetworth ordered two Bellini's and waited.

Finally Bella appeared. She could have been entering a high style, New York City club she was so elegantly dressed. She had still not caught on to the casualness of Santa Fe. She had yet to buy her first pair of cowgirl boots.

After sitting down she smiled. "Well, I have to say, you have me quite intrigued. Have been puzzling all day over what you might have to tell me."

"All in good time. I ordered you a Bellini. Know how much you like them."

"I do, indeed. Very thoughtful." She picked up and studied the menu. "I understand the lamb shanks are quite delicious here."

"Well, it's been awhile, hasn't it?" Chetworth said as he leaned back and contemplated Bella.

There had never been any romantic attachment between them, but rather close family connections. Bella's father, Frederick, and Chetworth had been best friends in college and were freshly recruited as OSS agents right after graduation, prior to the OSS becoming the CIA. They both stayed with the new agency for a few years, but Chetworth's interest turned to politics, and Frederick's turned to the family banking empire.

"So tell me," Bella proceeded, "what happened with you and Deloris? Always thought of you two as the perfect couple." She smiled, "Did somebody play a little hanky-panky?"

Chetworth laughed, "No nothing quite that exciting, I'm afraid. Simple, plain, old-fashioned boredom. Grew apart and saw no reason to go on. The kids grown. The house paid for. The lawn perfectly manicured. It was all just so....predictable - and boring. We both just wanted out.

"I see. And why exactly do you think there might not be a next election for you?"

"Well now, that comes more directly to the heart of the matter, but I'm not ready to go there quite yet. Why don't we order first?"

"As you like."

As they ordered and dined Chetworth kept a careful eye on the guests around them, and monitored everyone who came into the restaurant. Bella noticed this but did not comment on it.

Finally over coffee Chetworth became very still and quiet, then leaned over and spoke earnestly and softly to Bella. "Now, what you want to know. I have something very important to ask you. I need you to help me if you possibly can."

"Money problems? Do you need a loan?"

"No, nothing like that." He pulled back and regrouped his thoughts before proceeding. "Let me start by addressing your first question. There will be no next election because it is time for me to leave the Senate. I've had quite enough of the gridlock and constant political pressure to toe the Republican line. It's become as ruthless as a Balkan dictatorship up there. No more."

"I see. Yes, can certainly understand that. And what is it you need my help for?"

"Quite another matter. I've become involved... Well, better not go there. Just let me ask you to do me this one simple favor." He reached down and pulled a manila envelope out of a brief case. He laid it on the table in front of him. "I need you to deliver this for me."

"Am I to know what it is?"

"No. What I need is for you take this up to Bandelier..."

"The National Monument up by Los Alamos?"

"Yes."

"But you know I don't drive, don't you?"

"Oh...no, I didn't."

"Always living in New York City and Washington never needed to learn. And since I've come here I've hired a chauffeur. I would have to have him take me there. Is that a problem?"

Chetworth thought about that for a moment. "Can you make the trip seem like a sightseeing adventure?"

"I suppose so, though I am not much of the sightseeing type."

"But if he's a new chauffer he doesn't know that. Right?"

"I guess."

"Then just make sure the chauffeur stays with the car so you can be alone in the park."

"I can do that. When does this need to be delivered?"

"Thursday morning." He took a brochure out of his brief case, opened it, and spread it out before her. "In this is a map showing how to get up to Bandelier. Keep this. It's very important. At eleven someone will contact you at the gift shop and you are to give them this envelope. That's it - nothing more."

"How will I know this person?"

"Not important, he will know you, and make himself known. The less you know about it the better."

Bella was very circumspect. "Is this legal?"

"It's a national security issue. Can't say more."

"And why me? Why don't you do it yourself?"

"You – because you are the only one I know and trust out here. And not me – because it would be too dangerous. And I am too well known and could easily be recognized, which would cause complications."

"I see." Bella was considering all the implications.

"Can I count on you for this?" he pushed.

"I'm not sure. It worries me."

"Please, Bella. It's not dangerous for you. It's just a simple errand and I would be eternally grateful."

"I don't know, Chet…."

"Then in memory of your father…. He would have understood. We worked so closely together in the agency. Think of it as though he was asking you to do this."

She smiled slightly, "You can be very persuasive."

"Is that a yes?"

"All right. But then I have this little tax favor to ask…"

Chetworth laughed. "I'll see what I can do."

"Just kidding…." Bella was thoughtful then asked, "Will I see you again after the delivery?"

"I think it best not. The less exposure we have to each other the better. And I can't thank you enough for doing this."

"Well, you got me when you evoked my father. I would have done anything for him."

"And he would have been very proud of you - and grateful."

◻   ◻   ◻

"Do we dare ask her?" Olivia asked Connye and Sonora. "I mean, won't Honey be just horrified? Might we not risk losing Honey if we ask Bella to a part of the coffee circle?

Little, round, fluffy Roberta trundled over with a soy chai and an apricot Danish. "What's up ladies? Did I miss anything?"

Sonora replied, "We were discussing the Bella. Do we or do we not ask her to join us for morning coffee? There seems to be some hesitation."

"But does she even *do* her own shopping? I've never seen her here – ever," Connye observed. "It's my understanding she has her own housekeeper and *she* does the shopping. I for one would not care to offend Honey, who is, after all, truly one of us, and not to be slighted by inviting Bella."

The three looked at each other. "Well, that seems to settle it then," Sonora observed, "No Bella at coffee."

"And what are we to do about the opera gala? You have all heard about that, *n'est pas?*" Connye asked, hefting herself up to her full height of indignation. "Does anyone else feel she is trying a little too hard to make an impression?"

O-o-o, Sonora was just juicy with contempt for that. "Yes, Ruth announced that little bit of news to us at Pie just the other day. I, personally, have always felt that ostentation was *not* a virtue. I can understand her wanting to make a mark, but really, must she commence her residence here in Santa Fe by trying to put us all to shame? Not all of us have her multi-millions."

"Well, some of us do," Connye quietly added, sipping at her latte.

Just then Honey and Brenda Getgoode, the brash Texan with her lap dog, the Contessa, breezed out of the market, seeking any news that might be going today.

"Ladies, got any goodies?" Brenda asked as she shuddered into place at the table, rocking everybody's drinks and giving the Contessa a kiss of the top of her head.

"Honey, you will be happy to know that Mrs. H-C will *not* be invited to join us here at coffee, in deference to you, dear one," Connye announced.

"Indeed, much relieved," she sighed as she leaned back in her chair and shed herself of several bags of groceries.

"But whatcha gonna do about the opera gala?" Brenda asked Honey. "Can't avoid the New York Bella forever. It's way too small a town not to attend *anything* where she might appear."

"Yes, been thinking about that," Honey answered. "Any event with a crowd will be fine. I've decided to attend the gala, though I shall keep a safe distance from Bella. I'll have all my other dear friends to chat with."

"Most prudent. Would hate to lose your company forever. After all, I'm afraid we must contend with Bella for the foreseeable future," Sonora sagely observed.

Honey addressed Connye, "What's up with Jefferson, he's not been to visit you, and you've not mentioned him in ages."

"Yes, not good news, I'm afraid. His father is very ill, and Jefferson's been reluctant to leave him."

"Then will you visit him soon in Georgia?"

"Might. But don't want to distract him from his father either. Need to see how things play out for a while."

Roberta said, "You must miss him terribly."

"I do." Connye said quietly.

"Well this is getting morbid," Brenda brayed. "Think I'll skedaddle. The Major will be wanting ta go ta the casino. Gotta keep an eye on the old bugger or we'll be broke as wetbacks." Brenda was never one to pride herself in political correctness. She hoisted herself up and scooted off.

The rest of the group, each having urgent errands, soon scooted off as well.

◘   ◘   ◘

To deny that Bella was tempted to peek into the envelope would be a fallacy, but her father's rigorous discipline prevailed and she staunchly resisted the temptation.

It was Thursday morning and she sat at her dressing table staring at the envelope. What was she doing? Why had she allowed herself to agree to this folly? But she *had* committed herself and now needed to see it through. After all, it seemed to be very important to Chetworth, and she had agreed to do her part.

She had arranged for the car at nine-thirty. Half an hour – maybe forty-five minutes - to drive up, a reasonable wander around the park, pretending to sightsee, and then the eleven o'clock meeting at the visitor's center gift shop. She could discreetly hand over the envelope and then, thankfully, be gone.

Bella had been unsure what one wore on such an excursion, so she donned a Versace jumpsuit, thinking that would be sporty. She tied a silk scarf around her neck and rose from the dressing table. He picked up the envelope, stuffed it into her bag, and headed for the waiting car.

Bella actually enjoyed her wander around the monument. It was a quiet, relatively cool Thursday, with a light crowd, and she even climbed a few ladders peering into caves that had been the living quarters of the long ago vanished Ancestral Pueblo people.

She found herself browsing the gift shop at ten till eleven. She was not taking any chances on missing her contact, but she was surprised to see how nervous she was. You would have thought she was planning to pole vault the Grand Canyon. Her hands were sweating and she had to dry her brow with a tissue she had stuffed into a jacket pocket. She nervously eyed the cashier who was keeping an eye on *her* as though *she* was a suspected shop-lifter.

At five past eleven no one had approached her. Now she was even more nervous. The cashier was looking at her with open hostility and poor Bella had no idea what to do. The cashier picked up the phone, whispering, and a security guard entered the gift shop and conferred with the cashier, casting glances over at Bella. Bella was now so unsettled she wandered into the visitor's center where she could keep an eye on the gift shop in case someone new came in who might be her contact. But as it was a quiet day only a mother and daughter entered. Bella felt certain they were not her contact.

She paced. She perused the exhibits. She checked her watch. Eleven fifteen. How long was she expected to wait? Finally at eleven thirty, and with still no one approaching, she fled to the car and instructed the driver to take her home.

What was she to do? Dare she call Chetworth, or should she wait for him to contact her? And what about the envelope?

She was not pleased to think she must keep something so suspect safe in her house. It was a responsibility she had not agreed to. On the way back to Santa Fe she flipped through the caller identification on her cell phone hoping to find Chetworth's number, but then remembered he had called her on her land line. There was nothing more she could do till she got home. She resolved to immediately put the envelope securely into her safe. And then she wondered if she should have stayed longer? Or did she mix up the time? Had it changed to Standard Time without her realizing it? No, she was just panicking.

Back home, and with the envelope locked securely in the safe, she checked her land line caller ID but found nothing she could identify as Chetworth's number. He must have called from a public phone or an unlisted number. She did not know his hotel and could now only wait for him to contact her. She was very distraught. And on top of all that the gala opera reception was to be this weekend and she had to be stunning, gracious, and cool as a glacier.

Bell of the Ball

Lionel had to admit he was having a rather jolly, good time. He had decided that Sonora did *not* need to know about his exploits with Pinky right away. He had been put off by her rather snarly episode at Pie over Bella's gift to the opera. Rather, he was planning to host a surprise evening of his own at The Carousel Lounge to introduce his protégé, and his much to be admired costuming for this impossible dream.

He had finally gotten Pinky on a sensible diet and had constructed six splendid ensembles for the show. He had an array of new wigs that didn't look like they were specifically designed for hookers – no strawberry cream page boy, or lemon chiffon bouffant - although finding suitable shoes had been an entirely different matter. After searching through all the thrift shops in Santa Fe, there was nothing to do but order very expensive custom shoes from a website that specialized in women's shoes for men. Lionel could not finalize the order by himself though – feeling far too embarrassed to use his own name he'd had Pinky complete the order.

Today, however, the usually immaculately neat Lionel found his little condo a rampage of fabric, ribbon, and sequins. And Sonora had invited herself for tea in... oh, in *just* ten minutes. She had promised him *splendid news*, so he'd had to agree. And as he didn't want her to know about what he was up to just yet there was a storm of scurry as he threw everything into the guest bedroom and locked the door. He was still picking up threads and stray sequins when Sonatina knocked at his front door - and he hadn't even started preparing the tea and English muffins yet.

"My darling, what a treat to see you," Lionel greeted, somewhat breathlessly, ushering her into his living room, and surreptitiously picking up the odd thread, and kicking a rogue ribbon under the sofa.

Sonora surveyed the room, and like a host on the Antiques Road Show, uttered her estimation. "My dear, have you been entertaining? There seems to be an air of *dishabille* about the room. Quite unlike your usual calm, centered, and composed environment."

"Oh, just a little exercising before you arrived, I suspect."

Sonora looked at him like he had just committed a murder. "You... exercising? Really? I find that hard to believe."

Lionel completely refused to take her bait. "Let me just put the water on. Tea will be in a jiff." He disappeared into the kitchen.

Sonora sat in the one comfortable chair and called out, "Think I should like lemon today if you don't mind."

"Cherry or Raspberry jam for the muffins?"

"Oh my, decisions, decisions.....cherry sound cheery." She laughed at her little joke.

Lionel came in with the tea tray and served.

"Now, you've had me on tenterhooks all afternoon about this splendid news. Time to spill it all," Lionel demanded anxiously.

Sonora so loved dragging out the suspense, and sipped delicately at her tea, and took a bite of muffin before she began. "Well, my dear, I hope your passport is in order."

"Oh my, and why is that?"

"It's been quite some time since I last visited my lovely little mill in Provence and was thinking a couple of weeks during the grape harvest might be a nice little treat and was wondering if you would care to join us? My treat, of course."

Lionel grinned and twinkled. "I will have to check my schedule, but I believe I might be able to slip away." He squinted slightly, "And who exactly is this *us*?"

"Ah, well... yes. Quinto is to have a brief hiatus between pictures and I invited him along. You know what an exhausting schedule he has these days, what with all his film projects."

Now this Quinto is an interesting and enduring figure in Sonora's romantic past. They first hitched up for a brief fling several years ago. He was a thirtyish, rambunctious Native American chef with a wild but playful side that appealed to the more sedate Sonora. Their affair burned itself out quickly - as he was too much of a free spirit, and she was much too cautious to let anyone permanently into her life. However, there were re-occurring clandestine romantic episodes from time to time that Sonora refused to acknowledge to anyone – not even Lionel.

Nevertheless, they remained close friends, and even worked on a movie script together that had enjoyed a modest success. As a result, he had become quite a successful screenwriter, and was later introduced as an actor into one of his scripts – only to become a heart throb of a star.

Lionel loved to tease Sonora about Quinto. "My dear - the devastating Quinto? What is one to think about that? Are you prepared for a hoard of paparazzi buzzing around your charming *moulin*? I understand he has become quite the star, on top of his writing. Not to mention his *other* more familiar, and local, kama sutric talents."

"Yes, what have I spawned? Once just a charming lad, but now a beast of fame. Was so sorry when he moved to California.

So enjoyed when he was just a simple chef managing my little dinner parties. But now - ah, how mysterious the unfolding of one's divine destiny." Sonora became lost in the metaphysical contemplation of life's mysteries.

"Well I have a little surprise too," Lionel hinted, rousing her from her reverie, and deciding it was time to let her in on his secret.

Sonora nodded, "Really, and what might that be?"

"I am hosting an evening of glamour and entertainment at The Carousel Lounge to introduce my protégé, and my very own array of ravishing original costumes."

"Why Lionel, how splendid. When did this come about?"

"A few weeks ago."

"And you kept this a secret from me?"

"It was touch and go for a while - not sure if I would be able to turn a turnip into a Cinderfella or not."

Sonora laughed. "Well, this will certainly rival Bella and her gala event. What is the name of this protégé of yours?"

"Why, Bella, of course. Bella Le Balle."

◘   ◘   ◘

Connye was devastated to learn that Jefferson's father had finally passed away. But secretly - well, not so devastated. Jefferson's father had been the major impediment to their being together. Now that he was gone the only major issue left was Jefferson's art appraisal business. But after all, Connye reasoned, Santa Fe *was* a major art market. Might she be able to persuade him to relocate his business to Santa Fe? She had a splendid home that would suit the both of them beautifully, and they could finally be together - if not married, then, at least together. (Jefferson had steadfastly refused to encumber either of them with a second marriage)

It was a surprisingly short time after his father's death when Jefferson called Connye and said he wanted to meet with her. They decided to spend some time together in a spot that was neutral for both of them, so she picked him up in her plane and they flew to Jackson Hole, Wyoming, where a friend had lent Jefferson a cabin in the mountains. Neither had ever been there before, so they decided that would be a pleasant spot to be alone together.

Now, wipe your mind of the image of a simple cabin of hand-hewn logs, a potbellied stove, beds with lumpy mattresses on hard springs, and snow shoes hanging by the front door. We are talking here of a *rich* person's log cabin – central air, three bedrooms, a billiard room, a gourmet kitchen, a Jacuzzi hot tub, and a state of the art sound system, satellite and wi-fi. No one was going to suffer here, unless they cut themselves cooking or banged a knee getting into the hot tub.

After the two had settled in Jefferson asked, "You ready for a mess of supper. I'm starving."

Connye laughed, "Sounds like your down home boy is breaking through there. I'm certainly ready."

They drove into town for a smooth and mellow evening of fine dining, excellent wine, and candle light. As the meal was winding down Connye was busting to ask Jefferson about what he wanted to discuss with her, but she had learned she needed to wait until *he* brought up the subject on his own. So she launched into a subject she knew he *always* wanted to discuss.

"How's Sophie? Have you seen her much?" she asked.

"Ah my darling daughter, and the bane of my existence."

"Really, is she causing you trouble?"

"She's discovered boys."

"But she's only ten."

"Ten and three-quarters as she continually reminds me. And if she could count the hours, minutes and seconds she would do that too."

Connye laughed. "And your ambitious plans for turning her into the Belle of the South?"

"I might as well be trying to teach table manners to a vulture."

"That bad?"

"It's all about make-up, and texting, and the mall. And if you can believe, she's already pestering me to teach her to drive.

"Ouch."

"And I only ever see her once a month when I visit New Orleans, so it all comes tumbling down on me at the same time."

"She'll grow out of it - or into it. Not quite sure what the correct phrase should be."

As Jefferson was settling up the bill he flourished, "Enough, enough. Please, let's talk about something else. Something nice, and charming, and pleasant." He shook his head and sighed. He reached over and took her hand. "Now you - tell me all about *your* delightful journeys. I've missed you so very much."

"Ah, journeys.....well, there's a landscape I would love for you to explore with me, but that adventure will probably need to be undertaken when we get back to the cabin. I could go on all evening about *that* delicious journey."

"I'm certain we can commence that journey later. I want to explore it all too. You know how I love to travel."

The next morning over breakfast Jefferson asked Connye if she wanted to go for a little hike. That sounded pleasant so they set out on one of the well-marked trails near the cabin.

Now Connye was no longer that lithe, little Louisiana bayou girl who had wrestled alligators as a kid, and these days physical activity rated with her right up there with ingesting toxic waste, so she was hoping the hike would be short. She was already imagining, upon their return to the cabin, a freshly made pineapple and strawberry smoothie to calm the nerves and serve as a fortifying tonic, when Jefferson suggested they stop to admire the view. She quite readily agreed. A fallen tree served as their bench and they paused to take in the snowcapped mountains, the valley below, the river, and the fresh morning air.

"My darling, Connye," Jefferson began.

Always a good beginning, Connye thought.

"I suppose you wonder why I wanted to talk with you."

"It's all I've been thinking about since you called. And it was all I could do to keep my mouth shut last night. I'm usually not one to hold back when I want to ask a question – as you know. But I've also learned not to push you."

Jefferson smiled. "Yes. I appreciate that. Thank you. But now that the father's gone I thought we should re-examine our living situation."

"I was both hoping and dreading that might be what it was."

He took her hand. "I'd like to hear what your feelings are first. I know we both agree marriage is not right for us, but we've also discussed ways we might spend more time together. I'd like to know what you feel about that right now – today."

Connye thought for a moment. "Well, since you ask.... I know you have your wonderful home and business there in Augusta, but I was also exploring the idea that since Santa Fe is such a thriving art market you might consider relocating your business to Santa Fe. My lovely home is big enough for the both of us, and then we could be together full time. Sophie could, of course, come visit us anytime – since she resides with her mother anyway." She paused. "What do you think about that idea?"

Jefferson considered, then said, "I was thinking along similar lines, but to be honest I'm not sure I'm quite ready to give up the family home and entirely move my business to Santa Fe. But here's my idea. Let me open a satellite office of the business in Santa Fe: I still have too many clients in Georgia to abandon them entirely. And as for the house well, I would be willing to sell it eventually, if I could get the right price. But instead of moving in with you I suggest you sell your house and let's buy a new house together. I have a feeling I would be swallowed up in your identity if I just moved in with you."

Connye was momentarily speechless. "Oh my.... Sell my house?"

"If we bought one together it would reflect the both of us and we could furnish it together with the furnishings we both already own."

Connye had not contemplated this. "I don't know. I'd have to think about it. That's a big decision."

"Yes, but me moving to Santa Fe and leaving behind my life is also a big decision. Would it not be fairer if we both shared in that journey?"

Connye shivered. "Oh Jefferson...."

They sat for a moment in silence, each lost in their own thoughts, concerns, and feelings.

"You drive a hard bargain, buster."

"Or maybe what we have right now is best. Just think about it."

Connye laughed. "I doubt I'll be doing much of anything else."

◘   ◘   ◘

Bella was greatly disturbed. She had not heard from Chetworth and had no way to reach him. She was troubled to be still holding that damn envelope in her safe and was thinking she might have to contact some authority or other. The police? The FBI? The CIA? She had no idea.

Finally on the morning of the fourth day, and still not having heard from anyone, she decided she needed to open the envelope and see what was inside. Sitting at her desk she carefully slit the seal with a knife and pulled out the papers.

Laying them out on her desk she examined the first - a folded blueprint. She opened it up and studied it. It contained schematic drawings of several buildings. The names of the buildings had been blacked out, but from what little knowledge she knew of architectural drawings she understood them to be industrial buildings. One small section at the upper left corner had been marked out, but faintly, and she could make out the words "Los Alamos" underneath the marking. She remembered Chetworth had told her this was connected with national security and she immediately thought of the Los Alamos National Laboratory – the nuclear weapons lab where plutonium pits for atomic bombs were manufactured or reprocessed. She wasn't sure which. Now *that* certainly qualified as national security.

She refolded the drawings and looked at the next document. This was even more puzzling to her. It was a series of copied photographs containing a vast array of mathematical formulas. Some of the photos were of a long series of formulas from a blackboard. Others were of hand written documents and a few were from what looked like a three ring binder. She surmised they were from Los Alamos as well. This was serious business.

She quickly placed the documents back into the envelope and returned it to the safe and locked it securely. She was really pissed off with Chetworth. His imposition on her life really annoyed her, so she decided to just ignore the whole mess and put it out of her mind.

And she had no *time* for this crazy business either, as she was preparing for her gala reception at the opera. Today she was to pick up the gigantic poster-board mockup of the check she was going to present to the Opera for the new addition. She also needed a new dress for the occasion. And it was time to have her squirrel's nest of hair tended to; and because she was new to town, she was still searching for just the right hair-dresser. So much to do. Yes, preparation for the gala must now command her whole attention.

◘   ◘   ◘

"Lionel, I can't possibly attend," Sonora firmly announced.

"And why ever not?" he demanded.

"Because, my dear, you have scheduled your little party the very same night as the opera gala."

"Oh well, that…. You can skip that, surely."

"I am on the opera board, as you know. Even if I wanted to, and believe me nothing would please me more, I just *must* make a showing."

"Oh bother. Really…. What time is this lavish event, and how long is it likely to last?"

"It starts at eight o'clock - and heaven knows what Mrs. H-C has planned. My guess is it will go to at least midnight."

"Well could you breakaway early? I could postpone the performance till ten. Could you make that?" Lionel was desperately trying to salvage his blunder.

"I can certainly try."

"And gather the rest of the fold as you leave. I want so much for everyone to see the lovely work I've done." Lionel sounded on the edge of tears.

Sonora's firmness melted a tiny bit. "Yes. I'll see what I can do - but I think we'll probably be able to make it."

"So grateful." He hung up. Lionel was emotional because this project had become so important to him. He realized this might be his last great achievement - his swan song. He simply didn't have the stamina he used to have. Everything was such an effort now. And he just couldn't contemplate not sharing this with Sonora and his dear friends.

However, Lionel was now late for his appointment with Pinky at the club. They were going to have a final dress rehearsal with full costumes and lights. He gathered his sewing box, and a few last minute articles of clothing, and headed out the door.

The club smelled of stale beer. Nothing seemed more forlorn than an empty club in daylight. The black walls oppressed. The floor and carpet were sticky, and all that could be heard was the hum of the ice maker from behind the bar – no music, no gaiety.

Lionel worked this way through the club towards the dressing rooms. Norman, the stage manager and lighting designer, was up a ladder on the small stage fussing with the lights. Lionel nodded to him as he passed.

As Lionel approached Pinky's dressing room he could hear Pinky in a very masculine voice talking on his phone.

"It's just not that easy....the Senator met briefly one evening with some old hag for dinner but then he just disappeared....I've been investigating...." Pinky saw Lionel standing in the doorway of the dressing room. He returned to the phone, "Oh darling, you are just too much....let me know if you *ever* get rid of that bitch, then we can talk. Kiss, kiss, bye, bye." He closed the phone. "Lionel, are you here to make me absolutely *fabulous?*"

◘   ◘   ◘

When Bella returned to the house, her hair all done up for the gala event, Rene was upset.

"Is something wrong?" Bella asked.

Rene was twisting the kitchen towel in her hands. "Some man has been calling all morning. I ask him what he wants and he says he'll only speak to you. He's been calling like every fifteen minutes and has become very rude. I stopped answering the phone."

"I'll take care of it. Did he leave a number?"

"No ma'am and his caller ID is blocked."

Bella was not going to have any of this bullying. Whoever it was would soon be dealt with when he called again. They obviously did not know who they were dealing with. She absolutely would not put up with the shady shenanigans of some aggressive telemarketer.

Bella went to her room to lay out her new dress for the gala. She then went to her office and opened the safe to select her jewelry for the evening. There was that damned envelope. She had almost forgotten about it in the preparations for the opera gala. She picked it up. She was tempted to consign it to her document shredder – and good riddance. Then the phone rang. Oh, that pest, no doubt. She answered.

"Bella Harrington-Crenshaw, and who is this?" She saw the blocked caller ID.

There was a moment of silence. "You have something of mine," a hollow voice spoke.

"How did you get this number?" Bella demanded.

"Unimportant. You were to deliver an envelope from Senator Spangler. Where were you?"

"Where were you? I was there, exactly where instructed."

"What time?"

"Eleven o'clock."

"It was to be at one o'clock. Why did you leave?"

"Did you think I was going to hang around all afternoon when I was told to meet at eleven?"

"I need that envelope. Where is it now?"

"Don't think I care to reveal that. How do I know who you are? I think I need to speak to the Senator first, but I don't know how to reach him. Do you have his number? If I can confirm with him who you are then you can have it."

Again there was a long pause. "The Senator is unavailable."

"Then I have nothing more to say to you."

"Don't…"

Bella hung up the phone. She was furious. She threw the envelope back in the safe and locked it once again. Now she would turn her full attention to her splendid evening.

◘   ◘   ◘

Connye answered her phone.

"Oh Connye, I'm so pleased to finally reach you. Been calling for ages," Sonora cheered.

"Been out of town - a little romantic adventure with Jefferson at Jackson Hole."

"How charming."

"I assume I will be seeing you this evening at the gala?" Connye asked.

"You will, and that's the reason I'm calling. Lionel is hosting a special little surprise party at the Carousel Club this evening. And silly boy never bothered to check with me first. So he has scheduled his little event the same evening as the gala."

"That's unfortunate."

"It is, but we're working around it. I've rounded up an intimate few, and we are going to bolt the gala early and trot on over to Lionel's little event. Was so hoping you might join us."

"And just what is this little event?"

"Lionel has asked me to keep it a surprise. But I assure you it will thrill and delight."

"Well, how can I possibly miss out on that?" Of course, I'll be there."

After the conversation with Sonora, Connye stood at her desk lost in thought. She was not at all settled. She had barely slept since she returned from her trip.   Jefferson's little bombshell about selling her house had shocked and unnerved her. She could certainly understand his reasoning, but she had been surprised by how deeply it had affected her. Sell her house? But what about all her art? And how could they possibly co-mingle their furnishings?   How would Jefferson's southern antebellum antiques go with her ultra-modern furniture? And what he said about losing his identity if he moved in with her was certainly a valid point. Just as she was feeling she would lose her identity if she sold her house and had to merge her art with his.

This was not going to be an easy decision and demanded a raisin oatmeal cookie for immediate comfort and food for thought.

◘   ◘   ◘

Bella had heard about some of the lavish and stylish parties given by the Santa Fe elate, and not to be out done, arranged for a stunning performance of opera selections performed by the opera apprentices. She personally knew this season's orchestra leader, and had arranged with him to put together the ensemble for this presentation. He had rehearsed them and assured her it would be a splendid performance. The food had been superbly catered and just required her presence to make the evening complete.

Bella had contemplated inviting a male escort, but still being new to the Santa Fe scene, knew of no suitable single gentlemen. And besides, who could possibly be up to her standards - one who would complement but not compete with her. No, much better to shine on her own.

Her driver was ready for her at eight-thirty. She slipped into the back seat and they left for the opera without a word. Just down the street from the gate to her estate a car waited. When her car left the compound the second car started up and followed with headlights off until they reached the main road to town, then turning on the lights, the car followed Bella all the way to the opera.

Honey and Olivia had come together, and arrived early, so as to avoid running into Bella. They scampered to the buffet and bar, loaded up, and retreated to the backstage area to enjoy their food undisturbed, but had to be scooted off a set piece where they were sitting by the stage manager.

As they lived close together, Sonora had offered to take Connye in the limo she had hired to shuttle Lionel's guests from the opera to the club. It would facilitate a quicker get-a-way, and would eliminate the need to find downtown parking. Often referred to as the dynamic duo, their arrival immediately sparked the party and set the standard and tone for the evening.

Ruth, as president of the opera board and her husband, Howard, waited to greet Bella. As Bella's car pulled up, Ruth stepped forward and waited as Bella emerged from the car.

"Oh, Mrs. Harrington-Crenshaw, what a delight to welcome you on this glorious occasion."

Bella nodded, not comfortable with such effusive greetings. "My driver has the presentation check in the trunk. Perhaps you might have someone who can take it from him?"

"Of course," Ruth cooed. She relegated that task to poor Howard.

"Everybody, but just *everybody* is here for the presentation. I can't possibly thank you enough again for your gloriously generous gift." Ruth could just not let go.

Bella was missing the New York scene where acceptance was more modestly modulated. "I assume everything is in order and the evening is well under way?"

"Oh yes, my dear, everything is splendid, and the entertainment I assure you is going to be sensational."

"So glad to hear it." Bella marched ahead onto the stage, out distancing Ruth. Howard struggled with the presentation check, lugging it backstage.

The plan for the evening was to have a time of social mingling with plenty of food and drink. Then Bella would present the check, followed by the entertainment. Bella had purposely arrived late. And indeed, the effect of her arrival galvanized the guests. A hush fell over the crowd as she swept in. Now, Bella did not have a great deal of physical charm to work with, but she certainly knew how to dress for maximum effect. And this evening she was wearing a rose and deep fuchsia layered gown with a blood red lace trim and ribbons of patterned fabric, slit down the left side showing a deep burgundy stockinged leg. She definitely knew how to make an entrance. And she carried it off while taking no notice of the effect she was having – or at least, giving that impression.

Connye and Sonora, who were sampling the culinary delights, actually paused in their conversation.

"That can't be Mrs. H-C, can it?" Connye asked in astonishment.

Sonora peered in silence but for a brief moment. "She looks like a lavish Balkan wedding cake. What *was* she thinking?"

"Well actually, I think she carries it off quite well. Not everyone could wear something like that," Roberta observed.

"My Gawd, looks like the Lord has come in all his raiment and glory - must be judgment day," Brenda brayed as she balanced her plate *and* the Contessa in both arms.

Sonora and Connye chuckled. Sonora responded, "Brenda, my dear, you certainly have a way with words. I think you've captured the scene exactly."

Bella spotted the Sonora/Connye group and glided over like a pink regatta. "Darling ladies, I so fondly recall your lovely welcoming party. So pleased you could attend this evening."

"All our pleasure," Connye replied.

"And what a wonderful reason to celebrate. Just imagine the exuberant costumes just flowing out of the new costume shop," Sonora added, eyeing Bella's gown. "Such a lovely frock. You must tell me your designer. I don't believe I have *ever* seen such a creation."

Bella caught the insinuation in Sonora's remark. "I would, but she is *very* exclusive. She doesn't design for just *anyone*. However, I could give her a call, if you like, and she *might* be able to fit you in - with my recommendation."

"Yes. Next time I need something like *that* I will give you a call."

 Both smiled sweetly at each other and Bella wandered away towards another group of opera worshipers. But she was interrupted by a single, hard looking woman who took her arm and physically stopped her. Bella gave the woman a searing glare.

"Excuse me," Bella exclaimed, as she pulled free of the woman's grasp.

"We need to chat," the woman said quietly, almost whispering.

"Who are you?" Bella asked, with some suspicion.

"A colleague of Senator Spangler."

That certainly caught Bella's attention. "Oh really? Then perhaps you can tell me how I can reach him. It's somewhat urgent."

"The Senator wishes you to comply with his original request. I believe you have a certain envelope which failed to be delivered as agreed."

Bella stared at the woman. "This is neither the time nor the place for this conversation."

"Next time we call don't hang up. If this matter is not resolved tomorrow there will be consequences." The woman turned and disappeared into the guests. Bella did not see her again that evening.

Now Bella is not easily ruffled, but this certainly shook her. That the woman should accost her on her own turf was truly unsettling.

Ruth came up to Bella. "It's nine-thirty, that's when you wanted to perform the presentation ceremony, wasn't it?"

Bella was still unnerved. "Ah, yes. Yes. The presentation. I think we should get that underway now." Bella looked about, but could not see the strange woman in the crowd.

Meantime, Sonora was gathering the group together that was to be off soon for Lionel's little show. "I certainly thought the presentation of the gift would have happened by now. I hate to leave before, but Lionel begged us to be at the club by ten."

Roberta saw that Ruth was conferring with Bella. "I think they're getting ready now. Can we wait just ten more minutes?"

Sonora sighed and checked her watch. "Okay then, ten minutes, but then we really must scoot."

Back stage, Howard fumbled with the awkward presentation check. Ruth consulted her notes and Bella paced. Finally Ruth gave the signal, and taking the microphone from the stage manager, walked out with Howard and Bella onto the stage and into the spotlight.

Sonora again checked her watch. It was nine-thirty-five. She was becoming anxious. She knew the limo would be waiting, and while it shouldn't take that long to whisk downtown, they would have to leave within ten minutes.

Ruth was unsure how to turn on the microphone. The stage manager came out and turned it on. Ruth welcomed everyone and began a recitation about the opera and the history of music in Santa Fe.

Sonora could clearly see they would have to leave before the actual presentation of the check. She signaled to the group headed for the club and they tried to sneak out as inconspicuously as possible. But Bella saw. And she was furious. To be snubbed like this was inexcusable to her. She was not likely to soon forget.

◘   ◘   ◘

Lionel was pacing in front of the club. He had reserved two tables for the opera ladies. It was already ten. Sonora had *absolutely* promised to be seated at ten and ready for the show. Poor Pinky was nervous enough. He had worked himself up to performance pitch, and every moment of delay would begin to deflate his sparkle.

Finally, Lionel spied the limousine speeding down the block and screeching to a halt before the club. Lionel opened the doors and the ladies exited in a flurry of fine dresses.

Finally with the ladies settled in at their tables, and drinks being ordered, Lionel went back stage to prepare Pinky for the start of the show. Lionel entered the dressing room and Pinky, without his wig, had his head down on the dressing table banging his forehead repeatedly.

"I can't do it. I just can't," Pinky cried.

"Oh no, you don't," Lionel scolded. "Not after all the work I've put into making you a stunning but grouchy diva. There is no way you are not going out there to show off these marvelous costumes. You can groan, you can moan, and fall flat on your face for all I care, but my friends are out there, and they are going to see just how fabulous *I* can be. Capiche? Now, let me help you with this wig." Lionel took the wig and began fitting it on Pinky's shiny bald head.

"I ca-a-a-n't. I look like one of those pathetic ballerina hippos in Fantasia."

"Don't be ridiculous. There." Lionel completed fitting the wig. He took Pinky by the hand and led him to the wings. "Now, go out there and be so swell you'll make me hate you."

"42nd Street," Pinky laughed, touching Lionel on the nose.

"Correct. Now you're going out a frump but ya gotta come back a star." Lionel pushed Pinky towards the edge of the stage.

The stage manager cued the music and out went Bella Le Balle, microphone in hand, blasting out an Ethel Merman classic. Lionel dashed into the club and sat with the adoring ladies.

The drag Bella wowed. She pirouetted, she pranced, she belted out Streisand, Midler, Tucker, and even a few more Merman ditties, all in a series of magnificent costumes – worthy of any star. The crowd roared at the end. Bella bowed, cried, and took eight curtain calls. A new star was born. And Lionel knew *he* was the one who *really* deserved the bow.

Shall We Dance?

Sonora loved her gracious social life. She delighted in attending and giving parties. She adored her lavish and comfortable home which had been featured in a fine edition, coffee table book – <u>Romantic Houses and Gardens of Santa Fe</u>. She relished her charities and, of course, she was enchanted with her financial involvement in Roberta's wonderful shop – Pie in the Sky – but that hardly took up any time at all. These aspects of her life were very satisfying – but they were not *quite* enough. She still longed for a purely creative outlet.

Was it only last year Sonora imagined she would become an Academy Award winning screenwriter? Oh my. That certainly didn't work out too well, did it? She struggled for weeks, like an agonizing Kerouac, and achieved but a paltry 27 pages of drivel. But she had *so* built up excitement about her little hobby amongst the coffee crowd that she just could not admit failure and defeat. So she had bought a screenplay from a screenwriter friend of Lionel's, passing it off as her own; but when Connye found her a producer, and he requested rewrites, she was at a complete loss until she lassoed her buddy Quinto into completing it for her. It had been a fair success, launched Quinto as a screenwriter, but left her feeling empty and flat. The accomplishment was hers, but not the achievement.

So what to do? Before she married, she had been a very talented young dancer with the New York City Ballet. After her marriage to a very successful and wealthy businessman she left dance to concentrate on raising money for the arts, and particularly dance. And her interest in dance never waned.

She had attended a few dance concerts produced by local, semi-professional groups in Santa Fe, but they all left her unsatisfied and wanting more. Of course, she could go to New York City at any time, stay in her lovely art studio apartment, and gorge herself on all the dance, theatre, and art exhibits she wanted. But she longed for something of that quality here in Santa Fe.

What had recently captured her imagination was the idea of owning her own professional dance company. She would search the country, find just the right company with a stunningly talented artistic director, and invite them to relocate to Santa Fe – with her blessing, direction, and, of course, her money.

And ah, the joys of the internet. She had done a very thorough and exhaustive online search and had narrowed down her choice of companies to ten. She was looking for a group with eight to ten dancers and a genius choreographer/artistic director.

She approached all ten companies by letter, email, and telephone. Six of the companies expressed no interest in relocating, leaving her with just four possibilities. She had taken secret little weekend jaunts to check out each company. She had told none of her friends what she was doing, and had not notified the companies she was coming to visit. She wanted a clear unvarnished appraisal of each company with no special preparations or overly eager welcomes. She wanted to remain completely anonymous until she had made up her mind.

Of the four groups she thought only two were suitable. The first was a group in Orlando, Florida, run by a young black woman who had become known for what she called Kinetic

Kinesis. Sonora had no idea what that meant, but it sounded perfectly profound.

The second group was from Casper, Wyoming. (Who in the world went to dance in Wyoming?) And this group was led by a hot young choreographer who had catapulted to fame by winning several dance expositions with something he called Etheric Dance. Again Sonora had no idea what this was about, but was willing to give it a view.

Her first exposure to these companies was brief, giving her an overall impression of the group's excellence. But now she needed to go in depth – meet the company, get to know the artistic director, discuss their serious interest in relocating, negotiate terms, and finally strike a deal. This week she had booked a flight to Orlando. She planned to spend an entire week getting to know the company, seeing performances, and finding out all about Kinetic Kinesis.

Sonora had invited Roberta to accompany her. Pie was sufficiently staffed and managed so it was easy for Roberta to get away now. She was thrilled for a jaunt, and spent an entire day packing and repacking. They were to leave first thing in the morning and were booked to see that night's performance.

◻   ◻   ◻

Bella was grumpy. While her opera event had been a success, she was troubled by meeting that strange woman who threatened her, and was still upset with the group of ladies who had stormed out during her presentation of the check. What can that have been all about? Certainly Sonora had been bitchy about Bella's dress, but that can hardly have been the reason for the mass exit.

But she was not going to let any of this spoil her breakfast. She had a wonderful sunny conservatory just off the dining room where she liked to sit back, relax, enjoy the morning, and have her café au lait and croissant with gooseberry jam and clotted cream. She shook out the newspaper, preparing to catch up on the news and search for any mention of last night's event.

There. There it was – a charming article with color photos about her grant to the opera for construction of their new costume shop. Glowing, glowing - just glowing. She put the page aside to snip out the article to add to her scrapbook. But she was stunned when she turned to the front page and saw the name Chetworth Spangler in a headline. It seems the Senator suffered an apparent massive heart attack and died in his senate chambers. Of course, she was devastated at the Senator's passing, but she was also instantly suspicious. A heart attack? Truly? She thought not. There was far too much suspicion around the delivery of that confounded envelope. Was the Senator wrapped up in some intrigue? Some scandal? Had he been secretly assassinated? And, of course, she immediately feared for her own safety.

Leaving her breakfast untouched she scurried to her office, opened the safe, and took out the envelope. She needed to rid herself of this horrid envelope as soon as possible. She just wanted to hand it over to those thugs and be done with it. But then it occurred to her that she had a civic duty to deal with this correctly. After all, a crime may have been committed in securing those papers, and then there was the death of the Senator. No. She needed to contact the FBI. They could take possession of the papers and provide her with security.

She hastily called the FBI offices in Albuquerque. She explained the whole situation to an officer there and requested immediate action and protection. The officer said an agent Matthews would be contacting her from Santa Fe shortly. They said she must not leave the house, and if she had any firearms to keep them handy until Matthews arrived. This terrified Bella no end, as the deadliest weapons she possessed were a kitchen knife and a fireplace poker.

She went to the kitchen, gathered Rene, explained the danger, and they sat at the kitchen table ready to wield chef knives, heavy bottomed pots, and a sharply pointed vegetable peeler.

◘   ◘   ◘

Lionel was thoroughly exhausted after his club debut. He slept till eleven, took a very long, hot soaking bath, and treated himself to brunch at the Chamisa Springs club house. And, for later, he was planning a haircut, a manicure, a pedicure, and he might even splurge on a hot stone massage and seaweed wrap. Oh my, it was nice to have a "me" day.

Soaking in his tub before brunch, he ruminated on the joys of the past few weeks. How he had enjoyed his little project with Pinky. This led to thoughts of all the other wonderful projects he'd done throughout his career. Sonora had been after him for *ages* to complete the memoir he had started a few years back. He had tinkered with it on and off, but was unable to muster the punch and drive needed to complete it. Now, that might be changing. He had been so enlivened by Pinky's challenge he thought – yes, it was time to complete the manuscript. He had already had promises from several publishers that if he completed the memoir they would take a look at it. That would show Sonora. She was not the only creative talent in the bunch. He, too, had dreams. One day soon he saw himself seated at a small table autographing books to a long line of admiring readers stretching out the door of the bookstore. But he was roused from his day dreaming when he realized the bathwater had turned tepid.

◘   ◘   ◘

Back and forth. Back and forth. Poor Connye could just not settle the question in her mind about selling the house. Yes, yes, she wanted to spend more time with Jefferson. But to go through the rigors of selling the house, deciding what would be in a new house, packing, moving....   No, no, no - it was just too much to ask. Particularly when she already had *the* perfect house for the two of them. She just didn't understand why Jefferson couldn't see that.

Finally, it became clear to her she would have to refuse to sell her lovely home. If Jefferson wanted to move in with her that was just fine. If not, then they would have to continue their long distance relationship as it was. She had lived alone now for quite a few years. She was set in her ways, and she realized she just didn't want to share her life and accommodate all the compromises that living together would entail.

Resolute, she picked up the phone and called Jefferson.

"Jefferson, good morning," Connye sounded out in her commanding voice.

There was a slight pause Jefferson's end. "And good morning to you. You sound very determined about something today."

"Oh, I'm sorry. Didn't mean to sound unfriendly." She laughed. "It's just I've been wrestling with what we discussed."

"Yes. And?"

"Well, I've come to a decision and wanted to call right away while the iron was hot."

"Can't wait to hear." Jefferson was amused by Connye's determination.

"Well, my dear. I just don't feel right selling my house. Guess I'm just too attached to my life and my lifestyle. Don't really want to change it. Even for you. So sorry."

Jefferson laughed. "You know, my darling woman, I have come to the exact same conclusion."

Connye guffawed. "No, really?"

"Absolutely. I don't feel I can give up my home either. And the thought of relocating is just mind numbing. I think I would abhor Santa Fe. All that brown and turquoise. Would feel like I'm living in a cowboy movie. Too much John Wayne for this Georgia boy."

"Oh my darling, I am so glad."

"But that doesn't mean I don't want to visit. I quite like what we already have I've decided."

Connye added, "And, of course, I shall still visit *you* and spend all day on the veranda, rocking in the shade with a cool tall drink."

"Then I shall cancel my order for chaps and cowboy boots immediately," Jefferson joked.

"And I feel so good, think I'll go right out and buy myself another piece of art for my charming gallery."

◻   ◻   ◻

Bella's cell phone rang. She was terrified to answer, but took a deep breath and opened up the phone. "Yes?" She didn't want to commit much till she knew to whom she was speaking.

"Mrs. Harrington-Crenshaw, this is agent Matthews – FBI.

"Oh, I am so glad to hear from you. I have been frantic with worry. Where are you?"

"Just outside your gate. Wanted to call before I came to your door. May I come in?"

"Oh yes, please. I'll open the gate. Just a moment." She rushed to the front door and activated the gate opener. "Is it opening?"

"Yes, be right up."

Bella was so relieved. She stood at the front door peering through the little view window with the grill. She was not going to open the door till she was sure it was the agent.

Agent Matthews approached. He was nicely dressed in a dark suit, white shirt, and red tie. He knocked.

"May I see some identification, please," Bella asked through the view window.

"Of course." Matthews reached into his jacket and pulled out a folding identification wallet. He opened it and showed it to her. FBI in red letters flashed before her.

"Thank you." She unbolted the door and opened it.

The man pushed forward forcefully, knocking Bella off balance. He grabbed her and pinned her against the wall.

She screamed out, "Rene, the alarm!"

Matthews took out his gun and put it at her head, laughing. "My colleague disabled the alarm and your land line as soon as you opened the gate. Sorry, there is no way to reach anyone, once I take this." He wrenched Bella's cell phone from her, threw it on the floor and stomped on it till it was in pieces.

"How did you know I'd called the FBI?" Bella soured.

"Simple tap of your phones. We're not dummies, you know."

"What do you want?" Bella asked.

"The envelope, of course. Give me that and I'm out of here."

"It's in my office. This way." She was shaking as she led Matthews, or whoever he was, through the living room.

In her office she nervously rummaged through the stacks of papers on her desk, forgetting she had just taken the envelope out of the safe, placing it on top. She finally found it, and turned to Matthews and handed it to him with shaking hands.

"There. Now get out."

Matthews raised his hand with the gun and stuck her beside the head. She collapsed onto the floor, and he fled the house.

In the meantime, Rene had *her* cell phone and had called the police about the break in. She hid herself in the utility closet behind the H/C unit and waited until she heard the sirens before peeking out.

◘   ◘   ◘

On the flight out to Orlando Sonora cautioned Roberta, once again, not to tell any of the coffee group about the reason for her trip to Florida. No one was to know she was searching to buy a dance company. The flight also allowed the two of them to *finally* conclude the discussion about the franchise offer for Pie. Sonora was all for it. She could turn over the business management of Pie to the franchise operators and then just rake in the profits. And Roberta was finally satisfied when Sonora explained that Roberta would not lose control over her direction of the company. It was nice for both of them. Sonora's investment had paid off well, and Roberta was secure in the fulfillment of her little dream.

Sonora had provided Roberta with her own hotel room; for as much as Sonora cherished the dear dumpling, Sonora also cherished her solitude and privacy. No sharing rooms for her. Sonora was luxuriating on her Orlando hotel balcony - bathed, lotioned, and sipping a glass from a split of Champaign. There was a warm breeze, and the sun was low on the horizon. A wild parrot screeched by and landed in a palm tree by the pool. Yes, this was very nice. Sonora had invited Roberta to join her for a drink before dinner, and letting herself in the room, Roberta came out to the balcony all squeaky with excitement at being in Florida for the first time.

Sonora poured Roberta a glass of Champaign.

"Please sit if you like," Sonora offered.

"Oh, isn't this just dandy," Roberta exclaimed, enchanted with the view, the weather, and the adventure of it all.

After a moment's silence, while Sonora observed Roberta's rapture, she asked, "Are you going to be okay for a week here on your own? You know I'll have to spend most of my time with the dance company."

"Oh yes, I'm going to explore absolutely everything at Disney and Universal, and there's the beautiful pool, and I'm going to catch up on all my reading, and there are walks, and all this wonderful, luscious weather…."

"But remember we are no longer in Santa Fe, it might well rain here at any time."

"Oh, that would be wonderful too." Roberta looked at Sonora with such gratitude. "Thank you so much for inviting me along. I'd never do something like this on my own."

"But don't you travel with your husband?"

"Oh no, he's not inclined to travel. A real stay at home kinda guy."

"Well, I'm glad you could join me. And I hope you'll enjoy the dance concert this evening."

Roberta clapped her hands. "Oh yes, such a treat."

◻   ◻   ◻

Finally the police were gone after investigating the assault. The Matthews who was the *real* FBI agent had come, done his investigation, and gone. And Bella had managed to calm down Rene enough so that, at last, the house was quiet once again. Bella had a lump on her head from the blow that thug had inflicted, but an ice pack was helping with the swelling. But at least she was rid of that dreadful envelope.

Bella's first thought was for the Senator. She had been unable to give much thought to his death with all the recent turmoil. His funeral was to be held in Minnesota rather than Washington. The Senator and her father having been so close, she contemplated attending the funeral. But quite honestly he did not mean that much to her personally, and she was so angry at him for having embroiled her in this mess with the envelope. No, she would send flowers instead.

She was desperate now for something meaningful to distract her form the recent events. It had left a decidedly bad taste in her mouth and she wanted to cleanse her palette with something equivalent to a lemon sorbet. She needed a new interest. She wandered about the house contemplating her next project.

Since she had moved into the new house she had not given much thought to the décor. She had moved her east coast furniture and fittings, and settled in with those. But none of it seemed appropriate to the southwest themed architecture. That was it - she would redecorate.

She rushed to her office and dug out her address book. She knew just the person to handle the task – the Principessa Angelica Castelerri, an old friend from Bella's Washington DC days.

The Principessa was from an ancient Italian, aristocratic family whose lands were once adjacent to Perguia. However, a syphilitic great grandfather, and a cross-dressing grandmother, parading around the countryside as a *generale di corpo d'armata*, soon bankrupt the family, as they paid no attention, what-so-ever, to the maintenance of the family fortune, and it soon withered away along with their fertile valley estate that eventually became the property of Mafioso loan sharks.

The poor Principessa quickly immigrated to the United States, where she applied her aristocratic sense of fashion and design, and her amiable social qualities and connections to establishing a thriving interior design business, serving the often ephemeral politicians coming and going from the nation's capital. A sexual or financial scandal could clear out a Georgetown house faster than an EF5 tornado. And, of course, new tenants were always ripe pickings to employ her services.

Bella picked up her phone and dialed.

"Castelerri."

"Angelica, it's Bella."

"Bella? Where are you? Haven't heard from you for ages."

"I've moved to Santa Fe."

"Oh my, such recklessness. I hope you are sufficiently fortified from the encircling hordes. Wouldn't want you to be impaled with sharp arrow-like objects. "

"My darling, Angelica, you have a very outdated view of the American west. Santa Fe is a bustling, sophisticated, and thriving art community. No hordes here – except for the occasional flush of summer tourists."

"I am so relieved. I had visions of you being strung up with rawhide by your tits in the hot sun over a colony of fire ants."

"No, my darling, pleasant as that sounds, you've seen far too many trashy movies, or read too many cheap novels."

"So, what can I do for you today? Or is this just a social call?" Angelica asked, wanting to get on with her busy day.

"No, no. I need your services. I've bought this charming estate in north Santa Fe. Southwestern design, but all my furnishings are just *wrong*. I need a complete make-over."

"You or the house?" Angelica joked."

"Now, now. The house, of course. I am perfect just as I am."

"Of course, you are."

"What is your schedule? I want to get on with this as soon as possible."

Angelica checked her calendar. "I could come out the weekend of the 20th for a few days to inspect the property and go over details with you."

"Splendid, I will wire transfer a sum as a retainer and for expenses to your account straight away."

"Any idea what you might be looking for?" Angelica asked.

"I don't want any of that usual Santa Fe style crap. I want new. I want contemporary - but with lots of color and swirl."

"Let me review my publications and I will bring some ideas along. I will, of course, want to take measurements while I am out there."

"Splendid, I will have my driver meet you. You can stay here at the house in my splendid guest room with your very own private garden. See you on the 20th."

"Charmed. Such a treat."

There, that was certainly a good start. But Bella was still restless, and the fumes of this horrible event still lingered in the air. She needed something more. Her head hurt and she had bruised a hip and shoulder when she fell after Matthew's assault. Ah, a long soothing soak in her hot tub and then a massage. She called her masseuse and made arrangements for her to be here at eleven.

As Bella soaked, she contemplated her time thus far in Santa Fe. What a strange few months it had been. She was a little ashamed of her behavior towards Honey Trapp, who, as it turns out, is one of the *group to know*. However, she did save quite a bundle on the transactions, and in the end that made it worthwhile. Honey would get over it eventually, Bella figured.

And her opera event had been tremendously successful. Tons of publicity and good will in the community, despite the flight of those few women. What was that all about? But Bella also realized she had not made any intimate friends yet. Acquaintances, but not any real friends. This gave her thought.

Of all the ladies she had met thus far that Connye Andreatos seemed the most promising candidate. Yes, she decided to give her a call later that afternoon and invite her to a luncheon. She could pick her brain about the other ladies in the group, and at the same time solicit advice about her redecorating.

Bella slid further down into the Jacuzzi, sighed, and closed her eyes.

◘   ◘   ◘

Roberta, as her first adventure, arranged to take the hotel shuttle to Disney World. She was to spend the whole day there. Sonora was scheduled to meet with the young choreographer at ten. That gave her time for a leisurely breakfast, a facial, and perhaps a swim in the hotel pool. She stretched out under the covers, but was unable to will herself to get out of bed just yet. She patted the bed to summon her little impish dog, IT - but then remembered she was not at home. Oh well, then, best to just get up. Anyway, she needed to review the notes from her first trip to the dance company. She wanted to make sure she knew what questions she wanted to ask.

After bathing and dressing Sonora wandered leisurely down to the dining room for the breakfast buffet. She found a table she liked overlooking a jungled water feature, ordered her coffee and a papaya-mango-pineapple juice, and headed to the buffet table.

Let's see, what looked good today? The scrambled eggs looked over cooked and dried out. The waffles looked soggy, but the fresh fruit was inviting, and a chef was available to make omelets to order. A Spanish omelet with a side of bacon would just do the trick.

Sonora was spooning the fresh fruit salad into a bowl and topping it with yogurt and granola when she was jostled from behind. Indignantly, she turned. "Excuse me," she pronounced in her most offended manner, as she turned to confront the jostler.

"I'm so sorry," a kindly voice answered.

"Oz?" Sonora gasped.

"Sonora?" the man responded.

Oz and Sonora had an intriguing history. Both were in the same social circle in New York City. And both were married – but not to each other. Just recently, when Sonora was back in her apartment in New York she picked up a book with a mysterious, unopened letter as a bookmark. Upon reading it, she learned that many years ago, before Sonora moved to Santa Fe after her husband's death, Oz had left her a love letter which she, up until then, had never opened.

She was intrigued and interested, and contacted Oz to discuss his proposal. However, many years had passed since he had originally placed the letter in her book, and he had moved on and was now involved with another woman, the charming and fiery Melissa. Time and opportunity had passed them both by, and Sonora had felt a sadness and longing she couldn't explain.

"What are you doing here?" They both asked each other at the same time.

Laughing, Sonora responded, "I'm here to check out a dance company I'm thinking about bringing to Santa Fe. And you?"

"Grand kids, can you believe? Giving my daughter a break. Three days at Disney World with two kids are enough to fry all living brain cells of anyone over thirty."

Sonora looked around, "Where are they?"

Oh, out at the pool. Bribed a life guard to rein them in. A brief moment of peace and quiet," he said.

"And Melissa, is she with you?"

"Sadly, we're not together anymore. She ran off with a bar tender in Key West when we were there for the winter months."

Sonora was very adept at masking her true reaction to that bit of news. "Oh, I am sorry to hear that."

"Well...." He shrugged.

Sonora suddenly realized they were standing in the way of others at the buffet. "Are you seated yet? My table's right over there. Will you join me? Would love to catch up."

"Certainly."

While they were getting seated Sonora took a good long look at the still very handsome Oz. Tall, lean, tan, and with short cropped white hair, a gracious smile, and piercing, ice-blue eyes - one could tell nothing escaped his attentive gaze.

"Tell me, I never knew – your name? Is it short for Oswald?"

He laughed. "No. Not at all. My real name is Anthony, but when I was about seven, I think it was, I was given a wizard play set for Christmas. I danced around in my cape, casting spells with my magic wand, and was nicknamed Oz – as in Wizard of. It just sorta stuck - thus Oz."

"Charming.

"I just can't believe I ran into you like this. What are the chances?"

"There must be a reason," Sonora added, shyly.

"Yes, there must."

They both stared at each other, unable to ask the burning questions.

Sonora finally broke the spell, "So how is your lovely boat? Is it still your pride and joy?"

Oz hesitated briefly, "Sold it."

"Really? You seemed so comfortable and content on it. And you were writing a book about your adventures, I believe.... So have you taken an apartment or something in New York?"

Oz sighed. It was getting perilously close to truth time. "No, I'm leaving New York. I'm moving."

"That so? And where might that be?"

"Santa Fe."

◘   ◘   ◘

Pinky was between shows at the club. His act had been a huge hit. Patrons packed the club whenever he was performing - which was but three nights a week. He was seated at an out of the way, dark table near the back of the bar. He still wore his stage make-up, but was wearing his street clothes. A man came over and sat at his table without announcing himself.

"I would hardly call all of this keeping a low profile," the man said sharply, waving and indicating the club.

Pinky shrugged. "Yeah, but it sure as hell is a great cover. Nobody would ever suspect."

"It better be."

Pinky leaned in closer. "And what about that little incident with the Harrington-Crenshaw woman? You guys kinda screwed up on that one, didn't ya? You are hardly one to question my accomplishments."

"Yeah, and just what *are* your accomplishments, anyway? Haven't seen dozens of useful dispatches pouring in from your post in any case."

"Hey bro, it takes some time working in deep cover. Can't just go parading around flashing badges like an obvious snoop, ya know."

"So what have ya got so far?"

"Well, this Bella character... complete innocent. Her connection to Spangler is a family thing. Her father and Spangler both worked for the company back in the good old days. Spangler was just asking her for a favor. She had no idea what the drop was all about."

"You sure about that?"

"Yep."

"And how did you find that out?"

"Been tapping information from that gal that works for her – Rene. Slip her a bill or two and she gives me all kinds of shit. Much more than I wanna know, I can tell ya."

"What else? Seems pretty thin so far."

"Been scouting a few suspicious dudes from LANL. Digging around their security. Looking for leaks. Gotta be very careful. Don't want to tip anyone off and send them scrambling for cover before we're ready to pounce."

The man sat back in his chair and took a good long look at Pinky. "What is all this shit?" he asked, indicating Pinky's make-up. "How did you come up with this as a cover?"

"Didn't. Was always doing this. I got recruited in LA. They needed a drag artist for some undercover drug operation in the gay community and came to me. Trained me. Deloused me. The whole big deal. And I've been doing it ever since. You think I can make a living doing this drag shit alone?"

"Damn. Never heard a story like that before."

"Yeah, every time I get a new assignment and have to move – boom, a new drag act." Pinky laughed, "And it's all tax deductible."

The man slapped his hands down on top of the table. "Okay. Gotta get outta this joint. Don't know how you can stand all this fag stuff."

"Hey, none of that kind of talk. We are a fully integrated and LGBT friendly agency now, remember?"

"Oh, crap." The man rose and turned to leave, but turned back. "Be careful, hey. Those scumbags don't take prisoners, ya know."

"As long as the agency has my back...."

◘   ◘   ◘

Sonora could barely focus on her task. Melanie Washington was ragging on about what Kinetic Kinesis was all about. Something about "Klinokinesis and the frequency or rate of turning being in proportion to stimulus intensity." What kind of horse pucky was that? Sonora thought. This was just not working for her. Melanie was a sweet, sincere, and very talented young woman, but oh my, this was not something that was going to go over well in Santa Fe. And on top of all that, the dances she had seen last night were just too much sunshine and oranges. Everything was geared to a sweetness and sentimentality that had not registered with her when she first visited the company. Why had she not seen this before? Had it not been evident then or had she been so stunned by Oz's announcement that the center of her balance had shifted and she was now in a different universe?

She was still digesting the shock of Oz's earlier announcement that he was moving to Santa Fe. That was like a hydrogen bomb in a tea cup. Her whole world had been shattered. All kinds of questions, longings, and complications had been stirred up by this announcement.

Sonora kindly thanked Melanie for her time and wished her all the best, but told her that her group was just not the right fit for Santa Fe.

Sonora left the studio and went back to the hotel. She had booked her stay for a full week, expecting to spend that much time at the studio, and here she was, already finished by the end of the second day. And then there was dear Roberta expecting her full week of fun in the sun. What to do? What to do?

First she needed to sort out some things with Oz. At their first meeting, after she had recovered from the initial shock of his announcement, she had asked, "Why are you moving to Santa Fe?"

"To be near you, of course," he answered. "I'm a free man now," he grinned like a freckled nine year old who'd just climbed to the top of the tallest tree in the back yard.

"I see," she said, still guarding herself, "And with what expectations?"

"To sweep you off your feet, and make you deliriously happy. Why else?"

"And work? You have plans?"

"Of course, I expect to live quite comfortably off of you and your fortune for the rest of my life."

She blanched and stuttered, "Ah... ah... well... "

He leaned forward, "Ki-i-i-d-d-ding. No, I am quite well taken care of, thank you very much. Discovered currency trading, and am solidity growing my quite comfortable little nest egg at home with my computer."

"And what makes you think I am at all interested in you?" she asked, with just the faintest hint of a smile.

"Sonora.....you have blushed six times and blanched four. I'm not blind, you know."

She laughed, and nodded her head slightly to the side. "Perceptive. And when exactly do you plan this move to Santa Fe?"

"I have a few loose ends in New York, but I expect to be in New Mexico by the end of the month."

"Do you have a place to live yet?"

"Well I was going to rent a condo, but that was before we met here. Do you have any other suggestions?"

That was when Sonora had to scurry off, already late for her meeting at the dance studio. They arranged to meet in the bar later that evening after the kids were asleep. There was still much to discuss.

And now back in her room she tossed off her shoes, opened a bottle of white wine from the mini bar, and collapsed onto a lounger on the balcony. First she would have to deal with Roberta. Best to let her stay on and enjoy her holiday, even if Sonora returned to Santa Fe tomorrow. Sonora hoped Roberta wouldn't pout because she was being left behind. Roberta often behaved like an abandoned puppy if she was left alone for too long. And as for Oz, well….time would just have to tell.

She thought briefly about Quinto - once quite important in her life. But he had moved on. He had a new life as a major writer and movie star in California. They barely spoke anymore, and she was more than certain he had a quite fulfilling romantic life - quite independent of her. But then there was the trip to France. She had invited him along and she would have to deal with that.

She was certainly infatuated with Mr. Oz, but she was also in no rush to jump into any relationship. And certainly she was not ready for him to move in with her. He would definitely need to find his own accommodation. But at the same time she found that she was open, expectant, and ready for whatever might develop.

Molto Bella

Connie responded favorably to Bella's invitation to lunch. While somewhat conflicted about Bella, (after Honey's terrible report of what Bella had done to her), she was also intrigued to find out more about her. Connye was curious to see if Bella had any ulterior motives in inviting her, and she also wanted to see Bella's house, which was one of the premier residences in Santa Fe, and one which Connye had never visited before.

While Connye expected to be the sole guest, she was surprised to find a second lady present when she was greeted by Bella.

"So pleased you could join us," Bella greeted, taking Connye's hand like a soft cloth. "This is the Principessa Angelica Castelerri, a dear friend of mine from DC, and she's about to completely redecorate my entire home."

"Charmed, so charmed," the Principessa dangled her hand towards Connye without actually offering it.

Connye responded by bowing slightly. She presented Bella with a colorful bouquet of flowers she had brought.

"How lovely." Bella called out, "Rene." The housekeeper came running. "For the table if you please."

"Madam." Rene took the flowers and scurried off.

The three ladies stood looking at one another. No one seemed motivated to speak first. Finally Bella asked Connye, "Would you care for a tour of the house?"

"Oh yes, I've always admired your estate whenever I was out this way. Never thought I would have the opportunity to actually see inside. Such a treat."

As they toured, Connye noted the heavy, stodgy furniture and the rather cluttered effect of the array of porcelain knick knacks; numerous silver picture frames with photographs of noted politicians, entertainment stars, and other assorted celebrities; and numerous glass balls, candy dishes, and heavy ashtrays. It gave the overall feeling of oppressiveness – rather like being in a cluttered old family home of many generations.

However, Connye was stunned by the dazzling array of Impressionist paintings – all originals. Now while Connye collected art – it was all contemporary. Some very nice and expensive pieces, but nothing to rival the value of these masterpieces which Connye could only imagine would be valued at many millions of dollars each.

"I see you admire my art," Bella observed.

"Yes, I'm a collector myself." Connye was lost in admiration. "But nothing quite like these."

"Yes, many were purchased by my family from the artists themselves. Picked up in Europe for a song back then. Was fortunate to have a grandfather with grand taste."

"Yes, to have been a fly on the wall for those transactions...."

Angelica wandered over, holding a cracker and cheese as if they were about to explode. "I do think we need to consider rotating the paintings, my dear Bella. There are so many. Keep most in storage and bring out a few at a time for display. Keeps everything fresh that way. And so much less clutter. More *molto bella.* Don't you agree?" She turned and wafted off without waiting for an answer.

Rene came forward, "Madam, lunch is ready now."

"Thank you, Rene. Shall we?" Bella directed Connye to follow her.

The dining room was so charming - light and airy, with the conservatory doors open to allow the scent of jasmine to waft through to the diners. Connye's flowers were arranged beautifully into several low arrangements along the table. Rene had prepared lemony marinated jumbo shrimp as a first course, followed by a delicious cold avocado soup, and a Salad Niçoise.

The ladies chatted along lightly during the meal, but during the desert of an orange raspberry crème Brule, Bella turned to Connye and asked, "Any chance I could see your modest art collection some time? While most of my art is early 20th century, I also have an abiding interest in contemporary works as well."

"Would be delighted to show you. Both of you, of course." Connye nodded to Angelica.

"Oh, I doubt I shall be able to attend. I am leaving day after tomorrow. Balancing many balls in the air, you see. I have clients clamoring for my attention back home." She touched her napkin to her lips. "But Bella will always have my complete attention, as well."

Bella nodded to Angelica, then turned back to Connye, "Someone at the opera gala made a reference to the fact that you were from Louisiana. Is that not so?"

"It is," Connye acknowledged, "born and bred."

"You must be eternally grateful to have escaped *that* hell hole. A lady of your quality must have suffered so."

"Well, when one is young, one does not recognize they are in a hell hole. So busy wrestling alligators and chawing tobaccy I barely noticed."

Bella had no idea what she had just triggered. Now, Connye could disparage her tiny, distressed, hometown of Dauvin all she wanted – and she often did. But let someone from outside cast dispersions and Connye's back was up and she was ready to rumble. But being the lady she was, *and* a guest in someone else's home, she reigned herself in, and decided to seek her revenge in a more indirect manner.

"So, Bella, what brings you out west to Santa Fe? Seems an unlikely place to land for an engaged easterner like yourself." Connye had been determined to dig deeper into the mysteries of Mrs. Harrington-Crenshaw and had done a little internet search on Bella, coming across a few intriguing insinuations that needed clarifying, and now seemed to be the perfect time to pounce.

"Change of scene. Family ties kept me back east for so long, but when those loosened, I felt the need to spread my wings and fly."

"I see, and was your husband one of those ties?"

"My husband? But I have never been married."

"But you are *Mrs.* Harrington-Crenshaw, are you not?"

Bella laughed a little butterfly of a laugh. "Oh that. Just a little affectation, I'm afraid. Like an honorary title. And when dealing with Washington bureaucrats it is useful to have the clout of an imagined, avenging husband behind one occasionally. Not very enlightened in this day and age, I suppose, but useful in the macho world of DC."

Connye wondered what other "little affectations" Bella might have invented.

She had been intrigued by one stray reference in her online research that she now wanted to pursue. "Bella, I was doing a little reading online the other day and I came upon a most intriguing reference. I thought it might be one of the reasons you decided to move out west. I wonder if you could expound upon it for me?

"Of course, whatever might it be?"

"I came upon a very obscure, but very interesting, reference to a Harrington-Crenshaw who had been briefly incarcerated because of an act of lewd and immoral sexual solicitation. Does that ring any bells?"

There was a ver-r-r-y long pause, and the air seemed to crackle with electricity. Angelica lowered her eyes and dabbed at her mouth with her napkin. There was absolutely no facial reaction from Bella. "It must have been another Harrington-Crenshaw," Bella announced firmly.

Connye smiled. "I'm sure you must be right. I imagine the east coast is just rife with Harrington-Crenshaws. Almost as common a name as Smith."

"Well Mrs. Andreatos, you will have to excuse us," Bella announced, forcefully rising from her chair, "Angelica and I have an appointment at two-thirty to inspect draperies. It's been delightful." She extended her hand towards Connye like she was pointing a pistol, but turned abruptly to lead the way to the front door. Connye barely had time to collect her handbag before she was smartly ushered out the door - even before she had time to thank her hostess for the loveliest lunch.

◘   ◘   ◘

Lionel was fired up now. He dragged out his long neglected, unfinished memoir, <u>A Stitch in Time - A Costume Designer in Hollywood of the 50's and 60's</u>, and read through what he had previously written. He estimated he was about two thirds through the first draft, and with the passage of this much time, he was able to read it with fresh eyes. Yes - he announced to himself - he was very pleased with what he had written thus far.

But what he had not considered before suddenly became very clear; he should include photos of his life and films, and drawings of his designs. That would enliven the project no end.

Now while Lionel had a computer, he could not compose more than the simplest emails upon it. He wrote everything out in long hand on legal pads, then transcribed the text to his computer. He had a very specific routine when he wrote. He would brew a pot of coffee, select just the right pen, and prepare a stack of blank writing pads on the dining room table ready to compose. Oh yes, and he had to have one of his lovely orchid plants in full bloom stationed directly before him - even as he recognized he was a bit of a fuss.

But today he had a new task. Since he had a clear idea of what projects would be included in the memoir, he determined today was the day to search through all his flat file drawers to find the drawings to be included in the book. He would tackle the photographs another day.

The files were kept in a bedroom Lionel had dedicated as a work room. He was always working on something. Often it was a casual frock for Sonora, a new brocade waistcoat for himself, or occasionally a stunning gown for one of Sonora's splendid occasions.

This morning he was on his hands and knees going through each drawer and selecting the most interesting designs to illustrate the film projects he describes in the memoir. The front doorbell rang.

"Bother," Lionel exclaimed. "Who can that be?" Lionel was puzzled, as Sonora always called before she came over. He hoped it was not some annoying solicitor. But that would be unlikely, as everyone had to pass through security before they were allowed into the compound, and the guards were usually able to weed those nuisances out. Lionel had to rouse himself from the floor (not an easy task with his arthritic knees) and hobble to the front door.

"Yes?" Lionel asked forcefully, and not very friendly, through the locked door. He was not about to open the door until he knew who it was. "Who is it?"

"Darling, it's your eternal worshiper. The ever so grateful Pinky. Your devoted admirer and groveling supplicant."

"What?" Lionel exclaimed as he opened the door.

Pinky lay prostrate on the ground, hands clasped together in a prayerful attitude, his face gazing up adoringly at Lionel.

"Oh for heaven's sake. Do get up." Lionel reached down to lend Pinky a hand.

Once up, Pinky clasped Lionel in a forceful bear hug, squeezing him like a sumo wrestler winning a competition.

"Pink-k-k-y," Lionel bellowed, "put me down."

Pinky released him and swirled into Lionel's living room. "Oh my, such memories. This is where the pumpkin turned into a glittering queen and became a *Star!*"

"I think you've mixed a few metaphors there."

"Never mind," Pinky breezed.

"So what can I do for you today?" Lionel asked, piqued, and wanting to get back to his drawings search.

"Why, nothing. Nothing at all. It's all about *you* today." He paused and dug into his voluminous bag. "Well, there is just one *little* favor...." He pulled out one of his gowns. "There's just the tiniest little tear there...." He showed Lionel. Maybe if you have a needle and thread handy...." He gave Lionel his most winning grin.

"Oh Pinky...." Lionel scooted to the work room and returned with his sewing box. "You could have fixed this yourself, you know. It's not like facial surgery."

Lionel sat in his comfortable chair. Pinky scooted over to him and hovered over his shoulder. "Oh, but honey, you are *such* a master. Who else could *possibly* duplicate your expertise?" He fluttered and kissed Lionel on the top of his head.

"Oh stop that," Lionel fussed.

"But this is not the only reason I've come to visit you. Oh no, no, no."

"Really? I shudder to hear what the *real* reason is then."

Pinky pouted and moved over to the sofa and sat down, grossly offended. "I came to thank you for your most generous help with my act. Not only were the costumes *divine*, but you helped me shape my act, and provided me with invaluable feedback." He paused and dug into his bag. "And I wanted to thank you by giving you this." Pinky handed Lionel a magazine.

Lionel looked at it in sudden horror. "What?" Lionel waved the magazine back to Pinky. "This is your idea of a thank you gift?"

Pinky took it back gravely hurt, but looked at it and hooted. "Hard Boys? Oh no, not that. Silly me. That's a little something for later when I get home. No. Can't see anything without my specs." He dug again into his bag and pulled out a glossy presentation portfolio. "Here, *this* is what I have for you." He handed it to Lionel.

"Luscious?" Lionel asked, "What is that?"

"Why I've booked you a full day at the Luscious Day Spa, any time you choose. A complete spa treatment, lunch, tea, and your whole body attended to by ever so loving hands." He grinned.

Lionel was a little speechless. "Any day I choose?"

"Any day. And it's all paid for, treatment, lunch, tip, and parking. You won't need to come up with a single nickel."

"Well, that's very thoughtful. Think I will certainly enjoy that. Thank you."

"Oh honey, you are just one big bunch of begonias, and you deserve every special, precious, treat imaginable."

Lionel also smiled. "And I have a little surprise for you."

Pinky beamed, "Really? Do tell."

"Well, your show is so simply marvelous – as are my splendid costumes - that I've decided to make a video of the whole performance. With your permission, of course."

"Oh yes. I'd love that. With titles and everything?"

"Of course, I have a friend who's a talented videographer. I will have her contact you directly to make the arrangements to your liking."

◘   ◘   ◘

Bella had been so disappointed in her lunch with Connye. It was all she could do to convince Angelica that what Connye suggested was purely mean rubbish. To imply that there were any improprieties from an upstanding matron like Bella was patently ridiculous. Angelica appeared to be convinced, but who knew what she might do, searching on her computer in the privacy of her own office?

But now Angelica was gone. She had done all the required measurements, and the two of them had conferred on possible design themes, so all that was left was for Angelica to work her magic, prepare plans for Bella's approval, make all the necessary arrangements, and schedule a time to return to New Mexico to install the job.

But Bella was still ill-at-ease. Somehow she seemed unable to connect warmly with this Santa Fe crowd. She thought after the welcoming party they gave her that she would blossom into warm friendships with many of the women. And certainly her grand gesture and generous donation to the opera should have had the population welcoming her with open arms. But, alas, not so. That Sonora woman seemed indifferent to her if not downright hostile, and Connye, the other social leader, had just revealed her malicious nature. Could her treatment of that Honey Trapp woman have anything to do with all of this? Hmm. She would have to meditate on that. Some sort of readjustment was called for, but where to start? What was the poor put upon Bella to do?

Bella was in her bed room this morning, holding up the swatches of curtain and bedspread materials that Angelica had left with her. She didn't really want to make choices. She just wanted Angelica to come sweeping in with her workers, and her delivery vans, and take over and clear away all the old junk and leave her with a dazzling new look that would have everyone in awe. But somehow it didn't seem to work that way. She would never understand. After all, what do you *pay* people for?

Rene came into the room. "Miss Bella, the mail."

Miss Bella. What was it with this *Miss* Bella? Rene seemed incapable of calling her *Mrs.* Bella as she requested. No matter how hard Bella tried, she could not break Rene of this habit.

"I'll take it. Thank you." Rene handed her a stack of mail - mostly flyers, junk mail, and bills. But one heavy envelope raised Bella's curiosity. She looked at the return address. It was from Chetworth. She blanched for a moment and felt a brief pang of panic.

She went to her office, sat at her desk, and opened the envelope. Inside were a letter and a small ring box. She started with the letter.

Dear Bella,

I am writing this to you because I feel I owe you an explanation. I am so sorry to have involved you in this matter with the delivery of that envelope. I realize now I should not have asked you to do that errand. It should have been my task, and mine alone. But since I did involve you I feel I need to fill you in on the details.

I would not ordinarily reveal this information to anyone. But since I feel that my life may be in danger I wanted someone to know the circumstances should something happen to me.   I have instructed a trusted colleague to mail this letter only if I should die unexpectedly.   And just so you know, I am in perfect health.   My death in the near future would not be natural - or accidental.

Let me start by going back to the days when your father and I worked together for the company.   We were young, ambitious, and, I'm afraid to say, rather reckless.   And I am going to tell you something now that may shock you. It involves your father. I don't know if he ever told you or not, but under the circumstances, I believe you need to know the truth.

Back in the days when we were both young, unattached, and heady with the thrill of being a part of an exciting new agency, your father and I became lovers. I know this must shock you, but it didn't last long. And as far as I know your father never participated in any same sex activity ever again. However, for me it has always been an off and on situation.

As a result of our little fling, we found ourselves threatened with blackmail.   In those days, our sexual activity was very dangerous, especially working for OSS. Any exposure could cost us our jobs and any possibility of advancement within the elite Washington social structure.

In the post-world war II years, Europe was in turmoil, with intense jockeying for power within the rebuilding countries. There was a lot of reconstruction money involved at this time, with many shady characters vying for a slice of it.   Information was a hot commodity and timely information even more so. Your father and I were blackmailed into acting as couriers for some of these interests. We were not spies exactly, but used diplomatic immunity to transport documents from the US to the European underground. It was shady and illegal, but did not threaten any national security.

However, we were found out by our bosses and asked to resign from what had then become the CIA.   Our excuse to colleagues and friends was that we were both interested in pursuing our own careers elsewhere. Your father and I remained *distant friends but were never close after that, each choosing to put the past behind us.*

I thought I was completely clear of the past until I became a Senator, then the blackmailers stuck again, but this time for higher stakes. We are in the age of industrial espionage, and this time it is the Chinese who want the information. And since my shadow sexual activities with men had continued over the years, I was now quite vulnerable to blackmail again. I had my senate career, my wife, and my family now, and so I, sadly, succumbed to their requests once again.

This activity has carried on for several years, but having decided to leave the Senate I told my handlers that this was to be my last job. However, I learned that the material I would be dealing with this time would compromise our national security, and I threatened to blow the whistle, thus putting myself in grave danger.

That is when I approached you, as I felt I was an immediate target and could not deliver the envelope without jeopardizing my life. I sincerely believed it was a simple hand-over delivery and if you did it there would be no danger to you. However, there was a mix up on the time of delivery and, of course, you know the result of that.

Now, since you are reading this, it is because something has happened to me. I don't really know if this puts you in any danger or not. I have no idea what these people might be capable of or what their agenda might be. But I wanted to enlighten you to the facts and urge you to take whatever precautions you feel are necessary. If you still have the envelope then you might want to turn that over to the FBI. And please keep the Bandelier brochure as a souvenir of our friendship. It has special meaning for me.

I am so sorry to have involved you in all of this. Please accept my deepest and sincerest apology.

Ever your devoted admirer,

Chetworth Spangler

PS. I have decided to send you this university ring. It was actually your father's. If you look under the top you will see his name engraved. We exchanged rings when we were a couple. Thought you should have it.

Bella was stunned. She opened the ring box and examined the ring. Indeed, it had her father's name engraved inside, under the top of the ring. And underneath, on the band of the ring below the crown, was a second engraving, so small Bella had to take out her magnifying glass to read it. It read: A turn of the head and you will see. She had no idea what that referred to, but suspected it was some sort of romantic phrase between the two men when they were lovers, and was something about which she did *not* wish to know.

She immediately went to her jewelry box and looked for the ring her father had given her just before he died. She had never examined it closely before, and upon examination found it had Chetwroth's name engraved inside.

Bella collapsed onto the bench at her dressing table. What now? She thought since she had passed on the envelope to the thugs she should now be safe from any further repercussions. But could she be certain? She was furious to have been put in a situation like this. If Spangler wasn't dead already she would certainly find a way to dispatch him herself. This set her laughing. Oh my. What a situation. The only thing she could think of to do was to call the FBI again and give them this latest information, even if it meant revealing her father's past sexual exploits.

The Wizard of Oz

A few ladies of the coffee circle were seeing Roberta for the first time since she returned from Orlando. Having fallen asleep by the pool one afternoon with her sun glasses on, she now looked like a raccoon with her red face and white circles around her eyes.

Honey was the last one to come out of the market. She looked at Roberta and stopped in her tracks. "My dear, are you blistered?" Honey enquired.

"Oh no," Roberta said meekly. "It looks a lot worse than it feels. Silly me, I need a nanny when I travel, I guess. Can't seem to take care of myself outside of my familiar routine."

"And why were you alone? Thought you went on an adventure with Sonora?" Honey added.

Sonora spoke up, "I had to return early, so left dear Roberta to enjoy the whole week of her vacation."

"And why did you need to return early?" Connye asked, suspicious and wanting to get to the bottom of the mystery, suspecting there was a lot more involved than what Sonora was telling.

Now Sonora was not yet ready to reveal her quest for a dance company. There had been such a "to do" when she announced she was writing a screenplay, way back when. And she didn't want *anyone* to know about her dance company quest until the deal was finalized. She still had one more company to visit before she would know if she wanted to move forward with this little project or not. And she certainly was *not* about to spring Oz on this devouring crowd as she had absolutely *no* idea where that episode might be headed. So she politely answered, "Oh a slight domestic disturbance came up that needed tending to. I'd had quite enough sun, so I scurried home."

Now that was far too vague and deflecting for Connye's liking so she ploughed on. "Henrietta not ill, I hope? Or that delightful creature you call IT?"

Sonora continued to evade. "Not at all, just a few financial adjustments to be made. One's broker can often be such a pain, don't you agree?" Sonora smiled sweetly and plunged on to divert the direction of the questioning. "I heard the most amusing story about the Mrs. H-C. It seems there was some sort of ruckus up at her house and she was surrounded with police cruisers, FBI, and who knows what all? Rumor has it she has been growing pot in her conservatory. Don't believe a word of it, of course, as I'm certain she has never tried pot in her entire life. Way too uptight."

Connye lit up at this because it fit right in with the wonderful bit of news she had been hoarding. "Well ladies, guess what I came across about our Bella on the internet?"

A hushed silence fell as all attuned to Connye's revelation. Connye leaned in and continued, "Way back, who knows when, there was a blurb in the Washington Times about a Harrington-Crenshaw, first name not mentioned, who was taken into custody for lewd behavior of a sexual nature. I tried following up on this tidbit but various attorneys must have rushed in to intervene, as there was no further mention of the incident anywhere. I had an opportunity to confront her on this little story and you should have seen her face - stony cold. But she whisked me out of her house faster than ice melting in hell."

"Well, I don't like to speak ill of one of my best clients," Olivia spoke up, "but when I was up at her house showing her products I saw what looked like an altar of some kind. And there is even speculation that she prowls about the streets at night looking for children to abduct for her satanic rituals."

"Damn," Brenda brayed, "Gotta put the Major out at night. Maybe she would whisk him away and I'd be free at last." She laughed heartily at her own jest.

Honey was intensely interested in Connye's information. "Well, I certainly have no love for the Bella, but how likely is it that this Harrington-Crenshaw you read about is our Harrington-Crenshaw? It's not very often that women get picked up for lewd conduct unless they are hookers? Do you mean to say she was looking for johns?"

"Who knows?" Connye answered.

Roberta asked, "Might it be someone else? Seems like a woman with her resources would hardly need to walk the streets."

"Unless she's kinky," Sonora speculated.

"But how many Harrington-Crenshaws can there be?" Roberta asked. "Maybe she has a brother?"

"Well, this is all very charming speculation, but I for one must tootle off." Sonora announced. "I have an out of town guest I am entertaining this evening and I promised Henrietta I would be home early with the groceries so she would have plenty of time to prepare dinner."

"And just who is this out of town guest, may we ask?" Honey pried.

"A New York acquaintance who's just moved to Santa Fe. Settling into a lovely condo - but boxes everywhere, so I offered dinner."

"Male or female," Olivia inquired.

"Male."

"O-o-o-o," the crowd purred.

"Is this someone we might meet?" Connye asked, rather insistently.

Sonora hesitated, but replied, "If you are all very, very good." And she swirled away.

◘   ◘   ◘

Sonora was intensely nervous about Oz actually coming to dinner at her home. It had all been abstract speculation up to this point, with no way to nail anything down. But now they would be alone in an intimate situation with no crowds, no pretty girl friend intruding with an arm-load of groceries, or clanging hotel breakfast activity to distract them from the core issues.

One fact was clear to Sonora, however, Oz had come to Santa Fe to woo and win her. Was she woo-able? That remained to be seen. When she was married, she had lived a quite comfortable life. Her husband was wrapped up in his work. He supplied her with freedom and ample money to pursue her charitable activities. They were comfortable with each other, but never really in love. Not unlike a substantial number of other New York marriages amongst the wealthy.

Sonora was used to her own life now. It was arranged exactly as she liked it, and the thought of actually sharing her life with another person at her age seemed the height of folly. And yet....

She had often ruminated on her loveless life. She'd had affairs, dalliances, and sly sexual encounters, but quite honestly, she had never been enflamed with an all-consuming passion, and certainly not a lasting love.

Sonora still had Oz's letter - declaring his love all those many years ago when he left the letter in her book, and unopened for a few years more. This certainly made her look at him with new eyes. And she could not deny the flutters she felt when they met again at the Orlando hotel. To put it mildly she was confused.

Henrietta had made a lovely dinner. It was all ready to serve. Sonora gave Henrietta the evening off and she was alone in her house waiting for Oz to arrive. She had dressed simply - nothing formal. Just a modest strand of pearls and seed pearl earrings, accenting a plain navy dress. She lit the candles around the living room and at the dining table. She put on some unobtrusive music and waited. And waited. And waited.

Dinner was to be at seven-thirty. At eight-thirty Sonora finally called Oz's cell. It went straight to message. Now she was worried. Had there been an accident? Had he suffered a heart attack or stroke? Unlikely as he was so fit. Had he gotten cold feet? Now she was starting to get angry.

Dinner was probably ruined by now. She went to the kitchen to check. Yes, all dried up like a carcass in the desert. She poured herself a glass of wine and made a ham and cheese sandwich. She sat in the kitchen eating and feeling sorry for herself. How glad she was she had not made any big pronouncements at the coffee circle. She did not want to have to backtrack at the next meeting. Luckily she had remained vague and insinuated nothing.

After eating, she marched out to the living room, pulled off her earrings, blew out all the candles, and charged into her dressing room to change into a comfortable dressing gown. She marched into the media room, turned on the TV, and engaged herself by watching a slasher movie. Every victim was a version of Oz.

At ten o'clock she was ready for bed. Maybe a nice night's rest would calm her and restore her equilibrium. She went to the kitchen, turned out the lights and was turning off the lamps in the living room when the doorbell rang. On no - not possible.

She strode over to the entrance, switched on the outside light, and opened the door.

◘   ◘   ◘

Pinky stood at the door. Bella asked for his ID, and this time she had him slip it through the viewing window and studied it thoroughly before admitting him. Pinky was amused by the fact that he was visiting another Bella. He wanted to comment, but he was on FBI duty now and needed to be professional and butch it up. No shrieks, no flounces, no draggy gestures.

He was a bit annoyed his boss had called him and assigned him this visit today. This could compromise his deep cover, but he doubted that *this* Bella would ever be exposed to *his* Bella, so he felt it would be okay just this once.

"Thank you, Mr. Powell," Bella handed Pinky his ID and ushered him inside.

Pinky surveyed the living room as he came in. "Are those for real?" he shrieked, after seeing the gallery of impressionist artworks. But he caught himself and restated in a much deeper and more controlled voice, "Are those paintings the genuine article, ma'am?"

"They are indeed. Are you an art lover?" Bella asked, somewhat taken aback by Pinky's first response.

Pinky pulled on his inner warrior and answered, "Nah, soccer's more my thing, actually."

"A charming sport, I believe, though I am not an aficionado myself."

Pinky decided he needed to take control of the situation. "Ma'am, I believe you have some new evidence for us concerning the assault from the other day?"

"Yes, Yes. Just a moment." Bella retreated to her office and returned with Chetworth's letter. "Here's the original, and I made a copy for you." She handed Pinky the papers.

"May I?" he asked indicating he wanted to sit to read the letter.

"Of course, can I get you a refreshment while you read that?"

"Oh, maybe just a little tea and lemon with sweet and low, and do you have any luscious little cookies or cakes." He was reverting rapidly to the other Bella.

Bella stared at him for a moment, then answered, "I'll see what we have." She retreated to the kitchen, while Pinky read the letter.

By the time she returned with a tray of tea and cookies Pinky had finished the letter. And Bella was seriously wondering if she was dealing with another imposter. Who was this strange man?

But Pinky had butched up once again – sort of. "Very interesting document," he observed as he sampled the tea and took up the first macaroon. "Ummm. Tasty." He delicately dabbed his lips with a napkin. "Now then, I will have the Albuquerque office analyze this and we'll see if that moves the investigation forward. We'll give you a call if we have any further questions about this. I imagine the office will contact Senator Spangler's people as well. Seems like a good solid lead to me." Pinky finished the tea and picked up one more tasty little treat. He rose to go. "So your dad was a screamer? Really? And you didn't know?"

That really upset Bella. "I beg your pardon. I don't think that was an appropriate remark. Who is your supervisor? Think I will want to speak to him."

"Oh, I am so-o-o sorry. Just slipped out."

"What? Are you some kind of homophobe?"

Now Pinky just relaxed and let it all hang out. "Oh, my dear. Not at *all*. I'm a big ol' screamer myself. In fact you *must* come by and see my act. I'm at the Carousel Lounge. Bella Le Balle. And I'm a big Star, Star, Star! How about that? Another Bella. Just imagine. Guess we're just gonna take over the world, aren't we girl?" And with that Pinky turned, gave a little backward kick, and with his head raised high, regally left the house.

Bella was speechless, and quite at a loss.

◻   ◻   ◻

"Melissa?" Sonora gasped as she opened her front door.

"You are *not* taking my man," the woman wailed, bursting into tears, and collapsing after her initial defiance.

"Come in, come in," Sonora offered, taking Melissa by the arm and leading her inside. She directed her to the sofa where they both sat down.

Sonora had met Melissa but one time before. Right after Sonora discovered Oz's letter in New York, she went over to where Oz was living on his boat moored at the Hudson River boat basin. She and Oz were dancing around the issue of his letter when Melissa showed up with an arm load of groceries. Oz introduced her as his partner and that ended any further romantic exploration for Sonora.

Melissa was in her mid-forties, with fiery red hair, green eyes, and a charming smile, which was not evident this evening.

"I'm sorry. I'm sorry," Melissa wailed. "This is not like me at all. But I'm just *so* worked up."

"Melissa, Oz told me you left him for a bar tender in Key West – some time ago, I believe."

"Well, yes. Sort of. Yes. Yes, I did - but it didn't last. I was a fool. But now I'm back." She suddenly became defiant again. "And I had to track Oz all the way out *here*. What in the world? Santa Fe? Really? There's no water out here. How's he gonna use his boat?"

"Melissa, he sold it," Sonora tried calming her.

"But he *loved* that boat." Melissa wailed once again.

"Melissa, why are you here?"

"To get him back."

"Then why are you at *my* house. He's not here."

"I know-w-w... I was just at his place. He was just leaving to come here. Said he had a date with you. But I told him no - he couldn't go. We needed to talk. So we talked."

"And?" Sonora asked, puzzled by this whole business.

Melissa was silent, head down, brooding. "He says we're through. Said my actions cut all ties. But I don't believe it. I know he still loves me."

Sonora's phone rang. She answered. It was Oz.

"Is she there?" Oz asked.

Sonora was unsure how much to reveal in Melissa's presence so she answered simply, "Yes."

"I am so sorry about all of this. Sorry about missing our date. Sorry about Melissa. I don't know what to say to make this better."

Sonora answered. "Nothing right now. We'll talk about it later. I need to resolve this immediate issue before it gets out of hand. Good-bye."

"Do you want me to come over?"

"Absolutely not." She hung up.

Sonora went back to Melissa. "You know what? I think you need to take a big deep breath. And I think you need to have a good night's rest, and I'm sure things will sort themselves out in the morning."

Melissa began bawling again. "But I don't have any place to go-o-o."

"You can stay here. My guest room's right over there. Get a good night's rest and things will look different in the light of day."

Sonora led Melissa to the guest room, helped her get undressed, and tucked her in, turning out the light, and closing the door after.

She telephoned Lionel. "My darling, are you still up?"

"Barely, Lionel grumped.

"Well, have I got a story for you."

"Give me five minutes. Want a cognac?" Lionel asked.

"Oh yes – please – a very lar-r-rge one. Be right over."

Just then Melissa came charging out of the guest room. "I can't, I've got to go. I can't stay here." She headed for the front door.

"Wait," Sonora shouted. "Where are you going?" She ran after Melissa. Reaching the front door, Sonora stopped and peered out into the darkness. Melissa was already gone.

Sonora marched back into the house, picked up the phone, and called Oz.

"That screwy broad of yours, just charged out of here. I tried to settle her down. Offered to let her sleep here, but she dashed out again. She's probably headed back over your way. Thought you ought to know."

"She's not *my* screwy broad. That horse left the barn a lo-o-o-ng time ago."

"Then you better bar and lock the door."

Oz sighed. "Okay, talk to you tomorrow. So sorry about this crazy business. I promise I'll make it up to you."

Sonora paused. "We'll talk." She was not yet ready to forgive him entirely. "Good night."

Sonora hung up. Oh, that large cognac was sounding pretty good right about now. She went over to tell Lionel al-l-l-l about the latest.

◘   ◘   ◘

Now that she and Jefferson had decided not to move in together, Connye was somewhat at a loss. She had so focused her energy on their relationship that now there was to be no big event, she didn't quite know what to do with herself. She, of course, had her art, her charities, her social events, and visits with the coffee group, but she wanted more. She wanted to be thrilled and engaged. At one point she had thought of organizing a grand summer spiritual retreat with the crème de la crème of new age pundits and gurus, but that had come to naught when it had been far too complicated to organize properly without a huge staff.

She secretly admired Sonora for all her clever and ambitious little projects – her film script (even though Connye was certain it was a fraud) - her jaunts to her residences in Puerto Vallarta, Provence, and New York – and her dear Mama, who was *always* visiting. Connye had never once been able to persuade her Père and Mère to come visit her in Santa Fe. Those stubborn bayou folk would never budge more than ten miles from her little Louisiana hometown of Dauvin.

Connye folded her hands, gazed towards the heavens with closed eyes, and opened herself to divine inspiration. And oh, there it was – the perfect project to enliven her interest and commitment. She would establish a thriving garden based on the same principles as the famous garden started at Findhorn Scotland in the 1960's.

She had only recently read about this astonishing project. Connecting with nature and seeking cooperation from the nature spirits and devas, a couple established the most wonderful garden on a windswept plot of poor soil in a trailer park. They grew enormous cabbages, succulent tomatoes, and every variety of wondrous fruits and vegetables – larger, bug/disease resistant, and more flavorful than anyone had ever seen in that area before.

Connye sprang up from her meditation and immediately began planning her new project. Of course, it was too late this season to start the garden, but anyway, it would require time to prepare and work the soil for the first planting next spring. And she would have to woo the spirits and devas. That would take some thinking about. Maybe there was a book about that.

First, she ran through the names of all her friends who might be interested in working with her. Calling every single one, there were no takers. You can't imagine the excuses these folks came up with. Honey had a bad knee and couldn't kneel for long periods of time. Olivia was allergic to soil. (now that really stretched credibility) Roberta was tied up with her pie shop. And Connye wouldn't *ever* consider calling Sonora. She just *knew* what kind of reception she would get from *her*. The Getgoods laughed at her. The Gladscows had never even heard of devas and thought she was advocating some sort of devil worship, and lastly the boys were completely tied up with running their hotel, but said if she came across any free nature spirits they would be more than willing to offer them a home in *their* garden.

So, stalwart and determined, she would have to instigate the project all by herself. And instigate it she would. First she would need some land. Although she had a fine backyard it was very expensively landscaped like a woodland and mountain meadow. Best not to disturb that. She'd had nasty confrontations with the Chamisa Springs board last time she tried to be creative with her property. No, she must go elsewhere.

Now, New Mexico was hardly the garden center of America. The soil was called caliche or hardpan - an impermeable layer of clay and sand that only a cactus could love. Wherever she started her garden she would need legions of devas to make this work. And, of course, she would need water, another rather scarce resource in this high desert environment. And literally tons of organic material dug into the soil. But she was not to be deterred. But she also didn't want to travel long distances to take care of her garden. She would have to find someplace close by, preferably with a reliable water supply, and perhaps a handy little tool shed. Then she had a stellar idea. Perhaps Chamisa Springs might have an unused scrap of land they would allow her to utilize. She immediately called the manager.

◘   ◘   ◘

The morning after Sonora's aborted date with Oz she thought about calling him first thing. But not so fast, she decided. It was *he* that should call *her*. Sonora busied herself with making arrangements to travel to Casper to see her last dance company. Should she go alone? It had been a little inconvenient taking Roberta. Maybe she *would* go by herself. Or should she offer to take Lionel? - or Oz? But until this whole Melissa thing got settled, and she and Oz got to spend some alone time together, she'd better not consider going with him. Oh dear, she didn't know what to do. Maybe she should just wait to schedule her trip. Oh, this was ridiculous, why wait? She called Oz.

"Oh, Sonora, I'm glad it's you. I was just going to call."

"Have you heard from Melissa?"

"Ah.....she's here."

"Can you talk?"

"Mmm, not really."

"Then why did you say you were just going to call me?"

"I ah... I... Look, I think I'd better call you later. I've got my hands full right now."

There was shouting and noise, and then the phone was disconnected. Sonora was a little concerned. She started to call back but decided against it.

This was exactly why she had not considered any serious relationships. It was all just *too* messy. How much better was her cool and glassy life. She had Henrietta to care for her immediate needs. She had IT for companionship – and Lionel too, of course. She had her friends – at a distance – to round out her social obligations. She sighed and adjusted her thinking to the joys of a solitary life. Oz could call or not. She was now completely indifferent.

◘   ◘   ◘

It had been decided that Angelica would have to make another trip to Santa Fe before she could come out for the final installation. There were so many decisions to make, and Bella had been reluctant to make *any*. Angelica could not get her to settle on a single thing. She's sent dozens of samples and swatches, but Bella had rejected them all. Angelica had worked with difficult clients before, but they were difficult because they had *too many* opinions. Bella had none. It was like trying to wrestle cotton candy. And what with the added expense of this trip she felt she would need to ask Bella for additional expenses and a larger fee.

Now a curious thing had transpired when Bella met Pinky. After a day or two of reflection she found herself increasingly intrigued by him. She couldn't quite put her finger on why, so she decided she needed to go see his show for herself. She located the Carousel Lounge in the phone book and called to find out the show times for Pinky's act. Then she waxed hot and cold on whether she would actually go on not. But she found herself at loose ends one Friday evening and decided she would take the plunge and go.

Arriving at the club only ten minutes before Pinky's act, she found a dark table at the side of the club, obscured by post, where it would be unlikely she would be recognized. As she scanned the audience she did not see anyone she knew so she was able to settle a little more into the spirit of the evening without feeling self-conscious.

Pinky had been working on his act and was trying out a few new numbers. The act was spotty and hesitant in a few places, but he wowed the crowd with one of his new numbers – a Bessie Smith blues number – and he again received a standing ovation.

How refreshing, Bella thought. So far she had only met the stodgy Santa Fe social crowd, and this Pinky was so totally different. But she was quite unable to reconcile the FBI Pinky with the Bella Le Balle Pinky. What a contrast. She debated whether she should go back stage and say hello - but finally decided to do it.

"Knock, knock," Bella announced as she peered into Pinky's dressing room.

Pinky turned and screamed, "It's the *other* Bella! Oh, Precious, come in, come in." His dressing room was a tornado's swath of costumes, wigs, boas, pallets of make-up, and magazines, newspapers, and a large assortment of shoes. He scrambled to find her a place to sit. No one else was visiting this evening so she had his full attention.

"I have another show at midnight," he announced, "so I'm not able to go out for a drink with you or anything, but I can order one for you from the bar here if you like."

"Oh no, I had a couple during the show. And how splendid you were. I never imagined. And how is all this possible with you being an FBI agent? You *are* an agent, are you not? This is not all some sort of an elaborate ruse or scam is it? I just couldn't go through any more of this distressing business after the Senator and all.

"No, no. I really am an FBI agent *and* a drag queen. Go figure." He laughed. "What an age we live in, eh?"

"Well, I was just bowled over. Your act was wonderful. One would never guess, seeing you – say on the street – that you could be this totally transformed diva. I've seen a few drag acts back east, but nothing quite like this."

"You are too kind." He paused and looked at her. "And you are a bit of a wonder yourself. I never actually thought you would come see the show. I was afraid I'd made a complete ass of myself up at your place. Sorry about that. Not very professional, I know."

"To be quite honest, I *was* a bit shocked at first. But then I started warming up to the idea. Not met that many what I would call *real* people here in Santa Fe yet. This social crowd I've been exposed to here take themselves a bit too seriously, I'm afraid. And you are a breath of fresh air.

"Oh honey, we're all just lost little children underneath. Ya just gotta get past the drag make-up we all wear, and underneath we are all the same."

Bella thought about that for a moment. "Even me, I suppose."

"Yes. And even me," Pinky said softly.

Bella suddenly brightened. "Would you like to come to lunch some afternoon? I somehow feel we could become great friends."

"Well, don't know if that would be a conflict of interest with my FBI drag, but what the hell. I'll risk it."

◻   ◻   ◻

IT was knocking a rubber doggie toy against Sonora's ankle. It was the urgency of playtime. Sonora was tempted, as she was processing bills to pay, but then the phone rang.

"Sonora, I've finally got it all settled. Poor Melissa – so distraught. But it's done. It's over. And I believe she understands that now."

"Oh, Oz. What a trial for you."

"Yes. But let's put that behind us and move on. I really want to see you, as soon as possible."

Sonora checked her watch. "Coffee at eleven? There's a charming…."

Oz cut her off. "Oh no, I was thinking, it's such a splendid morning, how about a hike in the mountains?"

"A hike? Mountains?"

"Yes, there are some wonderful trails. I bought this very informative map."

"Trails?"

Oz, sensing some hesitation asked, "You do like to hike, don't you?"

Sonora had a moment of panic. "Oh yes, of course."

"Good, I can pick you up if you like."

Sonora hesitated just a little bit more. "But what about bears?" she asked plaintively.

"Bears? Real bears?" Oz asked. "You mean like lions, and tigers, and bears, oh my?" He laughed.

"Well, actually, yes."

"My dear, there is nothing to worry about. There will absolutely be no bears anywhere near where we will be hiking. I promise you a gentle and completely safe hike. Can you be ready in half an hour?"

"Yes, I suppose so." However, she did not sound all that convinced.

"Good, I'll see you then." He hung up.

Now, what in the *world* does one wear to go hiking? She scurried to her dressing room and rummaged through her closet and drawers. She managed to find a pair of khaki shorts she'd not worn since she'd bought them. She hoped they still fit. She found a loose white cotton top that looked appropriately sporty but casual, and she found some old boots at the back of her shoe closet that she remembered buying as part of a Halloween costume when she went as a great white hunter, and Lionel went in blackface as a tracker. And finally she found some plain white cotton socks from the box of clothes she was going to give to the Goodwill. But she would also need a hat. She found a baseball cap that Quinto had somehow left behind. And now she was ready.

Oz picked her up in his rented jeep. He'd not owned a car for years. Buying a car was on his list of things to do. With the top down, and the wind whistling round them, there was no conversation going up to the mountain.

Oz had selected an easy, wide trail that was gently sloping, without any obvious challenges for, what he rightly suspected, was an inexperienced hiker.

They started out on the trail and soon came upon a small stream that enchanted Sonora. "Oh, could we sit for a moment?" she asked. "This is such a pretty spot."

"Of course, and I have a little surprise for you," he added.

They sat by the stream. Sonora took off her shoes and let her feet play in the water. Oz opened his backpack and took out a thermos.

"You suggested we meet for coffee earlier, so I obliged." He poured them coffee.

"How delightful." Sonora was actually beginning to enjoy herself. She saw no lurking bears, and her fears of broken legs, or tumbling off towering cliffs now seemed farfetched.

Oz took this opportunity to launch into the little prepared speech he'd been working on for days. "Sonora, I just wanted to say how sorry I am for all this disruption with Melissa. I was so looking forward to our evening together. I had flowers and Champaign, and even a silly box of candy. I wanted to be the perfecto suitor."

Sonora smiled. "I understand." But she was still roughly reluctant to have this discussion.

"My darling, ever since I wrote you that letter.…."

Sonora turned to him. "Stop. Stop. I know what you're going to say. And I really do appreciate it. But I'm just not ready for this. I hope you can understand." She stumbled in her thoughts. She didn't want to hurt him. She didn't want to completely close the door, but she was doubtful anything could come of this.

"So, I don't understand, then. What is it you *do* want?" Oz pleaded.

She thought for a moment. "I want time."

He was becoming a little annoyed. "What are we talking about here? A month? Six months? A year?" He laughed. "I only took a six month lease on the condo."

Sonora laughed too. "I don't know. I don't know. I'm sorry. But I've got to go slow. I'm not ruling anything out just yet. I do care about you. But a romance? A relationship at my age? I just don't know."

"Okay, okay. Slow. Slow. I get it. You tell me. How do you wish to proceed? Shall I ask you out on dates? Wait by the phone for you to call me? Camp outside your house? What?"

Sonora shook her head. She was confused. She didn't know how to respond. "Okay, I'll tell you what. Let's go back to square one. Let's have that dinner you missed and go from there. Only this time *you* cook the dinner. I had to scrape the last one into the trash."

"Okay. Dinner. You got it."

◘   ◘   ◘

The Chamisa Springs management had reluctantly agreed to let Connye work a weed infested plot of land behind a work shed at the back of the property. But only after Connye religiously promised the General Manager she could have all the heirloom tomatoes she wanted. Connye grumbled a bit about that, but agreed, as the manager was not asking for any rent.

Now while there was a water hookup at the work shed, it would be city water with chlorine and fluoride, and Connye knew that would not work for the Devas. She either had to purify the city water or create a cistern to catch natural rain water. But as this was a region with almost perpetual drought she settled on putting in a water purification system to water the land.

During her first visit to the nascent garden Connye walked carefully, not wanting to disturb any nature spirits by stepping on them. She dug up a sample of the soil to have it tested to see exactly what nutrients would be needed, and she smudged the property with sage and sweet grass. Finally she said an evocation to entice the nature spirits to live there, and promised them that soon she would be transforming this sad little plot into a virtual Garden of Eden.

The New Girl in Town

It was one of those late summer - early autumn days when it could be a bit chilly one minute and uncomfortably warm the next. The scent of roasting coffee and freshly baked bread wafted from the market. The last of the summer bees circled around a honey sweet Apache Plume in its second bloom, with its delicate white flowers and tufts of pink plume. It would not be long now before the coffee circle would need to meet inside. But for now the patio was still inviting and the place to meet.

No one had seen Olivia at coffee for days. Where could she be? She was almost always one of the first to arrive - eager to catch, or deliver, any juicy new bits of spicy news.

Sonora was still not ready to subject Oz to this group of carnivorous gossips. She was moving slowly, seeing him occasionally, and had dared to invite him to go with her to Casper to check out her dance company. He had accepted, and they were scheduled to leave Thursday afternoon. But she had booked them separate rooms.

Connye would not *stop* talking about her garden. She seemed to be seeing dancing garden spirits, sprites, and devas everywhere. She was even inviting them into her back yard, like a colony of homeless bees.

Honey's kids were breathless, waiting for early acceptance letters from their colleges of choice. And that's all *she* talked about.

The ladies were gathered this morning, seeking shelter by a sun warmed adobe wall, and scooting their tables closer together to catch a spot of sun. While during the summer iced coffees and teas were the norm, today all had steaming hot drinks and sipped happily, holding the hot drinks to warm their hands.

Without a lot of news today, the ladies were chatting about odd, but mostly uninteresting daily events. Then around the corner came Olivia and a younger woman. They strode up to the group.

"Well, well, well," Honey announced. "We've not seen *you* in ages. Where have *you* been? Hope you have some splendid news for us."

"Hi, everybody. Yes, it's been too long, hasn't it? But I've been quite busy visiting with my sister. Everyone, this is Candelaria Lobata, my baby sister."

"Candice," she announced to the group, then leaning towards Olivia whispered, "I'm called Candice now, remember?"

"Oh, yes. Sorry," Olivia winced. Olivia introduced all the ladies, and added, "Even though we are sisters, Candice never actually lived in Santa Fe, so she is just now discovering this city's many delights."

"How long will you be visiting?" Connye asked.

"I'm not sure. Just staying with Olivia for the moment, but seriously thinking of relocating here."

"From where?" Sonora asked.

"Las Vegas - the Nevada one. Keep forgetting there's one here in New Mexico as well. I was Celine's nutritionist during her last show. But I really don't care for Las Vegas. Neither the weather, nor the cultural climate suits me.

"What would you like?" Olivia asked, ready to go inside the market for drinks.

"Let me think... a soy chai, please. And maybe a whole grain muffin of some sort. With soy butter and natural fruit juice sweetened jam if they have that. Thank you."

Candice was a younger and slightly prettier version of Olivia - dark black hair, exquisite skin, and bright eyes.

"And what would you do here? Don't imagine there are a lot of positions open for nutritionists – except maybe school cafeterias." Sonora observed a little wryly.

"Don't think that should be a problem. I've chatted with Val and Gene. They may need my services, and said they would certainly refer me to some of their friends. But for now I just want to relax, take in the wonderful prana in this sacred place, and enjoy the blessings of the spiritual vortex."

Connye lit up at this revelation. "Oh Candice, then you must come see my wonderful garden. I'm establishing a miracle garden. Working with all the nature spirits to recreate the magic of Findhron right here in Santa Fe. Can't get any of these ladies to join me though. Would you care to participate?"

Candice considered. "I'll have to see. It will depend a bit on what clients I line up and what their requirements are. Must give them priority, you understand."

"Of course," Connye replied, with some disappointment at the obvious evasion.

"Ladies," Sonora ceremoniously announced, "I think Candice's arrival calls for a little celebration. I want to invite all of you to a harvest gathering at my place. And, as promised, I will introduce all of you to my New York City friend, Oz Garfield. And I may soon have another announcement as well, but that will have to wait. Shall we say two weeks Sunday at noon? A lovely spread provided, of course."

◘   ◘   ◘

Sonora had come to Lionel's for tea at his invitation. She was anxious to tell him the news from coffee. And he had a little surprise for her as well.

"What have you heard from your new friend?" Sonora asked, as Lionel poured the first cup of tea.

"New friend? And who might that be?"

"You know, the one we saw at the club," Sonora replied, thinking Lionel particularly dense today, even though she had been unable to remember the man's name herself.

"Oh Pinky, yes. Well, hardly a new friend. More like a client really." But he stopped and considered for a moment. "But that might be a bit cold. Yes, I guess he would be considered a friend now. But he's always stopping by for me to sew the rips and tears in his costumes. Don't know *what* he does to them – unless he's introduced acrobatics into his act."

"That seems highly unlikely," Sonora commented, "unless he's lost considerable poundage."

"That, I'm afraid he has not. So, any news from coffee today?" Lionel asked.

"Oh my, Olivia has a younger sister. She brought her by today."

"Really? And...?"

"Quite pretty actually, though she seems a bit full of herself."

"Oh yes, but then aren't we all?" Lionel joked.

"Well, I don't know about that. You and I are quite modest, I believe. However, this new one, Candice her name is -

though I know for a fact it is really Candelaria. This Candice has a rather annoying habit of dropping little celebrity first names as though we were all part of some Hollywood cult. But it's probably just insecurity - being in a new environment and all."

"Does she have the potential to be one of us?"

Sonora considered that question. "Not sure. I'm having a little event in a few weeks - to which you are invited, of course. Calling it a harvest festival, but really it's to put Ms. Candice to the test. I think we'll find out *all* about her then. And I may have another surprise or two."

"And they are?" Lionel insisted.

"Now, now. What fun is life without a few surprises?"

"But my darling Sonatina, as you know, you *always* tell *me* everything."

"Not this time. I want to be certain of a few things before I announce, even to you."

"Well, I have a surprise for you. I must say, I too have been keeping a secret, but am now ready to reveal it." He got up and went to his workroom and returned with his manuscript. It was neatly printed out and bound. He offered it to Sonora.

"What's this?" Sonora beamed.

"What you've been after me for months about - my memoir. It's finally completed."

"Oh, my dear.... Really and truly?"

"Will you read it please? I have several publishers interested, but don't want to send it out till I have your feedback."

"I'd be honored."

◘   ◘   ◘

Oz was having a difficult time. He was trying very hard to be patient with Sonora, but she was sorely trying his patience. He was attracted to her and truly admired her, but he had come all this way out to Santa Fe, established himself here, and had wooed her persistently, but she was not responding. Now here they were about to take this trip to Casper, Wyoming, of all places, and she had insisted on separate rooms. How much could a red blooded American guy take, for Chriz sake?

Sonora, for her part, had had an idea, and was beginning to hatch her little plan. It would require some finesse, and a certain amount of strategy, but if the chemistry and timing were just right, it might work.

Sonora told Oz to bring along his cowboy boots if he had any, as she would be involved most of her time with the dance company. She thought it might be nice for him to go horseback riding, and, of course, there was always hiking. The hotel had a pool, a gym, and a spa, so there was no excuse for him not to be fully occupied. And they would have breakfast and dinner together.

This time she did not book her trip for a week, but for only three days, so she would need to determine quickly whether this company would work for her and Santa Fe. And as this was her last company if this didn't work out she would have to start all over again, or drop the project entirely.

"Are you sure you're going to be okay today? "Sonora asked Oz over breakfast their first morning in Casper. "You're welcome to come to the dance studio with me if you like."

"Nah, you're right. There's plenty for me do to. I wouldn't have anything to add if I went along, and would probably just be in the way."

"As you wish."

"But I saw an interesting steak house as we drove in from the airport. I could make reservations...."

"Of course, why don't you do that? Sounds fun," Sonora answered as she gathered her things to head off to the studio. I'll leave *you* the rental and I'll take a cab. That way you can go wherever you want."

She whisked off, leaving Oz feeling somewhat desolate - neglected and useless. He really had no interest in going horseback riding, and quite honestly wished he'd not come at all. So he had another cup of coffee and pulled out his paperback.

Brock Calisto was the artistic director of the dance company. Sonora was immediately taken with him. He had a winning, boyish smile, a shock of wiry brown hair that exploded in six different directions, and eyes that sparkled. He moved in bursts of energy when he danced, and he was discerning, direct, and yet patient with his dancers.

As the dance company was connected to a dance school, it was instructive to see how he inspired the young students, leading them by example, and prodding them to draw forth their best efforts. Everyone adored him.

The small dance company consisted of three men and three women. Sonora had hoped for a slightly larger group, but after seeing them perform again, she was determined this was the group for her.

Brock carefully explained what Etheric Dance was all about, but Sonora thought that Connye would be able to understand what he was saying far better than she could. It had something to do with tracks of energy, the unseen essence of matter, and manifestation of potential subtle archetypes. Oh yeah. He might as well have been speaking Swahili. He might not be unable to explain it to her so she could understand, but he sure could dance it, and that's all that mattered.

She was so excited at dinner Oz could hardly get a word in.

"You will come this evening, won't you? You've got to see what these people do. They're simply marvelous."

"Of course, I would love to," Oz answered.

"And I was thinking we might be able to be up and running in Santa Fe by next season. First thing I'll need to do when I get back is find a studio. We won't need a performance space right away - there are plenty of venues for rent. But they *will* need their own studio to work in. And I was thinking about a school. Oh, you should have seen how he works with the kids. They just worship him. And....."

Oz reached out and took Sonora's hand. She stopped speaking for a moment.

"I'm so glad you've found what you're looking for. But you might just want to take a breath."

Sonora laughed. "Oh my, am I rattling on?"

"Yeah, just a little." Oz laughed.

"So how was your day? I never asked, did I?"

"No-o-o, you did not. You know, horses really aren't my thing. I walked around town, did some shopping, had a barbeque sandwich in some joint - took a swim, and read most of the afternoon."

Sonora considered what he said. There was just the slightest edge to his voice. Maybe he wasn't having such a good time. Not the best plan to bring him along, especially as it was not the romantic trip he was, perhaps, hoping for. Sonora thought for a moment then spoke again. "You know I've had a wonderful idea. While I am certainly excited about bringing the dance company to Santa Fe, I would hardly call myself a business manager type. And since you are now without employment, I was wondering if you would consider managing the company for me. I'd pay a good salary – for a non-profit that is. And you could still do your commodities trading, or whatever it is you do. What do you think?"

Oz nodded as he thought about it. "Hmmm. Worth considering." He also thought it would give him more time with Sonora in a shared interest. Maybe she was warming to him after all, and this was her way of showing it. "Yes, I like the idea. Once you've clinched your deal we can talk more about it and work out the details."

Sonora stopped, "No, why don't you come with me tomorrow? If you are to be the manager it would be useful for you to be in on the discussions. And I would value your input."

"Yeah, sure."

Sonora was immensely excited the next morning as they met with Brock and members of the company to discuss moving to Santa Fe. Sonora soon realized, however, it was going to be expensive to move a troop of dancers to a new city. The cost of living in Santa Fe was a lot higher than in Casper, and the modest dancer salaries would have to be increased to compensate. There would be the transportation costs of moving six individuals with all their belongings, pets, and boy and girlfriends. Then there would need to be incorporation papers for the new artistic entity, the cost of a new studio, publicity, and the whole startup costs for the new school if that was also to be a part of the package. Now, while Sonora was enthusiastic, she was also realistic, and realized that some major fundraising would need to commence as soon as she returned home. She did not want to support a dance company all on her own. There would need to be active financial support from the community as well.

But despite her concerns, the deal was concluded. Sonora had brought a bottle of Champaign and there was a modest celebration as glasses were poured.

Brock was overflowing with excitement, "Mrs. Livingston-Bundt, can't begin to tell you how very pleased we all are that you have taken an interest in us."

"Oh please, Brock, call me Sonora. We can't be all formal now that we are partners in crime, as it were."

"Daniel and I are so excited about moving to Santa Fe. We visited several years back and just fell in love with it."

"Daniel?"

Brock pointed to one of the dancers. "My husband. Got married in California before Prop 8."

"The two of you should feel very welcome in Santa Fe. It's a very gay friendly town."

"I've got so many plans and ideas for the company and school. Can't wait to get started. Was thinking we could present the company to Santa Fe in a gala performance at the Arts Center next autumn. I'm sure I could persuade several principal dancers from major companies to join us. It could be quite an event."

"Sounds expensive," Sonora hesitated.

"But we could use it for, what I like to call, a 'fun' raiser. It would raise immediate cash, and we could sell season subscriptions, and perhaps start a capital donor campaign towards eventual purchase of a studio. What do you think?"

Sonora smiled and nodded, but thought, "*Oh Lord, what have I gotten myself into?*" But then she remembered Pie in the Sky, and how much money she'd made off of that little venture by selling the franchise. And the losses from the dance company would certainly help restore her tax breaks. Hmmm, not too shabby a deal, after all.

◘   ◘   ◘

All morning Angelica had been encouraging Bella to make a firm decision. She had presented Bella with a variety of delightful design ideas, but Bella just couldn't make up her mind. A sea of swatches were arrayed around the living room. A rainbow of paint samples were taped to the walls. But the more choices Angelica gave Bella, the more confused she became. Finally Angelica just collapsed in exasperation.

"Oh Bella, are you sure you want me to do this project?"

"What do you mean? Of course, I do."

"But, my precious one, you said you wanted color and swirl. I have presented you with half a dozen stunning design concepts and all you can do is sigh and ask to see more. I feel like Daffy Duck trying to explain quantum physics to an assembly of drug lords. Can you outline in any more detail *exactly* what it is you're looking for? Anything specific would help – photos - magazine articles - doodles on the refrigerator."

Bella thought for a moment. "More blue...."

"Oh thanks. That's a great help." Angelica started gathering up her rejected designs.

"Wait." Bella called out, "take a look at this," Bella announced after studying a lithograph in her gallery.

She led Angelica over to a splendid Picasso of a man in a black hat, strumming a green guitar in a riotous field of cartoon color. "There, that's what I want. Can you translate that into a room?"

Angelica lit up. "Absolutely. That's wonderful. I see exactly what you mean."

"Excellent, now we are having a guest for lunch. So relax and have a glass of wine with me."

Angelica felt with the eventual success of the morning, it was time to bring up the delicate subject of money. "My darling Bella, as we are now in such a sympathetic vibration over your lovely home, I was thinking it was time to get a little check."

"Oh really? Whatever for?"

"Well, there has been this unexpected *second* trip out to Santa Fe, and I have absolutely *slaved* away, many more hours than usual, on your sweet project, so I was thinking an additional five thousand would cover it."

"I see...." Bella had to think about that. "All in good time. Let us just relax and have a pleasant lunch for now, shall we?"

"But...." Angelica tried to pursue.

Bella stopped and glowered in no uncertain terms, "As I said – later."

Pinky wanted to have a little fun. He appeared at Bella's door dressed in exactly the same style as Bella herself. When Bella opened the door she gasped, and broke into a hearty laugh.

"Pinky, you are too much. My, you look exactly like me. How ever…?"

"I've always believed we should see ourselves as others see us."

"Well, in that case, I should dress up as you," Bella joked.

"But you have, and we look exactly the same – a hall of mirrors, endlessly reflecting each other."

.   "Well come in then, or I'll have the neighbors thinking I have a twin."

Bella introduced Angelica, who was momentarily, and uncharacteristically, speechless at seeing the two Bellas. "Charmed," was all she could eventually manage.

"No, it *I* who am charmed, Principessa," Pinky said, and landed a big, wet kiss on the back of her outstretched hand.

As Angelica withdrew her hand she discretely wiped the back of her hand against her leg.

"We must talk – FBI stuff," Pinky whispered aside to Bella."

"After lunch, let's not spoil a lovely occasion with unpleasantness beforehand."

"Of course," Pinky agreed.

Pinky suddenly, and playfully assumed Bella's identity and announced, "Angelical, Mr. Powell, I believe luncheon is now being served. Shall we retire to the dining room?"

Bella hesitated, then smiled, and entered into the game. "It's so nice of you to invite me to your home as a guest. Who would have thought a scumbag of an FBI agent like me would be welcomed into such a splendid home. What an honor."

Pinky leaned in to Bella and nudged her, "You don't have to go quite *that* far."

They both giggled. Pinky seated himself at the head of the table and rang the little bell that was placed just before him. Rene came in and froze in surprise.

"You may serve lunch now, whatever your name is," Pinky instructed.

Rene turned to look at Bella, who nodded.

"Yes, ma'am, right away," Rene answered, and returned to the kitchen shaking her head.

Poor Angelica had no idea what was going on. She looked down at her plate and hoped this would soon be over.

"Oh Bella, do tell us about your colorful life before you moved to Santa Fe," the real Bella asked Pinky.

"Ah well, the riches.... Of course, you know about my run for president. But alas, it was just too soon. The zeitgeist was not yet ready for a woman president, but I did manage to have a splendid but fleeting affair with the vice-presidential candidate. Too bad he turned out to have a nasty social disease."

Angelica was beginning to see the fun in the game and decided to enter in. "Well, I for one, have never been able to tell the difference between a social disease and social media. They both seem to have the same corrosive influence."

Now everyone at the table was set to laughing. Poor Rene was having a difficult time serving the soup.

Bella recovered first and asked a second question of the Pinky/Bella, "You must have been devastated at the presidential loss."

"Not at all, I picked myself right up and decided to reform the banking system instead. But, of course, as you know, that failed miserably. But not to be deterred, I become the dictator of a small South American nation rife with corruption. I almost succeeded in transferring all the nation's wealth into my personal account, but I kept being swept from power, and settled instead on raising race horses in the Argentine."

"My you *have* had a colorful life. Why ever would you decided to settle in such a quiet little town as Santa Fe? It seems an unlikely place for one of your expansive ambitions," the True Bella asked.

"Well, at some point one just wants to retire from the battle and strife and contemplate the eternal realities of the universe. And so I lead my quiet, but unimaginative existence, in the peace and solitude of my lovely home. And you, Mr. Powell, however did you become an FBI agent *and* a drag queen?" Pinky asked.

True Bella thought for a moment, "Marlene Dietrich inducted me into the French Foreign Legion and I quickly became a general. However, I was captured by a band of Bedouin Gypsies and was disguised as a princess in order to escape notice by the Germans in Casablanca. And well, after that, one thing just led to another."

The soup finished, Rene brought forth the main course, a chicken breast stuffed with Prosciutto and Fontina cheese, served with polenta and asparagus. The flights of fancy ebbed as the three began to enjoy their lunch and more normal conversation took over.

After lunch Angelica excused herself and began photographing all of Bella's paintings and art work. Pinky, who actually had a real job to do, needed to be on his way, but first asked if he might have a private word with Bella in her office.

"Bella, I need to be serious with you for a moment," Pinky began, once they were alone. "We've finally heard from the investigation into Senator Spangler's death. The evidence is conclusive. The Senator was murdered."

Bella gasped. "How?"

"Ricin poisoning."

"How dreadful. Have they identified the murderer?"

"No. But it seems likely it was the blackmailers, or someone they contracted to do the job. And it is clear from his letter that he knew he was in danger and wanted you to know."

Bella thought a moment. "Then why didn't he just hire some messenger to deliver the envelope? Why would he involve me? I really resent that he involved me in all of this."

"Yes, I've been wondering about that myself. Can you think of any other reason he might want to involve you? Did he give you anything, or say anything that seems out of the ordinary?"

Bella considered, then answered, "Can't think of anything. The only other thing he gave me besides the envelope was a map showing how to get to Bandelier."

"Do you still have it?

"I believe so. He asked me to keep it. Don't know why. Should probably just toss it now." Bella searched her desk and came up with the map. "Here." She handed it to Pinky. "You can keep it."

He examined it. "I don't see anything out of the ordinary, but you should keep it until this whole issue is resolved. But would you mind making me a copy – front and back."

"Of course." Bella complied.

"Thank you. And be careful. Keep a lookout for anything unusual. And remember, if you think of anything else that can be useful to the investigation please give me a call me, and I'll come a-runnin'," he joked, before turning and leaving.

◘   ◘   ◘

Connye scrambled excitedly around her new garden plot soon after she took possession of it. A hired a man with a motorized garden tiller had come over to dig up the hard soil, as she had given up trying to use a hand hoe ten minutes after she started. Besides digging up the soil, he had rototilled in six truckloads of horse manure, secured at what Connye considered was a rather considerable expense for what was, after all, only horse shit. By the time she added up all her startup costs, she estimated each tomato would eventually cost about twenty dollars. But what sublime tomatoes they would be!

Her next task was to "work the soil" her books said - carefully breaking up any clods and horse droppings that had not been broken up small enough to plant seeds along the rows. Somehow she had never contemplated the actual *work* required to prepare a garden for planting. She stopped every few feet, wiped her brow, and looked at how many rows there were left to hoe. She began to think seriously about hiring a student to do this type of work. She much preferred the task of making little maps of the garden, drawing in exactly where each vegetable would go, and constructing decorative row markers indicating each variety with its English and Latin names, with little drawings of each veggie. And *very* important tasks they were too, she concluded.

Connye did manage to get the garden prepped, however, by hiring Honey's kids to finish the hoeing for her. And very grateful they were for the extra cash with college looming in the not too distant future. *Now* the cost of each of her tomatoes had skyrocketed considerably.

But uncertain if the nature spirits and devas had gotten the memo on her garden, she decided they needed additional enticement. She collected a number of bottle caps from the empty jars and bottles in her recycling bins, and all the thimbles available from a fabric shop. She wanted to invite her spirits and sprites to a special feast. Carefully punching the thimbles into the ground in the perimeter of the garden she filled each one with a nectar mixture that was usually used to feed hummingbirds. The bottle caps she interspersed between the thimbles and filled those with raisins and nuts. She then chanted a little sprit welcoming song, and did a spirit dance that she felt would please the devas peering in from the outskirts of the garden. She was determined to make them as welcome as possible. And as a final enticement she engaged a priest from the local Tibetan community to come over and perform a blessing ceremony.

As autumn was now approaching, there was not a lot more she could do on the garden this season, except plant garlic, as it thrived being wintered over. Connye had gone to Portabellos and bought up most of the garlic available that particular day and when she went out to the patio everyone wondered what she had eaten the night before, as the garlic smell was so strong. But she went home and separated all the individual cloves from the heads and was on her hands and knees this morning pushing the cloves deep into the freshly hoed bed. Now all that was needed was a good watering and the nature spirits could take it all from there – until next season, of course, when she would plant the rest of the garden.

◘   ◘   ◘

Sonora had decided to invite Bella to the harvest celebration. Honey would just have to get over it. After all, one could only hold a grudge for so long before it became petty, and reflected badly on the one holding the grudge. And so Sonora felt the rift between the group and Bella needed to be healed.

Sonora had a gorgeous patio and back yard with enticing garden beds of southwest plants and trees – just inviting a leisurely stroll. And as the summer monsoon rains were over, and the early September days were still warm and inviting, she decided to hold her Sunday afternoon event outside. This was not to be one of her grander entertainments. She wanted to keep it intimate, as she was starting to implement her little secret plan and felt she could control the situation more carefully if she kept the group small. She'd decided on a barbeque, and hired a top New Mexico barbeque chef to come with his smoker and set up on the patio. Henrietta was making a multitude of luscious side dishes and a wonderful desert of fresh peach cobbler with accompanying scoops of vanilla ice cream. The bar would be set up on the patio, and she engaged a country music band to play for the afternoon.

Lionel had been bugging Sonora for her reaction to his memoir. She wanted to read it, but was being negligent, and kept putting it aside at bedtime. Not that she wasn't interested in his success - but quite honestly, she just didn't care that much about Hollywood during the 50's and 60's.

Oz had offered to come by early to help with the set up. Sonora thought that was a splendid idea – and yes, sometimes it *was* nice to have a man about the house.

"What do you think," Sonora asked Oz, "do we have enough ice?"

Oz surveyed the coolers and buckets stuffed with bags of ice. "Unless you're planning to entertain polar bears, I would say you have quite enough."

Sonora gave him a sour smile. "Then I think we're ready."

Sonora had her usual crew of servers and bar tenders, and she stood looking out across the patio and garden with satisfaction. The chef tended his smoker and the pungent, sweet smell of smoking meat permeated the air. Sonora was ready for the first guests to arrive.

As usual, Lionel was early. He was hoping for a word with Sonora about his book before she became too busy to pay him any attention.

"My darling, Sonatina, have you had a chance to read it yet?" Lionel asked, fluttering around her like a bird with a broken wing.

"Oh Lionel, I told you I would let you know when I'd finished reading it."

"But have you started it? Have you come to the any of naughty bits? Are you shocked? I certainly hope so."

"My darling, this is not the time. I have nothing to discuss with you right now. I've been just too busy preparing for this party and our trip to France. Tell you what, I promise to take your book along and read it on the plane and when we get to the mill. Please just be patient."

"Oh, very well." Lionel sulked and went over to the bar to get a glass of white wine.

By now the first guests were starting to arrive and Sonora went to the entrance to welcome them. The party was not to be a lot larger than the usual coffee crowd, with the exception of a few other regulars and, of course, Bella. Connye was somewhat unnerved when she learned that Bella was to attend, but in the grand Santa Fe tradition decided to forgive and forget.

Bella had called Sonora the day before to ask if she might bring a guest. Sonora had, naturally, agreed. So when Bella appeared at the door with her almost exact double everyone paused and stared. Both were dressed nearly identically, and wore large hats that partially shaded their faces. Of course, the second Bella was Pinky, but even Lionel did not recognize him at first.

Sonora gasped as she walked forward to greet the two ladies. "My, my. What have we here?"

Both replied simultaneously by extending their hands and announcing, "Bella." Sonora reached out with two hands and greeted both. "Such a pleasure, now, will the *real* Bella please step forward?"

They both did, and announced together, "I am the real Bella." Then laughing they removed their hats and Mrs. H-C announced, "I am the Bella you were expecting."

And Pinky followed with, "And I am the Bella you didn't expect. But I too am Bella – Bella Le Balle, *star* of the Carousel Lounge," he exclaimed, throwing his arms out and taking a deep bow.

"Of course, I remember your splendid performance opening night. Welcome both of you."

Lionel came up to Pinky. "You scoundrel, however did you meet Mrs. H-C?"

Pinky had not revealed to Lionel his FBI connections so he prevaricated, "Ah, a little secret. Let's just say destiny divined that our paths should cross."

"Oh Pinky that is about as likely as me playing national football."

"Okay then, she came to the show. Was so *thrilled* with my performance she just had to come back stage and meet me."

"But all of this?" Lionel waved his hand at Pinky's Bella outfit. "Must have been planned."

Pinky nodded. "Indeed it was. You know how I *love* a grand entrance."

"But however did you get her to agree to such a stunt? Seems completely out of character for our dear madam."

Pinky shook his head sagely, "Strange are the ways..." Then he drifted off towards the bar, giving Lionel a wicked wink and a wave, trailing the smoke of his mystery.

The real Bella had been surrounded by a number of guests, delighted with her entrance. She was making quite a hit, and was thoroughly enjoying the attention.

Meanwhile, Sonora corralled Oz, assisting at the bar, and led him to the center of the guests.

Sonora called out, "Attention everyone. May I have everyone's attention, please?" The group hushed. "I have a couple of announcements I'm sure you'll all want to hear." As always, Sonora loved to draw out the suspense. "First, I am so glad all of you were able to attend. Such dear friends…."

Olivia called out, "Oh Sonora, get to the point and stop beating 'round the bush like you always do."

That elicited laughter and light applause from the group.

Sonora laughed then proceeded, "You know me all too well. Very well, first I want you all to know that I have a little surprise project that is just now coming to fruition."

"And that is?" Olivia pushed.

"As you all know, I was a dancer in New York City before I retired to the life of luxury and leisure… "

"You retire? Fat chance," Connye commented.

"I know, so driven… However, I have decided to bring world class dance to Santa Fe." She paused for reaction. There was none. "So I am bringing a darling dance troop to take up residence here. And along with performance we shall also be starting up a dance school for children."

"What are they called?" Honey asked.

"The Calisto Kenetic Dance Group."

"Never heard of them," Connye added, "Where they from?"

"Casper, Wyoming," Sonora replied.

"Oh yes, dance capital of the western world, "Connye sneered.

"Well, just you wait and see. And I expect all of you to attend our inaugural 'fun' raising performance – to be announced shortly. And tell all your friends."

"Any cute guys?" Honey called out.

"Yes, my dear, but I know for a fact at least two of them are married – to each other."

"Yeah, yeah, yeah."

"But – as they say on TV - that's not all, folks." Sonora put her arm through Oz's and brought him forward. "I want you all to meet my dear friend from New York, who you've all heard about by now – Mister Oz Garfield."

"Howdy all, happy to be here," Oz waved.

"An-n-n-d he's agreed to be the General Manager of the dance company. Ever so much more accomplished at managing than I am."

"I doubt that," Connye laughed.

Sonora nodded at Connye and smiled. "In any event, the company will be arriving tomorrow. I will welcome them, and then I'm off to France and my lovely mill for a few weeks. Everything here will be in the very capable hands of our dear Oz." She leaned over and gave him a chaste kiss on the cheek.

That sent a few guests wondering just what else might be brewing between the two of them.

"And now I hope you'll all have a splendid afternoon. The barbeque is almost ready, there is plenty to drink, the garden is delightful to walk about in, and the music is ready to begin."

Lionel came over to Sonora and gave her a mock slap on the arm. "Oh, you are too wicked."

"Whatever for?" she asked.

"Not telling me about your little dance project. I tell you everything."

"Well, I seem to remember I only learned about the Pinky Project way after it commenced."

"Oh yes, but that's because I was unsure if it was going to happen or not."

"Well, I forgive you."

"Forgive me? Some nerve. You offend me to the core. I'll probably never speak to you again."

"Well at least until we fly to France. I assume there will be words between us then."

Lionel lit up. "Oh yes, so exciting. But I have no idea what to pack."

"Travel light. That's always been my motto. And be prepared to stomp about in vats of grapes. It is grape harvest remember."

"Oh, certainly I can be an observer for *that*. Don't imagine my arthritic toes would appreciate all the squishing."

Lionel turned to leave but then turned back. "My Darling Sonatina, just a quick question. Exactly why is Mr. Oz *not* coming with us and the exquisite Mr. Quinto *is*?"

Sonora thought for a moment before responding. "Timing." She turned and, grabbing Oz away from a group of inquisitive ladies led him over to Olivia and Candice.

"My darlings, how lovely you both look this afternoon," Sonora smiled.

Olivia's make-up was, as usual, flawless. Candice looked young, fresh, and unadorned. She eyed Oz with a welcoming smile.

"May I steal your adorable sister away for a moment," Sonora asked Olivia.

"Of course, but not for too long, I trust."

Sonora took Candice by the arm and led her and Oz away from the crowd and into the garden for a leisurely stroll. "Are you still planning to relocate to Santa Fe?" Sonora asked Candice.

"Oh yes, quite enchanted with this lovely little city."

"I am so glad. And have you found any employment as of yet?"

"Not really. Not an urgent rush."

"Well, I have a little proposition for you." She then turned to Oz, "With your consent, of course."

"What's that?" he asked.

In response she said, "Well, since I will be out of the country for a few weeks, and with the dance company arriving, and all the work of setting up the business end of things, I was wondering if Candice might be interested in working to assist you?" She turned to Candice. "Is that something you'd be interested in? I pay quite handsomely."

"Define handsomely."

Sonora laughed. "I was thinking of something in the fifteen to twenty dollar an hour range. And it need not be full time if that would suite you better. And if it works out, it can become a permanent position when I return." She turned to Oz, "What do you think?"

Oz gazed at the charming woman and answered, "That sounds splendid."

"Now, I don't want to rush your answer Candice, why don't you and Oz get acquainted and he can ask you any questions he might have about your background. Is that agreeable?"

Candice once again gave an admiring glance to Oz, "Most agreeable."

"Shall we?" Oz extended his hand and invited Candice to stroll with him.

"Excellent. Let me know what you two decide. And I look forward to working with both of you if that is the decision." Sonora smiled as she walked away from them. Yes, now her little secret plan had been launched. Only time would determine the final outcome.

When Sonora returned to the living room Pinky was at the piano. He played beautifully and was belting out rousing songs from his show. The crowd was entranced. Even the country music band had stopped playing, and the three were attending to Pinky's splendid performance. Lionel was beaming. He had to admit, the kid had class.

After the entertainment the chef announced the barbeque was ready to serve. The band commenced once again, and the guests surrounded the food table and bar. It was a delightful afternoon.

Eventually Oz came over to Sonora.

"How did it go?" she asked.

Oz smiled and answered. "Very well. Yes, very well, indeed."

Sonora smiled too, "Good. I thought she might be a good match."

Le Moulin

Quinto was up on the roof of the mill replacing damaged tiles.   Lionel was stretched out in a shady hammock by the stream, enjoying his afternoon nap.   Sonora was folding laundry – all very domestic.   But let us make one thing perfectly clear. Sonora had not hand washed the laundry in the stream, nor dried it on a line.   She had a fully functioning washer and dryer.   After all, there was a limit to how far Sonora was willing to descend into domestic bliss.

Sonora's lovely Provencal mill was set at the far end of a tranquil valley surrounded by rolling hills - the scents of pine, lavender, and wild thyme wafting down rocky slopes.   Rows of neat vines, bursting with ripe grapes poised for harvesting, trailed across the inclines of ancient vineyards.   A small village graced the top end of the valley.   Once used for grinding flour, Sonora's mill had been turned into a charming, but snug holiday retreat. The grind stone no longer worked, but the water wheel still turned when the gears were engaged, creating a symphony of falling water and creaking joints.

Sonora had purchased the mill on a whim on one of her many excursions abroad, when she was still living in New York City with her husband, Brandon - though they rarely traveled together.   She had been journeying through France on an art and wine exploration. And stumbling upon the mill, and finding it for sale, she nearly fell all over herself with eagerness as she scurried to secure it for herself. She rarely visited it these days, but rented it out most of the time during the summer months to travelers through an English agency. She was seriously considering selling it, but on an afternoon like this, after a lunch of fresh garden tomatoes from the local market, fine crafted soft and runny cheeses spread on warm crispy bread, all served with a chilled and delicate Pouilly-Fuisee - she was not so sure.

"Ooops, Quinto warned as a tile slipped from his hand and slid down the roof landing with a thump near Lionel. Poor Lionel sprang awake, heart pounding, and twisted in the hammock, falling on the grassy verge of the stream with a second thump.

"Sorry," Quinto shouted from above.

Sonora raced over. "Are you all right?" she asked, helping Lionel stand.

"Nothing damaged, but my dignity," he replied, brushing himself off and retrieving his glasses, which had rested on his chest as he slept, and were tossed aside as he fell. Luckily he didn't land on them.

Sonora started to laugh. "Sorry, but it really was very funny."

Lionel was not amused. "I could have injured something," he pouted.

"I know. So sorry." Then she started laughing again and pointed to the back of his pants which were quite wet and grass stained from the fall near the stream.

"Bother," he grumped, as he headed to the house to change. "It's not funny, now I'll have to do another load of laundry," he called back before he disappeared inside.

"Is he okay?" Quinto asked as softly as possible from his high perch.

"Oh yes, he'll live. Why don't you come down now? That's enough for today, anyway."

"Shall I cook this evening?" Quinto asked as he climbed down the ladder.

"Absolutely not, you are on holiday. And besides you are the BIG film star now, no more chefing for you, dear boy."

"But I like it," he said, as he came over, grabbing her, and planting a big kiss on her turned cheek.

"No, I made a reservation at this absolutely charming, and very hard to get into, little bistro in the village. Believe me, it's a very special treat. The wild boar is cooked for two days in local wine, herbs, and truffles, and served with a delicate pippin and wild current sauce. Not to be missed."

"Oh, you are just too good to be true. Why did I ever let you go?" he asked, as he picked her up and twirled her in a circle.

"We both know why. I'm afraid neither of us are the settling down types. And now, of course, you are a bi-i-g mo-o-o-vie star totally married to the Hollywood lifestyle. Wouldn't suit me at all."

"I'll give it all up and whisk you away," he joked.

"No you wouldn't. And beside it's usually me that does the whisking. I would never have seen you if I hadn't invited to you to come away with us to France."

Lionel came ambling out of the mill wearing pink shorts and a turquoise shirt. Sonora started laughing again.

Lionel grumped, "Well, you told me to pack light. I have nothing else to wear. All my good stuff is in your laundry basket."

"Well, here, it's all folded, pick out what you need."

"Hey there, Pilgrim," Quinto intoned in his John Wayne accent, "You gonna wrestle some bronks a-dressed like that?"

Lionel was not amused. He gave both of them a stony look, pulled out his laundry, and returned to the mill, mumbling under his breath.

Quinto stretched and sighed. "Oh my, this is just all *too* wonderful. I don't feel like doing much of anything right now. What time is dinner?"

"Eight-thirty."

"Man, that's my bed time when I'm shooting."

Sonora patted his cheek, "Well, you are in France now, my darling. Need to make adjustments."

Quinto eyed the hammock. "Think I'll work on my script a bit, then take a nice lazy nap. Care to join me?"

"I think we'd both end up tumbling into the stream if we did that."

Quinto slapped her butt. "Okay then, gorgeous. Call me when it's time to leave."

◘   ◘   ◘

Pinky would have *loved* to support himself by only performing his drag show. But that was just not possible. Three nights a week at a hundred, maybe a hundred-twenty-five on a good night, just did not make it. So the FBI gig was a necessary evil. And while, occasionally, he had to do the suit and tie routine, as an undercover agent he could usually get by dressing casually. When he was not attending to Bella, he was tracking some characters sniffing around LANL. His boss suspected the Chinese underground was involved in Senator Spangler's blackmail and murder, and there were definitely connections through the Senator to LANL, as he sat on both the Senate energy and defense committees.

Someone in LANL had been providing leaked documents to Spangler and he, in turn, was handing those documents over to the Chinese through a US gang. It was Pinky's job to try and discover all the points of contact along the route, identify the players, and then the FBI could swoop in and round up the culprits.

Pinky was working leads at two of the contact points. He had narrowed his search down to three suspects in LANL who might be providing the documents. And he was close to identifying the gang that connected with the Chinese through their consulate in Los Angeles.

Through his FBI software, and with top clearance, he was monitoring the emails of the three LANL suspects. Gabriel Kurchner, an Israeli guest scientist, was his prime target. This Kurchner had a dodgy background. He had traveled extensively to Africa, particularly Chad, which had a significant Chinese presence with a large energy development project. He'd worked for a time at Nikan, a Chinese nuclear processing plant - a highly secluded, fortified, and secretive establishment deep in the Chad interior with its own airfield and satellite tracking system.

Kurchner's expertise was spent nuclear fuel reprocessing, which could lead to enriched weapons grade uranium. He had been invited by LANL to consult on their nuclear pit refurbishment project. What made Pinky suspicious was that Kurchner had continued contact with a Chinese colleague at Nikan, and was sending regularly scheduled encrypted emails. Pinky did not have the expertise to untangle the encryption, so he sent those on to his cryptology colleagues at the agency. However, today he came across an email that sparked his immediate interest. Kurchner was to meet a Mr. Lu at the BioPark in Albuquerque at three this afternoon. He promised to have the "posole recipe" with him. Now to the untrained eye – no big deal – but what was a nuclear scientist doing meeting a Chinese man at the aquarium in Albuquerque on a weekday, to deliver a recipe for a green chili and hominy stew? Made no sense, whatsoever.

And now that the Senator was no longer in the chain, Pinky suspected Kurchner was going to pass his stolen information on to the Chinese directly himself. Pinky immediately jumped into his car and headed for Albuquerque and the BioPark. He knew what Kurchner looked like and would be able to track him to the meeting with Mr. Lu. He called the ABQ FBI office and alerted his boss, and requested back-up in case this was a serious drop and an opportunity to apprehend Kurchner passing secret information.

◻   ◻   ◻

The streets of Chéniers sur Verdon were quiet and deserted. The church bell had just struck eleven. The three amigos were wandering back from the restaurant towards their car parked at the edge of town. Most the town was pedestrian friendly with the town center closed to vehicular traffic. With no large cities in this part of Provence, the night sky sparkled like all the riches in a pharaoh's newly discovered tomb.

Quinto had wandered into the only shop still open for some chewing gum. Lionel took Sonora's arm as they proceeded down the darkened street, lit only by a few faint lamps attached to the tops of stone buildings.

"Well, have you finished it yet?" Lionel asked.

Sonora hesitated, but finally answered. "Most of it. Just a few more chapters to go."

"And?"

"Well, it certainly is colorful," was all Sonora would concede.

"That's it? Colorful? That's like saying the ugly girl has nice hair and a charming personality."

"Oh Lionel, really….'

"No, I want you to tell me what you really think."

"Do you?"

"Ooo, that doesn't sound too good," Lionel winced.

"Oh darling, what can I say? If you really want the unvarnished truth, then I think it's a mess."

"Damn...."

"It's not that the material isn't interesting – to a film buff perhaps - but the structure is just a jumble. You jump all over the place, and you linger over long drawn out descriptions of bits that aren't that interesting, and rush over what needs more examination. And my dear, you really need to check your spelling and punctuation."

"So what should I do?"

"You might want to engage a professional editor. I'm sure there are plenty available on the internet."

"Do you think it's salvageable?"

"I would think so. But *remember* I'm not a professional, and while everything you do is eternally fascinating to *me*, I am not really a film history buff. I'm probably not the best person to give you a reliable opinion. I would certainly ask others to read it too - perhaps some of your Hollywood friends."

"Yes, good idea. Thanks."

Just then Quinto came charging down the street and grabbed Sonora by the waist. "Man, you were right about that restaurant. That was some damn good eats."

"I'm glad you liked it because I made us another reservation for our last night here."

"You think of everything, don't you?"

"We try."

"Is somebody maybe just a little too controlling?" Quinto squeezed her arm.

"I think not," Sonora replied, pulling away.

"You are too," Lionel said, agreeing with Quinto, as he was still bruised from Sonora's harsh assessment of his book.

"Very well then, I shall not make another suggestion during the rest of the trip, and then see what little fun we shall have." Now it was Sonora's turn to pout.

"Awww," Quinto sidled up to her and pulled on her ear. "Somebody's hurt. Come on give us a smile. Want some gum?" He skipped ahead towards the car. "Last one to the car's a crybaby."

"Oh what to do with him - such a kid." Sonora shook her head.

"Oh, I imagine you can think of any number of things," Lionel joked. "That old mill sure creaks a lot at night or is it a bed?"

Sonora slapped his shoulder.

◘   ◘   ◘

Something kept nagging Bella. It took her awhile to realize there was something in Chetworth's letter that did not quite make sense. She went to her desk, found the letter and looked through it again. The first thing that caught her attention was his request for her to hold on to the Bandelier map. *And please keep the Bandelier brochure as a souvenir of our friendship. It has special meaning for me.* Now why would he say that? Once she had been up there why keep it? What special meaning did it have for him? After all, it was only a brochure with a map on it - unless the map had some hidden significance. She opened the brochure and studied the map again. He hadn't made any markings on it. She studied both sides of the brochure but found absolutely nothing of interest or note.

She put the brochure back on her desk and sat back in her chair to think this through. She reached for the ring box. She opened it and took out the ring Chetworth sent her. She played with it in her hand, rolling it around in her palm like a marble. The telephone rang.

"Yes?" Bella was distracted and very abrupt answering the phone.

"My darling, are you ready?"

"What? Who is this?"

"After all the time we've spent together and you still don't recognize my voice?"

"Oh Angelica... How are the designs coming?"

"So splendid. They are done. Do you have a color printer?"

"I do."

"Then I am sending you an email with all the yummy designs. Get back to me as soon as you've made a decision, then I can get the orders in, and arrange for the installers. Can you do that?"

"Yes, send them along."

"Check your email, they should be there already."

Bella checked her inbox, "Ah, yes. Let me take a look and I'll call you right back."

Bella downloaded and printed out the designs. She spread them out before her on the desk. Yes, now here was finally something she liked. She picked up the phone and called Angelica.

"Well now, think you've got it."

"So relieved. Which one?"

"Hmm, the second and the fifth. Let me study them for a few days and I'll let you know which one I like best."

"Splendid. Yes, thought you'd like the second one. It's my favorite. But live with them for a while and let me know. Bye."

Bella hung up. She spread the two designs over her desk. A light breeze from an open window ruffled the papers. She set the ring she was still holding on top of the papers to settle them down. She turned on the desk lamp to brighten the colors. The way the ring lay on the papers it caught the light from the lamp and cast a prism effect across one of the designs. This was strange and Bella picked up the ring again to examine it more closely. She looked at the top of the ring which had a large amethyst stone set in the center. She turned the ring around and remembered the inscription on the band and re-examined it. It read: "A turn of the head and you will see." Yes, of course, how obvious.

Bella turned the ring over and twisted the head of the ring with the stone. When she did that a bright beam shot out through the stone. It looked like a laser beam but might have been anything for all she knew.

She suddenly got an idea and reached for the brochure, opening it up. She turned the light from the ring onto the map. Immediately she could see the hidden writing. Next to the map in the margins of the brochure was a list of names, addresses and contact phone numbers. The list was named "Scumbag Blackmailers." Chetworth had a sense of humor right up to the end. And he had counted on her to figure out how to use the ring to find the hidden message.

Oh, she *had* to call Pinky.

◘   ◘   ◘

Quinto insisted he would cook dinner this evening. He had completed his task on the roof and wanted to play. And for him that meant preparing a scrumptious meal, and what better place to gather the ingredients for such a meal in France than at the local street market and the wonderful specialty food shops in the village.

Quinto was in the car and ready to go. He was waiting for Sonora to get herself out here. There was a knock on the side of the car. Quinto looked up to see an elderly man with a basket peering in the window at him.

"Monsieur," the man greeted, "Madam Sonora, is she here?"

Quinto slumped his head as he knew their journey into the village would now be delayed. "Yep, she's inside, should be out any minute. Is there anything I can do for you?"

The man shrugged and ambled towards the mill. Quinto got out of the car. He thought if he brought Sonora out that might hurry along this interview.

Sonora emerged from the mill and seeing the old man, exclaimed, "Monsieur Bonnet, ça vas?

"Eh…" the old man shrugged again and offered her his hand. "Hip still not so good."

Sonora gave a French looking shrug and asked, "What can one do? Life is like that, no?"

Bonnet handed the basket to Sonora, "A little something from the farm. Killed the summer pig last week." He leaned in, "Very good sausage. And Madeleine sent a few eggs to go along with them."

"How thoughtful." Sonora stared after Bonnet who wandered towards the mill, examining it with a critical eye.

"See someone's been working on your roof."

"Oh yes, my friend Quinto did a fine job."

"Hmm, does he know about the mistral? - wicked wind. Hope he secured them good."

Sonora was looking nervous. "Oh, I'm sure he did."

Quinto came over to Sonora and whispered, "We've got to go. All the best produce will be gone if we don't get there early."

"Just a minute." She turned back to Bonnet. "Monsieur, excuse me, can we chat about this another time? We don't want to be late for the village market."

"Ah, how's that water heater holding up? My great nephew is a first class plumber. He could set you up just fine. Don't want to be in a cold snap with no hot water."

"Sonora, we've got to be going. If we don't get to the shops there'll be nothing left but the old cheeses," Quinto nagged.

Sonora turned to him, "Well the old cheeses are the best cheeses."

Quinto smarted back, "Then there will be nothing left but the new unripe ones."

Bonnet carried on oblivious of their desire to go. "Oh, that pine tree by the chimney, that's got to be at least seventy-five – maybe a hundred years old. Look how it leans. If that fell during a storm could cause terrible, terrible damage. My niece's husband could have that down in couple hours."

"Sonora, do you want dinner tonight or not?" Quinto pushed again.

Sonora commanded, "Here, take this in the house. Empty the basket and fill it with green gages from the plum tree. Give it to him and maybe he'll leave."

Quito looked in the basket as he headed towards the mill. "Well, at least we'll have breakfast."

Sonora went up to Bonnet and tried to steer him towards the driveway. "Monsieur, so kind of you to visit us. Perhaps before we go next week you and I could sit down together and discuss our arrangement. It's so nice to have a caretaker one can rely on."

"How was the drainage during that last storm? See you got what looks like mud on the patio. If water sits there, could get into the foundation. Nasty bit of work if that goes. Got a nephew could level that out and put in a nice retaining wall for the drainage right over there by that hill."

Lionel came out of the house and straight over to Sonora. "There was a rat in my room last night," he announced with a great deal of indignation.

Sonora just stared at him for a moment. "Couldn't be. Must have been a squirrel.

"Oh no, I know a rat when I see one. It was *not* a squirrel."

Bonnet spoke up, "Rats, eh?" He shook his head. "Old mill – grain – bound to be rats."

Sonora turned to him. "There's been no grain on the premises for fifty or more years."

"Rats don't know that," Bonnet stroked his chin. "Now, my good friend, Jean-Claude he sure knows about varmints. Could rid them for you good and forever. Just need to give him a call. He'll be right over."

"Are we going to town or not? I need a shoe lace," Lionel fussed.

Quinto came over with the basket filled with plums. He handed it to Sonora. "Can we go now?"

Sonora's phone rang. It was Oz. "Oh Oz, not a good time. Can I call you later?"

"Sonora we have a serious issue. Needs to be addressed immediately."

Bonnet leaned in, "Driveway needs some gravel. I got extra behind the barn, could bring a truck load over. My wife and I could rake it out for you."

Oz continued, "The studio we'd hoped to rent has fallen through. I've got a dance company here ready to work and no place to go. These guys are on salary now. Can't just have them sitting around and doing nothing. And they are dancers, and need to be doing a daily class."

"Have you called around? Any other places available?"

Quinto was now in the car and honking the horn. Lionel was tugging at Sonora's sleeve and nodded his head indicating they should go. Sonora whispered to Lionel. "Just a moment. Go to the car. I'll be right there."

Oz answered her question. "I've called everywhere in the phone book. Nothing available for at least six weeks."

"Not even short term, till I get back?"

"I can get two hours in the afternoon at the Fort Marcy gym on the basketball court. I can get the stage at Sweeney Elementary in the morning *before* school starts for an hour and a half. And the mall can let us use the food court after hours."

"Oh, Lord...," Sonora sighed in exasperation.

Quito honked the horn again.

Sonora handed Bonnet the basket with the plums. "Here enjoy. Hello to your dear Madeleine and we'll talk another time. So sorry, but I've just *got* to go." She dashed to the car leaving Monsieur Bonnet without a single work order.

"Oz, listen." Sonora turned back to her call. "Call some movers. Get them over to my place and have them clear the living room. It's quite large and even has a sprung wood floor. Had it put in when I remodeled. Love to dance on my own sometimes. The company can use that till I get back, then we'll sort something out. Okay?"

"But they need mirrors too," Oz added.

"Rent some, and the dancers can use the guest bed room and bath for changing. It's the best I can do from here. Oh, and call and alert Henrietta so she doesn't have a heart attack when the movers show up."

"Damn, you're good."

"I know. Bye."

Sonora slipped into the back seat of the car and pushed back her hair. "Now then, how about some shopping? And I know of a lovely little place for lunch."

◘   ◘   ◘

Pinky fumbled with his phone. It had an annoyingly loud disco ditty for a ring-tone. He was trying to be inconspicuous as he followed Kurchner. He ducked behind a saguaro cactus in the desert section of the botanical garden at the BioPark while trying to keep an eye on his query.

"Hello," he whispered, answering the phone.

"It's the other Bella."

"Can't talk right now, my dear, can I call you later?"

"It's very important. I've found a list – all the names and addresses of Chetwroth's blackmailers."

"Oh my, yes. That *is* important, but I'm actually tailing a spy right at the moment."

"Oh Pinky, you are too funny."

"No, I am. Really."

"Oh sure, and I'm dancing naked in the Santa Fe plaza."

Pinky laughed at the image, then cringed. "Okay, you win. But I really have to call you back. Soon as I can – I promise."

"Oh, very well. Soon as you can, then."

"Yes, yes." Pinky closed his phone and scrambled to catch up with Kurchner who had disappeared out of the garden house and was headed towards the aquarium. Pinky slowed his pace as he was advancing too quickly now. He was also pissed because none of the Albuquerque agents had identified themselves to him. He didn't know if he had any backup or not.

Entering the aquarium, Kurchner headed for the men's room. Pinky started sweating. This was getting far too complicated. There were too many people coming and going, and it was becoming increasingly difficult for him to keep track of his man without being detected. Dare he go in? Or should he wait and catch him on the way out? He decided it would be too obvious if he followed him inside so Pinky browsed a rack of post cards and waited.

Finally Kurchner came out. He did not seem to be aware of Pinky so Pinky followed. They entered the glass tunnel that cuts through the center floor of the aquarium, allowing underwater viewing from all sides. As Pinky and Kurchner entered, a troop of school kids came screaming from the other end of the tunnel, swallowing everyone in a swirl of rainbow activity. Pinky, in an effort to not squash an infant took his eyes from his query, and when he looked up again, Kurchner was gone. Pinky hoped Kurchner hadn't seen him and been spooked, as he needed to keep his cover to be effective.

It was not easy getting out of the tunnel, and when he did, Pinky could not find Kurchner anywhere. He combed the entire building and grounds but he was gone. What a fucking waste of time and energy. He immediately called his boss to ask where his back up had been.

"Well, they were all out to lunch," was the reply.

Pinky was pissed, but Pinky still had Bella. Perhaps what she found might wrap up the case without the need to keep tailing Kurchner and the others. He opened his phone and called her.

◻   ◻   ◻

It was not the disaster Quinto had feared. Despite all his anxiety over being late to the market, he had found everything he needed for his feast – all fresh and properly ripened - vegetables and assorted cheeses. In addition, he's secured fresh bread from the boulangerie, and the perfect leg of lamb, which he would debone himself, from the boucherie.

Sonora had treated them to a delightful lunch in a café on the town square. Now Quinto was playing pétanque – the local version of boules. He had ingratiated himself with the locals, and was pretty sure he would score big, but these old guys were the true experts. He would get his ball well placed close to the target but some old geezer would come along and knock his ball from hell to kingdom come – sending it scurrying to the next county. Sonora and Lionel looked on, amused, but not about to participate. No, they were quite content sipping coffee and cognac at their table after their very satisfying lunch.

"Are you really thinking about selling the mill?" Lionel asked, "Don't know when I've had a better time - despite the rodent over-population in my bedroom."

Sonora had her head back, her eyes closed, letting the warm afternoon breeze flow around her in utter peace. She heard what Lionel asked, but was in no rush to answer. "Ah-h-h. Yes. The mill....no, I don't believe so. It *has* been marvelous, hasn't it?"

"I know you don't get over here often. But what a shame it would be to let all of this go. Don't you think?" Lionel encouraged.

"As much as I love Santa Fe, think I could stay here forever. No, cannot even *begin* to think of selling the mill now."

"But then you'll need to learn French, don't you think?"

Sonora left her reverie and sat upright. "Yes, well there's the rub. I'm not much for languages, I'm afraid. My language abilities are limited to restaurant French and dress sizes. Never been able to go much beyond that."

Where they were sitting at the café they were in the shade. A portion of the square was brightly lit and Sonora was suddenly struck by two teen-agers sitting on a low wall eating ice cream. She leaned forward. "Lionel, do you see what I see?"

"And what is that?" he asked, adjusting his glasses.

"Those two kids over there. Aren't they Honey's boy and girl?"

Lionel peered over. "Aaron and Rachel. Yes, I do believe you're right. Hello!" He shouted and waved frantically, and when they turned to him, he motioned for them to come over. He was not about to get out of his comfy chair to go get them.

"Oh my God," Rachel bellowed as they approached. "Sonora? Lionel? What in the world are you two doing here?"

"Staying at my lovely mill for a few weeks," Sonora replied. "And how do you happen to be here?"

"Our first trip to Europe. High school graduation present. Mom sprang for us to travel in Europe this summer. We've been everywhere," Aaron answered. "We've just come from Spain and are backpacking our way towards Italy."

"Gotta be back home soon. College starts for both of us end of September," Rachel added.

"Where you staying?" Sonora asked.

Aaron turned and pointed, "The hostel over there." He pointed down a busy street. "Bit of a dump - but hey, we're traveling on the cheap."

"How would you like a nice quiet bed and a clean room tonight?" Sonora asked, suddenly animated. "I have a guest bedroom with twin beds, and we're planning a wonderful feast for this evening. Care to join us?"

Their faces lit up. "Would we *ever*," Rachel raved. "But we'll have to get our things. They're locked up at the bus station."

"Not a problem, we can pick them up on the way home. Come sit down. Do you want anything to eat or drink?"

"Would love a coffee," Rachel replied.

"I'd like a *citron pressé*," Aaron said scooting up to the table.

Quinto came ambling over. "Hey gang, just got my ass kicked by those old dudes over there. Think I'll stick to swinging in the hammock rest of the trip."

"Quinto do you know Honey's kids?" Sonora asked.

"Oh my God, you're that movie star guy," Rachel gushed.

"Yep. But just some regular guy too."

Rachel and Aaron introduced themselves. The waiter brought the coffee and Aaron's lemon drink.

Quinto sat down. "Hey gang, we gotta get goin' soon if we want to eat before midnight. I gotta get back and start cookin', pronto, pronto and sooner."

"We'll help," Rachel offered for the two of them, both being good cooks in their own right.

"Great. Can use all the help I can get. These two are useless in the kitchen," Quinto joked, indicating Lionel and Sonora.

Sonora stretched and yawned. "Oh my, look how lazy I've become. Okay, then, finish your drinks and let's be going."

After picking up the kid's gear they headed back towards the mill. Quinto was driving and Lionel sat next to him in the passenger seat. Sonora was actually dozing in the back seat. Lionel leaned over and spoke softly to Quinto. "Do you think I could ask you a favor?"

"If it involves power tools might be able to help. If it requires kitchen expertise - absolutely. If it's anything else - we'll have to see."

Lionel laughed. "I'm afraid it's in the 'anything else' category."

"Shoot. What ya need?"

"I've written a memoir of my Hollywood days. I'm afraid Sonora doesn't think much of it, and was wondering if you would mind reading it and giving me your opinion. After all you are the 'Hollywood dude' now, and might appreciate it more than Sonora does with her *very* provincial ways."

Quinto thought for a moment. "Hey guy, I'm working under a deadline on my script right how. And I'm in a blind alley. Unless I can break my writer's block don't think I'll have the time. Sorry."

"I understand. But thanks anyway," Lionel replied sadly.

Back at the mill, Sonora showed the kids their room. Lionel helped Quinto unload the groceries, and Quinto immediately set to work deboning and trussing the lamb, before starting to make a tomato flan as a first course.

Sonora ambled over to the kitchen. "So I'm useless in the kitchen, am I?"

"Oh yes you are, absolutely."

"But there must be *something* I can do." She picked up an onion. "What do you do with this, for example?"

Quinto leaned over and planted a kiss on her cheek. "My darling that would only confuse you and make you cry. And I don't want to spoil those pretty little cheeks."

"I might become frustrated at my lack of expertise but I doubt that would make me cry."

Quinto retrieved the onion from her. "No, my dear, that is not why you would cry. It's the fumes from the onion that would make you cry. And if you don't know that then I certainly don't want you creating havoc in my kitchen."

"Well, what about this?" Sonora asked as she picked up a fennel bulb. "I can certain do something with this funny looking celery."

Quinto laughed, turned to her, and taking her by the waist, escorted her out of the kitchen with a kiss on the top of her head. "Oh you *are* a lovely lass, but let's just leave the kitchen help to the kids. Okay?"

In the guest bedroom Aaron and Rachel were settling in. They had unpacked their backpacks. Rachel went to Sonora with an arm load of dirty clothes and asked if she could do some laundry. "Of course," Sonora replied, pointing to the laundry room.

Aaron took his backpack, having repacked most of it, and tossed it on the floor at the back of the closet. As he did so he heard a click and a snap. He turned on the room light as there was no light in the closet. When he went back to look inside he saw a panel at the back of the closet had opened. It was still dark but he could see there was something inside. He immediately rushed out to where Sonora was now sitting at the dinner table folding napkins.

"Sonora, do you have a flashlight?"

She thought a moment. "Check in that drawer," she said pointing to the sideboard. "Why do you need a flashlight?"

Aaron found it and took it out. "Come look, I've discovered a secret compartment in the closet." He called out, "Rachel, come look." Rachel came from the laundry room.

They all traipsed into the guest room. "Look," Aaron said, shining the light into the compartment.

"How did you find that?" Sonora asked.

"I threw my backpack on the floor and it must have struck a trigger or something and that panel opened." He reached in and pulled his backpack out of the closet and examined the wall and floor with the flashlight. "Here, it must be this." He said as he pushed on a peg in the wall. As he did that they could hear a clicking in the wall. "There, that must be the release."

"What? What's going on?" Lionel asked as he came into the room. "I heard excitement afoot."

"Aaron's found a secret compartment," Sonora announced.

"There's something in there," Aaron added, shining the light closer. "Looks like a manuscript," he said, "Shall I take it out?"

"Yes, but be careful," Sonora cautioned.

By now, sensing the commotion, Quinto had joined them. Seeing what was going on he cautioned. "Wait, wait, wait. Don't put your hand in there yet. Scorpions just love dark little hidey holes like that."

"There are scorpions in Provence?" Sonora winced.

"Sure are. Saw lots when I went hiking up in the hills the other day," Quinto answered. Here, let me." He was carrying a pair of kitchen tongs and carefully grabbed the manuscript and slid it out. No scorpions, though there were a few mouse droppings and nibbled edges. He held it carefully and everyone craned in to examine it closely.

"It's music." Sonora exclaimed. She took it and examined the pages. The paper was brittle and the music was hand written. There was no immediate identification as to either the title of the piece or the composer. "This is really old. We need to take great care. Let's take it to the desk where there's better light."

Sonora led the group into the living room. She placed the manuscript carefully on the desk and turned on the lamp. "Now let's see what we have here." She carefully turned each page. There was no significant damage and each page was clear and intact. When she got to the last page there was writing. It was in fact the title page. The composer was Marin Marais and it was titled Motet – *domine salvam fac regem – pour le rétablisserment de le Dauphin*, and was dated 1701.

"Good Lord," Sonora exclaimed. "This is really significant." She turned to the kids. "Can you do an internet search on this?"

Aaron replied, "Sure, let me get my tablet. You got wi-fi here?"

"I believe so." She turned and looked at Quinto.

"Yeah," he nodded. "Don't need a password."

Go ahead, give it a try," Sonora told Aaron.

Aaron went to the room and came back already searching on his device.

"I'd better get back. I'm at a crucial stage." Quinto excused himself. "Let me know what you find," he called out, disappearing into the kitchen.

"Here, here, here. Listen to this. Marin Marais was this composer dude in the sixteenth-seventeenth century. He was at the royal court and all that shit. Here, it lists his works. Ta da, ta da, ta da," Aaron mumbled, as he perused the list. "Wait, wait. Here it is. Read that title again." Sonora read it to him. "Yes, here it is. And it says the music was lost along with a number of other works. Think they might be here too?"

"I'm sure you'll look."

Sonora sat back in her chair, dumb founded.

"That's got to be worth a whole lot of shit," Aaron exclaimed.

"I'm sure it *is* worth a whole lot of shit," Sonora added with an edge, "However, it should not be for sale. I intend to get it into the right scholarly hands. This is a very important find and it rightfully belongs to the people of France."

"And I bet it would be illegal, in any case, to take such an artifact out of the country without some kind of license," Lionel suggested.

"Hadn't thought of that, but you're probably right. But who should I contact? I have no idea."

"I'll do some research for you," Aaron offered, turning back to his tablet.

Sonora smiled at the two kids. "I'm so glad we ran into the two of you. What an exciting afternoon we've had and it's not even nap time yet."

Quinto came back to the group. "Hey this little incident has given me just the idea I need for my script. Solves a big problem I was wrestling with, and should be able to finish up now." He turned to Lionel, "Hey bud, should be able to take a look at your book, if you still want me to."

"Absolutely, let me go get it."

"Hold on there, cowboy, I'm right in the middle of cooking. It can wait till after dinner, can't it?"

"Sure - sorry," Lionel said a little sheepishly.

"Hey guys, I know you're treasure hunters, and all that, but where's my kitchen help when I need it," Quinto addressed the kids.

"Gotta put a load in the dryer, and I'll be right there," Rachel answered.

"Yeah me too, soon as I finish this search," Aaron added.

"Okay, get your butts out here, then, when you can," Quinto laughed, returning to the kitchen.

"Here ya go," Aaron addressed Sonora, handing her his tablet. "That's who ya gotta contact."

"You're such a good boy," Sonora cooed as she wrote down the address and phone number. "I just hope someone there speaks English."

"Think I'll go check my room for more secret compartments," Lionel brightened. "Let me know if you guys need help with anything." He headed towards his room.

Sonora regarded Aaron as he was preparing to go help Quinto in the kitchen. "Thanks so much for your great help. And what a thing to find this manuscript. Just want you both to know you are welcome to stay here as long as you like before we return home."

"Thanks. Might stay a couple of days. But we have a lot of places to visit yet. And don't want to wear out our welcome. But it's sure nice to have a comfy bed and a private shower." He headed to the kitchen.

Sonora sat back and contemplated the manuscript. Yes, as soon as she returned home she would need to issue a press release. Not just for the local press, but for the national media as well. Might there also be interest from the Today Show, Good Morning America, or Entertainment Tonight? Hmm.

My, how Connye would wiggle and squirm. Her paltry little archeological expedition last year, when she believed she'd discovered buried treasure in her back yard, just paled in comparison. And Sonora knew for a fact it was not real treasure at all, but debris from the construction of her house. To cover up her disappointment after the loudly trumpeted initial find, Connye had gone on a shopping expedition to a few select antique stores and bought up artifacts to display in her specially constructed showcase, passing them off as her "found" treasure.

It was a pity Sonora couldn't keep the manuscript. She could have it framed in a shadow box for all to see. But Sonora was far too ethical. She could *never* allow herself to cheat the French of their national heritage. And maybe there would even be a *Légion d'Honneur* for the noble sacrifice she made in the nation's interest. Now that would be an achievement indeed. She just knew Connye would turn beet red. Now a shadow box for the medal *would* be impressive.

"Madam?" Monsieur Bonnet called out from the front door.

Sonora snapped out of her reverie. "Oh Monsieur, so glad you stopped by again. I want to go over a few things with you before we leave. Is this a good time?"

"Oui - yes. May I come in?"

"Of course." Sonora welcomed in the caretaker, and they sat by a window where the late afternoon sun was pouring in.

"Thank you for the plums, they were very nice and my wife sends her regards."

"Merci. And your sausages look scrumptious. Planning to have them for breakfast tomorrow morning."

"Pardon? I do not know that word – scrumptious. What is that?" Bonnet asked.

"Especially delicious. That's what it means."

"Ah, thank you."

"Now I just need to go over our caretaking arrangement with you," Sonora began.

Bonnet was looking around the room. "Have you had the chimney swept? In old places like this it needs to be done at least once a year."

Sonora took hold of both of Bonnet hands to draw his attention back to her. "Dear Monsieur, I understand this is an old building, and it needs constant attention. And that is exactly why we need to talk and come to an arrangement. Do you understand?"

"Oh yes."

"Please listen to what I have to say. Previously our agreement only covered you looking out for the mill and calling me if there was a problem."

"Yes, yes."

"But now I want to extend our agreement. I am going to leave a sum of money in a bank account in the village. This money is to be used for the care of the mill. I really love it here and want to come back more often. And as you have pointed out, there is a lot of maintenance to be done. I want you to direct the work and I will give you authority to use the money for repairs as you see fit – with a salary for you, of course."

Bonnet's eyes lit up. "Madame, that is very wise and generous of you."

Wise or not Sonora knew she had a good caretaker, and wanted to help him, his family, and all his friends who would benefit by the work he could supply them. "Very well, I will make the financial arrangements and will stop by your farm next week with the details. Is that agreeable to you?"

Bonnet nodded. "Perhaps I could raise a pig for you during the summer and come next fall I could fill your freezer with fresh cochon." He gave a sly smile. "For an extra fee, of course."

Sonora smiled. "Of course."

◘   ◘   ◘

Pinky marveled at the magic of the ring. He kept turning the head and playing with it until Bella told him to focus on the map.

"Oh yes, let's take a look here." Pinky focused the laser from the ring on the map till he discovered the writing – the information on the blackmailers. "Oh my, that is impressive. May I take the ring and the map to my boss?"

"Yes, but I want the ring back. It was my father's," Bella emphasized.

"Of course."

"I hope this means the end of this frightful business for me. This whole ordeal has been truly traumatic."

"I understand. But I can't see how it would involve you anymore. After all you have nothing the blackmailers could want, do you?"

"I don't believe so, unless they want to seek revenge for me revealing this to the FBI," Bella worried.

"Then you be extra careful, sweetie. Can't have you feeding coyotes and their pups out there in the desert, can we?"

"Oh Pinky, don't even go there. How could you…?"

"Well, I'll be off then. Need to get this to headquarters right away. Now I'll have to make a second wretched trip to Albuquerque in the same day. I need my own helicopter."

"Were you really tracking a spy?" Bella marveled. "I didn't know you were that butch."

"Oh honey, you have no idea. You should have seen the training they put me through for this job. My hair was just a mess."

"What hair?" Bella teased.

"Now don't be mean. A girl's got pride." He started to leave, but had another thought and turned back. "Seriously, Bella, you be careful. Don't hesitate to call me if you have any concerns at all."

"I will."

"Promise?"

"Yes."

◻   ◻   ◻

"Bernie, what's up?" Quinto asked as he answered his phone.

Dinner was nearly finished. All that was left was for Quinto to bring out the fresh wild strawberries with the dressing of Balsamic glaze, and the selection of cheeses he'd purchased that morning.

"I never knew vegetables could be so yummy," Rachel commented. "And what was that incredible sauce?"

"I believe it's called aioli," Lionel answered, "I saw him making it with a mortar and pestle and asked him about it."

"What a revelation France has been. I want to learn to cook like this when I get home."

Sonora gazed after Quinto as he chatted on the phone in the living room. "Yes, but of course, it helps to have one of the best chefs I know prepare our dinner." She sighed, "What a waste to have such a talented guy go out to the coast to be a movie star."

"He might disagree," Lionel said. "After all there's a lot more money in films than in itinerate part-time cooking."

"Oh yes, I know. But if I were Queen....." She trailed off into thought.

"Sorry gang," Quinto announced as he returned to the table. "You kids help me clear up and I'll bring in desert."

"Who's Bernie?" Sonora asked, as Quinto disappeared into the kitchen.

"My producer," Quinto answered. He returned with the cheese board and fresh cut bread. Rachel brought a tray with bowls of the strawberries. "And I'm afraid I have bad news."

"No..." Sonora groaned.

"I have to go back to LA tomorrow."

"Not fair. You promised I'd have you for the full two weeks."

Quinto came over and patted the top of Sonora's head. "I know. But can't be helped. Crisis on the new movie - but as I'm one of the producers, they need me back pronto. So sorry."

"Poo," Sonora grumbled.

Quinto turned to Lionel, "And you, Mr. Lionel, if you give me a copy of your book I'll read it on the plane. It's a dreary long flight to LA, and I'd love to take a look at what you've written."

"Oh yes. Lovely," Lionel beamed.

Later that evening, everyone had gone to bed but Sonora and Quinto. Music played softy in the background with a smoky bourbon note. They sat by the fire drinking cognac. A sudden turn in the weather had brought on a cold wind. Outside the hammock, once a comfy spot for a nap on a warm afternoon, now swung in the wind, leaves falling and blowing around in spirals. Sonora and Lionel would be returning back to Santa Fe in three days. The hearth was warm and Sonora, wrapped in a wool shawl, gazed into the fire.

"Well, my darling woman, the summer is certainly over now. The trip is almost complete - and soon we all go back to our 'other' lives."

"Yes, yes. And I have such a lot to do when I get back. My dance company... Whatever was I thinking?"

"Oh, you'll be fine. You love a challenge, and once you get back into it you'll just thrive."

"I know. But for the first time, I've seriously considered relocating here. It's been such a special time."

"But you can't always just recreate a moment like this. It was a magical combination of factors that made it so special. And holidays always have a way of collapsing like a failed soufflé if we try and extend them, or make them work for us on an everyday basis."

"You're probably right. I don't know. Why can't life always be just like this?"

A log collapsed into the fire, and a spray of sparks sizzled.

Quinto looked intently at Sonora. "So tell me about this Oz dude. What's his story? You've said hardly anything about him. I know he's from New York. What brought him out to Santa Fe?"

Sonora looked up and over to Quinto. She calculated just how much she wanted him to know. "Me."

"Oh yeah? Business or pleasure?" Quinto smiled.

"Ah, the sixty-four thousand dollar question."

"And the answer is?"

"He came a-courting."

"Really? Then why am I on this trip instead of him?"

"I said he came a-courting, I didn't say I'd accepted."

"Uh huh, interesting. And the outcome will be…?"

"Yet to be determined."

Quinto studied her. "Sly. So sly."

"I've been working on something which I believe will determine the outcome."

"Care to tell me?"

"Not yet. But I'll let *you* know when *I* know. In the meantime, he is taking care of business back home. I made him Administrative Director of the dance company. Otherwise I'd never have been able to get away to France."

"You are too ruthless for me. I'd never be able to dream up a character like you for one of my scripts. I'd have to name you Divastation – Empress of the Underworld."

"Ouch. Is that really how you see me?"

"Not at all - but that's how I believe you see yourself."

"Hum. Interesting. Could be."

"I've often wondered," Quito treaded softly, "what might have happened between us if things had been a little different."

"Oh, you were so young and wild. Don't think there was a coral big enough to contain you. And me? Well, too independent and strong willed. Like things my own way, and have the capacity to follow any personal whim without consideration for anyone else." She thought for a moment. "Yes, Divastation – aptly named. That's good."

"That's why I get the big bucks."

They both laughed, then lapsed into silence, as they sought comfort, gazing into the depths of the fire.

How Ya Gonna Keep 'Em Down on the Farm?

Henrietta was frantic. Not only was the house in an uproar, but there was loud thumping music all day long – every day. Poor IT was frightened and confused, and refused to go through the living room, when the rehearsals were taking place, to use the doggy door. Henrietta retreated with the dog to her quarters over the garage and stayed there the whole time Sonora was in France. She occasionally escaped to the club house for tea in the afternoon and found excuses to linger till she knew the dancers would have gone for the day.

Sonora's return was a God send. Now things could start getting back to normal. Or at least that's what she hoped. But Sonora informed her that until they found a suitable studio, the rehearsals would have to continue in the house. Sonora compensated by giving Henrietta a paid vacation to visit her family in upstate New York.

And Sonora? Well, there was no way she was going to share her house with constant rehearsals, so she checked into Quacking Aspen Inn for the duration. The boys gave her a terrific deal and the best suite, and the most delightful breakfasts in bed, plus room service on call. Why would she ever want to leave?

Oz had rented office space to manage the company till they got their own quarters. Sonora checked in on her second day back from France. While the office was cramped, it was neat and efficient. Oz and Candice looked up with surprise when she entered, as she had not called beforehand to say she was coming.

"Sonora," Oz exclaimed. "Boy, is it good to have you back." She was surprised he didn't jump up to give her a hug, but put that down to being in the work place.

"Hi Sonora," Candice welcomed, and Sonora detected a fleeting look of anxiety and concern from her.

"Well, I'm ready to jump right in," Sonora offered. "Seems we have some problems to solve."

"Good news," Oz grinned, "I think I've found the perfect studio space."

"Excellent."

"But just one little problem…" Oz hesitated slightly.

"Yes?"

"We'd have to buy it." Oz winced slightly as he told her.

"How much?"

"One point five."

"Million?" Sonora gasped.

"I'm afraid so. Do you want to see it?"

Sonora considered this for a moment. "Yes, I suppose so. But it better be gold leafed and have Angels on High in attendance for that price."

"Oh it's a great place. Three studios, tons of office space, men's and women's changing rooms, and one of the studios is large enough to hold performances in if we wish. Think you'll love it."

"Okay, let's take a look."

Oz laughed. "I have the keys so we can go right over if you like. And just in case, I put a five thousand dollar deposit on it so we could hold it and move quickly if you decide you want it."

"Well aren't you the Johnny come quickly." Sonora neglected to realize the sexual overtones to that little remark.

Oz cast a quick look at Candice. "We'll be right back. You okay?"

Candice nodded.

Oz glanced nervously at Sonora as they drove in near silence for a while. "How was France? Did you have a good time?"

Sonora looked over at him. "Yes." She paused a moment. "What's going on? Is there something you want to tell me?"

"Well, just the studio, and, of course, the company is working hard for the fun raiser." Oz kept his eyes on the road. "Hey, here we are. Looks great from the outside, doesn't it?"

"Nice. Let's see what we got here."

They went inside the studio. It was conveniently located with plenty of parking and adjacent to major roads. The studios were beautiful – good natural light, great mirrors, beautiful sprung floors, and an ample entrance and office space - suitable for both the performing company *and* the school.

"Who was here before? How come this is for sale?" Sonora asked.

"Husband and wife team were going to open a yoga and qi gong studio and then they broke up. He was messing around with some student and she nailed his ass. This is part of the divorce settlement it seems."

"Could we make an offer?"

"Real estate agent thinks we could get it for a million two. But they did all this renovation and pumped a bundle into it."

"Let's offer a million and see what happens. Let my friend Honey represent us if you haven't signed with a buyer's agent yet."

"Certainly."

"And any idea when we can close if it's a cash deal?"

"The listing agent said maybe two weeks. It's not that complicated if it's cash."

"Good, although I am enjoying my suite at the boy's inn, I really want to get back into my own house as soon as possible. And poor Henrietta will be ecstatic. I had to send her away to preserve domestic harmony."

Oz beamed. He came over and gave her a hug. "That's great. And I believe it's a great investment for you as well."

As they separated, Oz couldn't look Sonora directly in the eye.

Sonora reached over and took Oz's hand. "Something's happened, hasn't it? Tell me all about it. What's going on? And I don't mean about the company."

Oz looked down and struggled. "Oh Sonora, I am so sorry. I know I came out here to be with you. But while you were gone, Candice and I worked really hard together to get everything up and running. We were together all day, every day...and a few evenings as well. And then one thing led to another and it just happened."

"She *is* a very attractive woman," Sonora added.

"Yes, she is. I am *so* sorry. I hope this doesn't devastate you. And I hope it doesn't destroy our working relationship. If you want me to leave – us to leave, I would certainly understand."

Sonora smiled softly. "Oh no, I wouldn't think of either of you leaving." She stifled a manufactured sniffle and a tear. "And I think I'll survive - somehow."

How well her little plan had worked. Now, she just couldn't wait to tell Lionel *all* about it.

◘   ◘   ◘

Lionel was having a hard time adjusting to being back home from France. It had been so nice to have everyone else do the cooking and cleaning. All he'd had to do in France was go to bed early, sleep late, take naps in the hammock, feast on wonderful fresh food, and mildly entertain the other guests with his dry wit. Sonora had even done his laundry without his asking. But that was *never* going to happen back home.

And since Sonora was camping out at the boy's inn while her house was in an uproar, they had not had tea together for several days. But Sonora had called late morning and said she was coming to tea this afternoon with some really stunning news. *Now* it was finally beginning to feel like old times once again.

Lionel wondered how Pinky was getting on. They had not spoken since his return. "Perhaps I'll stop by the club unannounced," Lionel schemed. He loved creating little surprises. He had brought Pinky an outrageous Chanel vintage hat from a second hand shop in the village just before they left France. It was *so* Pinky. Lionel couldn't wait to surprise him with it.

Lionel's phone rang. "Hello."

"How ya doin' guy?"

"Quinto... You get back all right?"

"Sure did."

"You trying to reach Sonora? She's not here."

"No, I wanted to speak to you. Read your book on the plane."

Lionel's stomach seized up a little. "Oh... And?"

"I loved it."

191

"Really?" Lionel was suddenly giddy.

"Got some spelling and grammatical problems, but nothing a good editor couldn't fix. I could recommend a few, or if you get a publisher they should be able to take care of it for you. Oh, I'm sending the manuscript back to you FedEx. Should get it tomorrow."

"Oh, I'm so pleased. Thank you so much for reading it."

"Man there was a lot in there I didn't know about Hollywood in that era. Very informative. Was a good read for me."

"Great. Then I guess Sonora just didn't know what she was talking about."

"Yeah, when I worked with her on the script we did together she was clueless, and more importantly, didn't really give a shit. Not the best constructive critic I've found. You got a publisher yet?"

"I had a few express interest before I wrote it, but nothing lined up definitely yet."

"I'm with a great agency. They handle books as well as film. I can talk to a few dudes at the agency if you like. Would be great to have an agent handle your deal."

"I'd love that. Quinto, you are a real doll."

"Okay, then let me grab your manuscript before it gets sent out and I'll hand it over to the agency to take a look at it."

"Really appreciate your help."

"Okay, gotta go. I'm sure someone will contact you from the agency soon as they've taken a look. Bye."

◘   ◘   ◘

Connye had spent the morning at her garden. Last night had been the first light frost. She wanted to check on things. First thing she did was examine the treats she'd left for the devas.

All had been eaten – whether by the nature spirits or the prairie dogs and squirrels she didn't know. But she favored the devas. Good. Everything was progressing as planned.

As she surveyed the garden it struck her that she didn't have to wait till spring to do some planting. There were plenty of hearty plants that just loved the cold and frost. Yes, she would go immediately to the nursery and pick up some kale, collards and mustard greens. Was probably too late to select the larger vegetables like cabbages and brussel sprouts. And they would have to be already established plants, there was not enough time to expect seeds to germinate and grow before the really hard freeze.

After running to the nursery she proudly planted her little plants, watered them thoroughly, and was prepared to be mama to her new babies. She was so excited she wanted to stand there and watch them grow, but realized that would be a futile exercise, even for her super animated Findhorn garden.

When Connye returned home there was a message on her phone. It was from Jefferson. She called him right back.

"My darling, you called?"

"I did. Besides missing you I was thinking," Jefferson greeted.

"About?"

"I was just checking the Kaiser Sister's website, and am so pleased to see how well they're doing with the sales of their paintings. And you know, they must both be about eighty now. Was thinking what fun it would be to throw them a surprise birthday party."

"What a lovely idea. When?"

"I have to be in Denver early October, so was figuring I could stop by right after that. Does that give you enough time to organize it all? Sorry to have to ask you to do it, but you're so good at it, and I'm so far away…."

"Of course, I'll take care of everything."

"You *are* an angel."

◘   ◘   ◘

Pinky sat at his mirror in the club. He stared at the new hat Lionel had brought him from France. It was *so* nice – so Pinky. Poor Pinky pondered his situation. How much longer would he have to do this dreadful FBI job? Why couldn't he make a living doing what he loved? He folded his arms on the dressing table and lay his head down. The hat toppled off.

The problem was he actually was a really *good* FBI agent. Pinky had taken the list of the blackmailer's names to the agency, and within a few days the whole group had been investigated, rounded up, and charged with conspiracy, spying, and the murder of Senator Spangler. Of course, these thugs had plenty of clout behind them and they got all lawyered up and were out on bail within a week.

Meanwhile, Pinky had been given the assignment of leading a unit to take down Gabriel Kurchner before he could cause any more trouble. One problem was that he was an Israeli national, so they had to move carefully, and observe proper protocol so as not to rattle the Jewish lobby. Everything was so political these days.

But Pinky had some good smarts, and worked carefully to set up the perfect sting. He knew they needed to catch Kurchner with the goods. It was no good just picking him up off the street. They needed iron clad proof of espionage if they were to make their case stick.

Now Pinky had discovered that Kurchner had a penchant for zaftig women of a certain age. And Pinky, with his internet savvy, created a charming character named Rosa Zeitwig of Oklahoma City. Pinky had been corresponding with Gabriel, as Rosa, for about a month, and finally hinted that if Kurchner was *really* interested she would come out for a visit to Los Alamos so they could meet in person. However, she had just one stipulation. (Pinky was just delighted with this little wrinkle as he had done his research and knew exactly what to ask)

Rosa's story went like this – Her maternal grandfather, Milton Spink, worked for the Manhattan project when it was first established. He was an architect and a builder, and was responsible for constructing two of the first labs where the atom bomb was researched and built. Now what Rosa wanted from Gabriel were her grandfather's original drawings and plans for the labs. She said her grandfather had died a pauper, but was much beloved in the family. If she could just have those plans it would mean so much to her and the family. Could Gabriel do that one *little* thing for her? If he did she would be ever so grateful, and would show her deep appreciation amply and fully when she came to visit him.

Well now, how can one say *no* to an offer like that? And Kurchner readily agreed, as he already had access to the architectural archives, and could easily purloin what no one ever looked for, as the original labs had been torn down and replaced years ago.

And so the rendezvous was set. Kurchner made a deluxe room reservation for Rosa at the historic Los Alamos Kingston Hotel, a grand old institution in the community. Besides its fine rooms and service, it was known for its fine dining restaurant and lounge where the atomic scientists used to meet and drink after exhausting days of research.

Pinky, as Rosa, arranged to meet Gabriel in the lounge. Pinky spent all afternoon on his makeup. Every detail had to be perfect. This could not be some crass drag act – pounds of mascara, glitter, and an orange fright wig. He/she had to be convincing in lounge light, and stand up under the scrutiny of a sex hungry Israeli spy. How thrilling. After his careful work Pinky examined himself in the mirror. Yes, truly convincing.

Of course, Pinky had arranged for backup. He was not about to take Kurchner down all by himself. He could be butch but not *that* butch. The other agents were to be stationed throughout the lounge, and would arrest Kurchner as soon as he handed over the architectural plans to Pinky.

Rosa sat sipping a Black Velvet, as Gabriel approached. Needless to say, Pinky was a little nervous. Would he pass the test of the first inspection?

"Miss Zeitwig?" Gabriel leaned in inquiringly.

"Gabriel, I presume." Pinky replied, trying to find Rosa's voice.

Gabriel stood back and looked Rosa over with a great deal of admiration. "My, my, aren't you just the sweetest tasty, little morsel."

Rosa batted her eyes and lowered her gaze. "Not so bad yourself. Won't you sit down? Shall I call the waitress? Would you like a drink?"

Gabriel sat opposite, his eyes devouring Rosa's every sensuous curve. "I was thinking perhaps I could order a bottle of the best Champaign and we could retire to your room to savor its sweetness. What do you say to that?'

Now this was not what Pinky had in mind at all. "Well, we have a little matter to settle before we go *anywhere*, Gabriel."

"You mean the plans?"

"I do."

"Oh, you know, I left them in the car. I was thinking we could get them later after we get to know each other better. I have reservations at a wonderful little French restaurant. Shall we sample the Champaign up in your room first?"

Rosa wagged her finger at him. "Now, that was not our agreement, Mr. Kurchner. A nice girl does not just rush into things. You understand?"

Gabriel studied her a moment, then leaned forward and whispered in her ear.

"Why, Gabriel, you would do that – to me?" Pinky asked in somewhat of a panicked surprise.

"Every inch." He beamed.

Pinky was starting to get nervous now. He sent furtive glances towards his backup. They seemed ready to pounce once the plans were passed, but Kurchner was not passing any plans. Pinky had to think what to do.

"Then I propose a compromise."

"And what is that?" Gabriel asked.

"I'll go to my room and prepare myself. And you go to your car and bring me the plans. How does that sound?"

"Hmm. Okay."

"Room 210. Shall we say fifteen minutes? A lady needs a moment to prepare herself."

"Very well." Kurchner rose and stood looking at Rosa. "You won't disappoint me now, will you?"

Rosa nodded coyly and smiled. "How can you even imagine such a thing?"

Kurchner turned and headed for the hotel entrance. Pinky bounced up and headed directly to the closest agent.

"Change of plans. Doesn't have the plans with him. He's agreed to bring them to my room – 210. You guys need to hide in the room and charge out when I call out 'Oh Gabriel'. That will be your signal that he's handed over the plans."

"Okay," the agent replied.

The agents followed Pinky as he headed towards the elevator, but Pinky turned and said. "And don't you dare be late. My virtue is depending on you."

The lead agent laughed. "Okay, stud."

◘   ◘   ◘

Connye was appalled and started crying. She stood gazing out over the expanse of her empty garden. Not a single plant that she had planted was left. Every single one was gone. Where could they have gone? Did someone steal them? Seemed unlikely. Gophers? Prairie dogs? Rabbits?" Why weren't the devas protecting her garden? She was pissed. She went over and kicked a bush where she believed her sprites were sheltering. That would teach them. She was not going to plant again this season. And for sure next spring she would have to put up a fence. Or maybe this whole idea was nutzy cuckoo. What did she really need with cabbages the size of hub caps? After all, how much coleslaw could one consume anyway? And besides, she had a birthday party to organize.

◘   ◘   ◘

There was an agent hiding in the bathroom. There was another one in the closet, and there was a third on the balcony, ready to burst through the sliding door. Pinky had changed into a super-sized negligee. He looked like spinnaker under full sail. The lighting was dim. He was taking no chances. He was sweating like a race horse, and it felt like his foundation was starting to run. There was a knock at the door.

"Come in, it's unlocked," Rosa called out in an uncertain voice.

Rosa adjusted herself alluringly on the sofa - the Champaign was opened and poured into flutes on the coffee table.

"My darling, are you ready for papa?" Gabriel came greedily into the suite.

"Oh daddy, yes. Champaign?" Rosa held out a glass for Gabriel, hoping to delay the inevitable just a little.

"Yum, yum, yum," Gabriel chanted as he approached Rosa waving the plans at her.

"Oh, you've got them. Thank you," she said extending her hand for the plans. He handed them to her. "Oh, Gabriel," she called out rather loudly, ready for the agents to swoop in and sweep up the now ravenous and lurking Kurchner.

No one came.

"Oh Gabriel!" Rosa shouted out even louder. Seeing this as a sign of passion and encouragement, it enflamed Gabriel even more, and he advanced and pounced on her, tearing at her negligee. Pinky struggled to fend the invader off.

Now as we know Pinky has some considerable heft, so when Gabriel attacked, Pinky took a huge swing, landing a firm kerchunk-a-punch right on the startled Gabriel. "Sorry Squire," Pinky consoled.   Kurchner tumbled to the floor, and Pinky bounding up, squatted on top of Gabriel, pinning him by his arms to the floor.

"GET THE FUCK IN HERE YOU DUMB ASS AGENTS!" Pinky shouted out at the top of his voice.

At that the agents burst into the room and pulled the panting Pinky from the trembling and startled Gabriel who was now totally subdued.

After Kurchner was handcuffed, read his rights, and carted him off, Pinky, furiously tearing off his wig, charged up to the lead agent and asked, "Why the fuck didn't you come in when I gave the signal?"

"I didn't hear the signal," he replied.

"I shouted 'Oh, Gabriel' several times."

"Oh… I thought you said the signal was 'No, Gabriel'."

◻   ◻   ◻

"Sonora, we got a counter offer," Oz announced to Sonora on her cell phone. Sonora was still in bed at the inn finishing her light breakfast and being deliciously lazy.

"What is it?"

"One point three five."

"Thought we were going for one point two."

"It will take another couple of days to counter. I thought if you were anxious to get back into your house you might want to accept this offer."

Sonora thought about that. It would still take another week or so after signing before the closing. Then the dance group would have to move out of her house with all their rehearsal gear and into the studio. Then the movers would have to come and move her furniture back into the living room. At least a couple of weeks total – or even more. Was she willing to wait that long to get home? Was it worth fighting for that other hundred and fifty thousand? "Go ahead and accept the offer," Sonora announced. "I rea-a-ally want to get back home."

"Okay, I'll call Honey and tell her we accept."

After speaking with Oz, Sonora thought it was time to try and raise some serious money for the dance company. It was shocking how much all of this was costing her. And while she *could* fund the whole operation herself with hardly a dent in her capital, she didn't *want* to. She thought about how she might proceed and decided to call Bella first. After all she *had* funded an entire wing at the opera.

"Bella, it's Sonora Livingston-Bundt."

Bella had not completely forgiven Sonora for the comment about her dress at the opera even though Sonora had invited Bella to her harvest party. "Oh yes, Sonora, what can I do for you this morning?"

"Was wondering if I might stop by for a visit sometime soon - at your convenience, of course."

"And what might be the nature of this visit?"

Sonora was finding this somewhat of an uphill climb. "I have a little project that you might find interesting and I'd like to discuss it with you. Or if you prefer we could meet for lunch at a restaurant of your choosing. My treat, of course."

This sweetened the proposition a little, but Bella was determined to be recalcitrant. "Let me check my schedule. I might be able to spare you half an hour sometime this week." She held the phone away from her ear as she pretended to consult her calendar. "How would Thursday afternoon at three be for you?"

"Perfect. Will see you then."

"Do you need my address?" Bella asked.

"Oh no, *everyone* knows where *you* live."

Bella was unsure how to take that remark, but decided to let any innuendo slide. "Till then."

No sooner did Sonora hang up with Bella than she got a call from Connye.

"How was the visit to your lovely mill?" Connye asked. "Seems like ages since we've spoken."

"Suburb, I almost didn't come back it was so enchanting."

"And I understand your dance company is here now. When will we have the pleasure of seeing this little group?"

"Am planning a little fun raiser quite soon. You will have a premiere invitation, of course."

"Did you say 'fun' raiser?"

"I did. The director of the company likes to use that word. Sounds a little more festive than 'fundraiser,' don't you think?"

"Indeed."

"Was there some reason you called me, other than to say hello?" Sonora pushed politely

"Oh my, yes. Must be losing my mind. Forgetting things right and left. My adorable Jefferson had a splendid idea and I wanted to discuss it with you and see if you might want to help."

"And that would be?"

"As Jefferson rightly observed our darling Kaiser Sisters are both around eighty now. I believe Kate turned eight-one last year, and Helen will be eighty in just a few weeks. It was Jefferson's idea to throw them a surprise birthday party. What do you think?"

"Oh, what a grand idea. How charming. Would love to assist however I can."

"Then could we meet say Thursday at three? We can have a little planning session over tea."

Sonora laughed. "I just made another appointment for that exact time. Would another time work for you?"

"Don't think we should leave it too long. How about this afternoon, same time?"

"Splendid. See you then," Sonora agreed.

◘   ◘   ◘

Pinky was receiving all sorts of commendations from the FBI. Not only was he an extraordinarily successful agent, but he had become the poster boy for alternative life styles within the entire agency. If there were any other drag queens in the FBI (except for the late J Edgar, of course) no one else was coming forward. So Pinky was in line for a promotion and a raise. And while he was pleased with the extra money and the praise, he was still not satisfied. As with so many circumstances in his life, it was not what he consciously chose to do that made him successful, but the silly random accidents that had led to his glory. And while the blackmailing and LANL incidents appeared to be resolved he was still worried for Bella. So he gave her a call and she agreed to meet with him.

When Pinky arrived at Bella's he was dressed in his street clothes. No Bella drag today. And to be quite honest, he looked like a fat assed plumber in his civvies. He looked so much better as Bella le Balle.

Pinky was surprised when he entered Bella's house to see the living room almost empty. Bella noticed his reaction and said, "Getting ready for the remodel. Angelica is almost ready for the installation, so needed to get rid of a lot of things. Thought it would be easier to do it before she arrived."

"Yes, looking forward to the new look. What's it going to be?"

"I'll show you the drawings after we have a little refreshment."

Bella led Pinky to the conservatory, where coffee was waiting on a low table before two wicker chairs. They sat.

"Oh my, I've been reading all about your exploits in the paper. What a hero you've become," Bella said as she poured Pinky's coffee.

Pinky blushed. "I wish I could be as successful with my act."

"Oh, but you *are*. You pack the club every time you perform."

"Yes, but it's still not a steady or reliable living."

"You should go on Ellen's show."

"Oh yeah… sure."

"I don't see why not. She's a dear friend. I could give her a call."

Pinky was stunned and without words.

"Well?" Bella was waiting for a response.

"You'd do that for *me?*"

"Of course, why not? I can't guarantee anything will come of it, of course. But I'll give her a call and tell her all about you."

Pinky fell to the floor and prostrated himself in front of Bella. "You would have my undying appreciation and affection for life."

Bella laughed. "Oh do get up. It's nothing. "I'll call her this evening. You do have a video of your act don't you? Get that to me and I'll send it along if she's interested in taking a look at it."

"Oh yes, I do. I'll get to you immediately." Pinky wiggled up closer and kissed the tops of Bella's shoes. "Yum, um, um. I'll be your slave forever."

"Now, now, don't be silly, get up." She was becoming embarrassed.

Pinky got up, sat down, took a deep breath, and finished his coffee. "Now then, down to business. I have a few things I need to talk to you about – in my professional FBI capacity."

"Very well."

"I wanted to update you on what's transpired with the investigation so far." He proceeded to lay out all that had happened with the case to date – including his ordeal at the Los Alamos hotel with Kurchner. "But now, what I'm concerned about is you." he added.

Bella blanched a little and a look of worry came over her face. "Why me? It sounds like it's all wrapped up."

"Yes, but our culprits are out on bail. Who knows what they might get up to, or how they might feel about your involvement in their capture."

"But I did nothing," Bella protested.

"They might not see it that way. After all, you *did* give us their names which you found on the map, remember."

"Oh, I wish I'd burned the damn thing."

"Oh, and by the way here's your father's ring back." Pinky delved into his bag and brought out the ring box. "Very neat little contraption, by the way. Didn't know they had such advanced technology way back when."

"Thank you." Bella took the box and looked at it wistfully. "So what am I to do to protect myself?"

"I plan to keep an eye on you. And, of course, if anything suspicious transpires, call me immediately. You have my cell number."

Bella thought for a moment. "Why don't I also give you a key to the house, and the alarm code? I want you to be able to get in any time if there's an emergency."

"Good idea. Now, let's forget all about that nasty business and show me your plans for the décor."

◘   ◘   ◘

Soon after speaking with Connye, Sonora received a call from Honey to say that Oz had signed the contract, and she would expedite the process so they could close on the studio in a week and a half. And - Honey emphasized - they would be able to take possession of the studio the very next day after the closing. What a relief. Soon Sonora would be back in her own home, Henrietta could return from her vacation, and all would be well and back to normal – whatever *that* was.

Now, Sonora could begin to think about her next project. Aaron had taken very careful, high resolution photographs of each page of the Marais manuscript. He emailed them to her, and now she was having them printed out and bound into an exact size replica of the original.

Before they left France, Sonora, Lionel and Aaron had thoroughly combed through the mill to see if there were any more secret compartments, or lost manuscripts - but nothing further was found. They had already discovered the mother lode.

After calling the Ministry of Culture, Sonora received a personal call from the Deputy Minister the next day who, speaking flawless English, announced he would be coming down from Paris, personally, to accept the manuscript on behalf of a grateful and appreciative nation... etc, etc, etc. My, how the French loved to formally rattle on.

Indeed, early the next afternoon a limousine pulled up before the mill. A phalanx of dignitaries and minions spilled out of the car, and with much ceremony, and snapping of cameras, the manuscript was accepted, a certificate of appreciation with an official seal was offered to Sonora, and the group reentered the limousine, sped down the driveway, and disappeared.

There was a fifteen second announcement on the national news that evening, and a small article in the arts section of a major Paris newspaper – and then silence.

Now, that was about to change. Besides having a stunning shadow box constructed for the replica, and the certificate of appreciation framed, Sonora was preparing a press release to go to all the major networks, music blog sites, and the national press. She rented a room at the Hotel Santa Fe for her news conference, and prepared handouts with photos and all the details of her significant musical find.

And now it was time for tea with Connye.

The Kaiser sisters, had been in a spot of trouble not long ago (they had been rightly accused of forging their famous father's paintings and selling them for big bucks), and within the Santa Fe social circle only Sonora and Connye had come forward with substantial help. However, it was Jefferson who had come up with the idea that finally rehabilitated them. He arranged for them to paint under their own names, and secured a major gallery to represent them. Since then they have thrived, and become known as the duel Grandma Moses of the southwest.

"I really am so happy to have your help," Connye greeted Sonora at the front door.

"Well, they are a darling duo and deserve a little festive surprise. So glad you called me."

"Instead of tea, I thought a little glass of sherry might be appropriate to plan a surprise event. Hope you don't mind."

"Not at all, but I hope I can keep my head," Sonora cautioned. "I don't usually drink in the afternoon as a rule - but what the hell."

Connye led the way to her garden room. They both settled down and Connye poured the sherry.

"And how was your wonderful trip to France? Is your lovely mill still standing snug and secure?" Connye teased.

"Sturdy as a rock. They certainly knew how to build back then. And the trip was a delight. In fact I will be holding a press conference shortly regarding a rather remarkable find in the old mill itself. It is of international interest."

"Oh do give me a hint."

"Not yet. I'm still preparing the presentation. It's better if it's revealed in its full glory. I'm sure you understand."

"Of course," Connye nodded.

"So tell me, how are things between you and Jefferson? Any announcements pending?" Sonora asked.

Connye considered before she replied, "We've come to a mutual understanding. Neither of us is quite prepared to sever our roots, so we've decided to keep things as they are. Travel back and forth for special occasions, and keep it fresh and romantic - without settling down into a dreary co-habitation."

"Can certainly understand that. When it came right down to it I couldn't see living with anyone either – neither Oz nor Quinto. I guess we are both just too independent, you and I."

They smiled sweetly at one another, then Sonora asked, "And your lovely garden, are we to expect any juicy tomatoes anytime soon?"

It was actually in this moment that Connye made her decision about the garden. "I'm afraid it's too late in the season to start anything this year. And you know it seems so much easier to just hop over to the Farmer's Market and get whatever I need there without all that toil and trouble. Think I'll turn it into a community garden, and then anyone who cares to may grow a plot."

"Ever so much more practical. And greatly appreciated by the populace, I'm sure."

"It's just how I am," Connye smiled.

"So what did you have in mind for the sisters?" Sonora asked, as she settled down to business.

"I want it to be nice, but nothing strenuous as the ladies are a bit wobbly now. No amusement park jaunts, or boisterous clowns, you understand."

"And how do you plan to make it a surprise? Anywhere we would take them - wouldn't they be a little suspicious?"

"Good point," Connye added as she poured a second sherry.

"Was thinking, what if we held the party at their place? It's so nice, and if the weather holds we could have it outside on their lovely grounds."

"But how would that be a surprise?" Connye asked.

"If we took them somewhere first, the party could be set up, and when we bring them back – surprise. Don't think they would suspect that."

"My darling Sonora, you are, as ever, a true marvel. Don't think I will ever be able to plan another event without you."

Sonora smiled and nodded. "Will you use your delightful caterer, or shall I have my Henrietta help with the food?"

"Oh no, don't want to put her to any trouble. My caterer is used to my eccentric requests and will accommodate us perfectly."

"Do you have a date yet?"

Connye poured them each a third sherry. "I was looking at the 11th – a Saturday. And was thinking I'd take the Sisters out for their weekly grocery shopping, as I often do. Surely that would divert suspicion from our real purpose."

"My precious, you think of everything," Sonora crooned.

By now the sherry was beginning to take effect, and both ladies were becoming a little tipsy and a bit maudlin.

"But it's you who are the inspiration," Connye plied, mawkishly, "I really don't think I could do any of it without you."

Sonora became pensive. "You know all these years we have always been in such fierce competition with one another, and here we are co-operating much more than we are opposing. Are we getting old?"

Connye laughed. "I don't know about old. But maybe a little wiser?"

"Well, let's not get too complacent. After all, I think it's the battle that keeps us sharp."

"You certainly get right to the *point*, don't you?"

They both started laughing.

◘   ◘   ◘

Lionel had invited Sonora for a little celebration. He had not told her why yet, but had prepared, all by his own hand, a delightful lunch with a bottle of Champaign on ice.

"You are too mysterious. You fixing lunch? My, what *is* the occasion?" Sonora asked, as she was greeted at Lionel's front door.

"Just be patient," he beamed, as he escorted Sonora into the living room. "I'll just be a moment. Need to attend to the quiche."

"You made a quiche? How ambitious. I thought tomato soup was your forte," Sonora teased.

"Now, you be nice or tomato soup will be exactly all you'll get."

"Well, I have a little surprise for you, as well. I brought it along and will share it later after your surprise."

Sonora heard the pop of a Champaign cork from the kitchen. Momentarily Lionel came out with two sparkling flutes.

"Oh my, this *must* be a special occasion indeed."

Lionel handed her a glass, they clinked and he said, "To the publication of my memoir. I now have a publisher, thanks to the charming agent Quinto introduced me to."

"Oh Lionel...   How marvelous. And when did this transpire?"

"Yesterday." Lionel marched over to his desk and came back with the contract. "I would love to say I couldn't have done it without you. But that would be untrue, now wouldn't it?"

Sonora blushed, "Oh Lionel, I *am* sorry. I wasn't much encouragement was I?"

"No, you were horrid. If it hadn't been for Quinto, I probably would have thrown it in the trash and gone to bed for a whole week."

"Well, you know, literature is really *not* my forte, dear. As you know, my little film episode would have failed miserably if it hadn't been for the vital assistance of you and Quinto. I'm a terrible old fraud, aren't I?"

"Yes. But you *will* be forgiven," Lionel added, "if you throw me a grand book release party."

"Oh, I think that can be arranged. When's the release date?"

"Not for a while. There's editing to do and assorted odds and ends that I don't completely understand just yet. But that's what agents are for, aren't they?"

"Then you let me know when, and we'll hold a grand old splash up on the date."

"And now, Madam, luncheon is served. If you'd care to take your place at the table…"

Sonora seated herself, as Lionel served the quiche and a green salad. Nothing fancy, but quite nice and well meant.

Sonora chatted, "I see your protégé has made quite a name for himself. He's been in the paper and on TV. I had no idea he was an FBI agent."

"Yes, isn't it outrageous? Next thing you know vampires will be elected to the Senate."

"Aren't they already?" Sonora retorted in mock astonishment.

Lionel giggled. "Too true. But Pinky an FBI agent? What *is* the world coming to? No doubt powder puffs are his weapons of choice."

"Now be nice. He's obviously quite accomplished in his profession. I read he subdued a dangerous international spy who'd been stealing secrets from LANL. And there was that business with the murdered senator. Gracious. How do you suppose he copes?"

"I have no idea. But I'm certain he *lives* for his club act."

"And he is awfully good, isn't he?"

"Yes, he really is. I was quite surprised." Lionel rose. "Desert? More Champaign?"

"Oh yes, both please. And then we'll have my little surprise, shall we?"

Lionel served fruit tarts – obviously from the bakery at Portabellos – and poured more Champaign.

"Now," Sonora said, leaning down by her side and pulling up a thick envelope. "Here is what I have for you." She handed the package to Lionel.

He opened it and pulled out a copy of the music manuscript. "I thought you gave this to the French."

"Oh, I did. This is a copy. I had it made up and thought you'd like a copy. And I hope you'll attend my press conference when I will announce to the whole world about our extraordinary find. Should make for a good story, don't you think?"

"There's just no end to how marvelous you are."

Dancing in the Dark

"Bella."

"Sonora."

Bella held the door as Sonora entered.

"You'll have to forgive the mess. Doing a major redecoration and the painters are everywhere today. I suggest we retire to the conservatory. It's nice and quiet in there, and we won't be disturbed."

Sonora looked about as they headed towards the garden room. "Bold colors," Sonora observed. "Should make quite a statement."

"That's my intention."

Bella offered Sonora a chair, but did not suggest any refreshment. She wanted to keep this short and as impersonal as possible.

"Now what can I do for you?" Bella asked, as she seated herself.

Sonora was not insensitive to the icy air, despite the warmth and breathing moisture of the greenhouse.

"I know how interested you are in the arts."

"Yes, I have dabbled from time to time."

"And how gracious you were with your generous donation to the opera."

"Obviously not gracious enough to keep the attention of a number of guests at the reception – who walked out during the presentation."

So this is where this was going. Sonora could see she would need to make a few adjustments in her presentation. "Yes, I am dreadfully sorry about that. My dear friend, Lionel, was hosting a very special event, and we just could not disappoint him by not showing up. Silly of him to schedule his event at the same time as yours, but he didn't consult me before hand and didn't know."

"And what, exactly, could be more important than a major donation to the opera for an opera board member?"

"Lionel had made some spectacular costumes for an act that was premiering at a local club and he so desperately wanted his dear friends in attendance."

"What kind of act?" Bella asked.

Sonora was unsure exactly how she should characterize Pinky's performance. A drag act would seem insignificant next to the power and glory of the opera. "An entertainment of music and impersonation," was how Sonora finally described it.

Bella was intrigued. "And the name of the entertainer?"

Sonora hesitated but stated, "Bella. Like yourself. Bella le Balle."

Bella lit up. "Oh Pinky. You mean Pinky Powell."

"You know Pinky?"

"Oh yes, he's such a doll."

Sonora was stunned. "How? Doesn't seem to me he'd be a part of your inner circle."

Bella waved the concern away. "FBI. He was investigating an incident where I was involved. He invited me to his show. What a talent, don't you think? And incidentally we became friends. Unlikely, but true."

"Will wonders never cease...."

Bella was conflicted. She didn't want to like Sonora or support anything she was pushing, but now they had her charming friend in common. She would have to be careful now. "So what is this art project you wanted to talk to me about?"

"As you may or may not know, I was a dancer with the New York City Ballet. Years ago, of course. But I've always maintained my interest in dance. And I believe dance is under represented here in Santa Fe. And as a result I just sponsored a marvelous professional company to relocate here to Santa Fe."

"Ambitious."

"It is. And as a result, I'm trying to build a support group for the company. I'm sure you can appreciate that without wide community interest and support the company won't flourish. And the reason I am coming to you is to see if you might be interested in joining me as co-chair of the support group for the Calisto Etheric Dance Group – that's its name. What I'm looking to do is build awareness and support for the company throughout the whole arts community. Might you be interested in helping?"

Bella considered this request. While she was certainly interested in the arts generally, she was not that much of a dance aficionado. And she had a nagging resistance to helping Sonora in any way.

"I don't believe so," Bella responded quite coolly.

Sonora was genuinely surprised. "Oh. I thought certainly this would be something that would appeal to your artistic sensibilities."

"I have to say, I have not felt all that welcome here in the Santa Fe social world. And after the lavish donation to the opera I expected a much warmer outreach from all of you."

O-o-o now this really rankled Sonora and she just had to respond. "Well you shouldn't be surprised after the way you treated our dear friend, Honey Trapp. We in Santa Fe are not in the habit of cheating one of our own out of a legitimately earned commission. I know for a fact she was counting on that to help with her two children's college education."

"Very well then, I believe our interview is concluded." Bella rose presenting an acid smile.

Sonora gathered her things together and prepared to leave. "I can assure you that if you think your reception up to now has been cool, then prepare yourself for an arctic blast."

"And I can assure you it will make no difference to me whatsoever. I have decided that I really have no wish to be a part of your paltry little social scene here in Santa Fe. You are a nasty, catty bunch, and I am quite relieved to be outside your vicious, insignificant little circle."

Sonora did not wait for Bella to see her to the door, but charged out of the garden room and found her own way out with thoughts of murder on her mind.

◻   ◻   ◻

Roberta called Sonora and asked if they might have lunch together. "I have something really important I need to discuss with you." She said it in such a way that Sonora was concerned that Roberta might be ill, or have a grave financial problem that might need Sonora's immediate attention.

They were to have lunch at Mango's, one of Roberta's favorite restaurants.

"You know this is where we had lunch the day you asked me to help you with Pie. Do you remember?" Sonora asked.

"Of course I do, and that is why I chose to meet here today."

"Oh really? Do you have another wonderful project for me?"

Roberta giggled. "Well, not exactly. I'm afraid I'm a little scared to talk to you about it. Do you mind if we eat first? I need to work my way up to it."

This only reinforced Sonora's concern for Roberta, but she acquiesced. "I always have the jerk chicken. It's quite my favorite item on the menu."

"And the hibiscus iced tea," Roberta added.

"Quite so."

Roberta nibbled at her food but did not seem all that hungry. She kept looking up at Sonora like she was facing the Inquisition.

Finally Sonora jumped in. "Roberta, my darling, you look like you are about to jump off a bridge, please tell me what's bothering you. Nothing can be that bad."

Roberta took a deep breath and said, "Very well. But you probably won't like it."

"Oh, my dear, nothing can be *that* terrible."

"I want to retire from Pie in the Sky."

"Really?"

"I know you must think I'm awful. I know you'll think, there's Roberta losing interest in her current project and on to her next little adventure, but that's not the case at all."

"Okay, then tell me why."

"Well, I'm exhausted. We've both worked so hard on Pie, and it's become a huge success. And while I still love what I'm doing, I just can't maintain the same pace. And now that we've become franchised, and the business is run by a corporation, I want to step back, enjoy the success, and go on to other things. We've become quite rich from it, haven't we?"

"Well, you have. I was already rich. Now I'm just richer."

Roberta laughed, much relieved. "Then you're not mad at me?"

"Not at all. You've done a remarkably wonderful job, and your wanting to retire is completely understandable and justified. But do you still want to maintain an active interest in the business? Maybe you could be on the advisory board or something."

"Yes, that would be nice. I was even thinking I might bake pies at home, to try out new recipes for the store."

"So what will you do with all your free time?"

"Nothing for a while. But after our little trip to Orlando was thinking I just might do some more traveling. Don't know if I can ever get hubby to go along, but hey, I can be a traveler all on my own. And maybe you'd like to join me occasionally."

"You never know. When do you want to leave?"

"Within a month. Will that be enough time to find a new general manager?"

"Don't see why not. You've got a great assistant we should consider."

"Oh yes, Jessie, would be great. Was thinking that too."

Sonora reached over and took Roberta's hand. "I really hope you'll be happy. And don't you worry about a thing. I'm sure we can work all out all the details."

"You are, once again, my white witch," Roberta smiled.

◘   ◘   ◘

The cottonwood trees shimmered golden in a light breeze. It was a delightful October morning. Jefferson had flown in the night before, and Connye and Jefferson were preparing to launch over to the Kaiser sisters. Connye had arranged to take the sisters grocery shopping to get them away from the house. Sonora was to come separately to meet the caterers and supervise the set-up of the birthday treats. She had also arranged for music, and to have a few members of the dance company perform for the guests. Everyone was to arrive in plenty of time before Connye, Jefferson, and the sisters retuned to the house.

The catering was set up behind the house, so as the sisters arrived, they wouldn't see any of the party activity. The guests were shepherded inside the house so everyone could all yell *surprise* at the same time.

After all the guests were safely hidden and stowed away Connye's car drove up to the house.

"Here, let us help with those," Jefferson said, as he took a couple of grocery bags from Helen and helped her out of the car.

"And I'll take the rest," Connye offered.

"Oh you two are too kind," Kate giggled. "Don't know how we would get by without all our dear friends."

"How are your sales, these days?" Jefferson asked the sisters.

"Oh you know - we can hardly keep up. The Denver gallery sells everything we send them right away."

"That's wonderful." Jefferson gave Connye a look and a nod to indicate they were ready to go inside the house. Connye responded with an answering nod.

"Ladies, we'll put the groceries in the kitchen so you two can have a little lie down and rest. We'll take care of putting things away," Connye offered.

"Oh yes, that sounds nice," Helen said.

Connye and Jefferson led the way, shielding the view from the sisters till they were inside the house.

"Surprise," roared up from the guests, and the sisters were speechless, not understanding what was happening at first.

Connye came to them. "It's a surprise party to celebrate you both turning 80 recently."

"Oh my…." The sisters were still recovering.

"But I'm already eighty one," Kate said innocently.

"I'm sure that doesn't matter on little bit," Connye reassured her.

"Come - we have a wonderful party all set up outside," Jefferson offered to help them navigate to the back yard.

Roberta had made a stunning cake at the shop. There was a table with birthday presents, and a bar where wine and Champaign was already freely flowing. Connye and Jefferson settled the sisters into comfortable chairs in the shade where the guests could come and visit with them.

Meanwhile, Sonora was gathered with a few members of the core coffee group, regaling them with her horror story of Bella's shocking behavior.

"I could have strangled her with my bare hands," Sonora snorted as she shook the neck of her imaginary opponent.

"What a ghastly woman," Honey added. "I would have gladly paraded her body through the streets like an African Warlord and left her body hanging from a bridge."

"Now ladies, let us remember the grand gift she bestowed on the opera," Ruth cautioned. "She may not endear herself readily, but I do believe she has a good and generous heart."

"If she has a heart at all," Sonora cautioned, "I doubt if anyone could even find a ticking pulse."

"Well, from what you say we needn't give her another thought. I suggest we forget all about her and move on," Olivia offered. "We are quite content with our own cozy little group, are we not?"

The others agreed.

Connye was preparing plates for the sisters, when Jefferson came over.

"I've been thinking," he said, as he put his arms around her waist.

"Something nice, I hope."

"Very nice. I think you'll like it."

"Good. Then just one moment. Let me take these plates to the sisters and I'll be right with you and then you'll have my full undivided attention."

"As you wish, my lovely."

Connye attended to the sisters and returned, refreshed with a glass of Champaign. "Now then, what are you thinking?"

Jefferson took her arm and led her to a secluded area of the yard that was quiet and shady. "You know how we both agree we cannot sell our houses and move in together in either Augusta or Santa Fe?" Connye nodded. "Well I think I might have come up with a solution that could work for both of us."

"And that is?"

"What if... we bought a house together in New Orleans? – or even rent, if buying is too much for you. We could decorate it together, and live there part time. We could keep our own places, and come and go as we needed. That way we could have the best of both. We could live together, and live separately. Pretty neat idea, huh?"

Connye smiled, "Well, that *is* a very attractive idea. I shall have to consider that."

"Oh please, do more than just consider it. Let's *do* it." He leaned forward and rubbed his nose against hers.

She stepped back. "Now you know I don't like to be rushed into quick decisions. Please, just let me consider it for a while."

"Of course, just as you wish." Jefferson bowed slightly. "Now shall we attend to our lovely guests of honor?"

Just then Sonora called for everyone's attention. "Ladies and gentlemen, we have a real treat for you this afternoon. As some of you know I have brought the most delightful dance troop to Santa Fe. It's called the Calisto Etheric Dance Group and we will be holding a premiere performance and fun raiser at our new studio shortly – to which you are all invited. And to whet your appetite we have a preview performance for your entertainment this afternoon." Sonora raised her hand, the music started, and four dancers sprang forward, and the dancing began.

◘   ◘   ◘

Should he or shouldn't he? Pinky sat at his dressing table the day of the FBI awards. Some big FBI honcho was coming in from Washington to present Pinky and several other agents with pretty little ribbons for valor or some such horse shit. All Pinky cared about was his raise. For the first time in his adult life he had been able to put some money aside on a regular basis. Could he ever save enough to free himself from the drudgery of the working-world slob? Probably not. But at least he still had the relief of his drag act on the weekends.

Pinky stared at his mug in the mirror. What a face. He reached for the foundation.

The FBI headquarters in Albuquerque was in a nondescript office building on a busy commercial street that looked like any other commercial street in any other medium size city in the country. There was nothing unique or southwest about the building.

On the small stage were American and an FBI flags. A podium was set up and there were rows of chairs for the agents and office staff. For most in attendance it was a break in an otherwise tedious afternoon. There was a table on the side with a coffee urn and several boxes of stale cookies. Florescent light washed out almost all color in the room. There were no windows, the room was stuffy, and the assembled crowd was getting restless.

Finally, the head of the Albuquerque agency stepped up to the podium.

"Excuse me for being a little tardy, folks, but the recipient of the coveted Hoover award appears to be missing. But not to keep you all waiting, we'll begin with the awards to those who *are* present and maybe he'll show up by the end."

It was difficult for most in the audience to keep awake. Several folks had their hand shading their face as they took a few winks of nap time. The Washington presenter was particularly long winded and had an annoying way of phrasing that broke up the sentences and made listening even more tedious.

All of the awards had been presented except for Pinky's. The presenter was becoming nervous and began glancing at his watch. A young woman appeared at the door, caught the presenter's attention, and went up to him and whispered. The man looked somewhat startled and headed towards the door.

Just then a boom box began to blare out a ballsy show tune, and Pinky appeared in his Ethel Merman drag, arms wide, belting out, "I had a dream, a dream about you Baby. It's gonna come true baby. They think that we're through baby." The presenter was so startled he reeled back against the wall, knocking down the FBI flag. Pinky was unfazed and continued to sparkle and shine. He presented three songs and ended with Don't Rain on my Parade.

The room went wild. The whole audience rose as one, shouting and cheering. Pinky did his deep diva bow, turned to the presenter, kissed him on both cheeks, ripped the award from the presenter's hand, and swept off the stage to shouts of "Brava."

"Thank you darlings," Pinky said, pausing and turning at the door, "much appreciated." And then he disappeared.

◘   ◘   ◘

Angelica was screaming at the movers not to scratch the new paintwork. The furniture was *finally* being unloaded from the truck. It was several weeks late, and poor Bella had been reduced to sitting on crates and garden furniture. She was so relieved this redecorating was finally coming to an end.

Bella closed her office door to keep out the noise, and provide some privacy. Connye's discovery about Bella's intimate and embarrassing past still rankled. The episode with Sonora made clear the peril she was in - here in Santa Fe. Bella felt she needed to take some preventative action.

"What do you mean there's nothing we can do?" Bella was on the phone to her Washington attorney.

"Bella, it's a public document. They have a constitutional right to publish it."

"But that's why I have you. To take care of these matters for me."

"I know it's frustrating, but my hands are tied."

"Then is there some way to affect the search engine so it doesn't come up in a search of my name?"

"Oh Bella, I'm truly sorry, but you are asking me to do things that are just not possible. It doesn't work that way. I can't just expunge the article about the lewd and immoral sexual solicitation charge. I'm afraid you're just going to have to live with it. But the good news is, it is very low down on the search page. Someone would have to know what they were searching for to find it."

"But the court records are sealed at least. Is that right?"

"Yes, we were able to do that. It would require another court order to release those files to the public."

"Excellent."

"And what about the court records on the name change?"

"That is taken care of as well. We were able to seal those records *and* keep them off the internet. You should be fine there."

"Good. As keeper of my deepest, darkest secrets I rely on you, you know."

"I know."

"Good. Now I'd like to take a minute to discuss updating my will."

◘   ◘   ◘

Poor Sonora. Her much heralded news conference had been a complete flop. She'd had the hotel prepare a table with tasty French treats, glasses of wine, and colorful handouts detailing the wonders of her musical discovery. The hotel had been instructed to put out fifty chairs.

Three people showed up. Two were from local newspapers and one was from an Albuquerque blog. No national press attended. No TV. No musical magazines or blogs. Sonora cut her presentation from half an hour to fifteen minutes. And while the food and wine were much appreciated, the three guests quickly fled after the presentation.

Lionel attempted to console Sonora, pointing out that she still had her certificate of appreciation from the French government. And she had her shadow box with the splendid reproduction of the manuscript.

But Sonora had other concerns, and being the trooper she was, quickly transitioned her interest to the dance concert scheduled for the next Saturday.

The concert was being held this evening in the large studio at their new dance complex. Sonora had, of course, provided a lavish spread of food and drink. This was a fun raiser, after all. She figured, get the folks a little sloshed, and they would be more likely to open their checkbooks and increase the size of their donations. However, because this was also a new dance school, dozens of kids were running around, excited by their studies with Brock. Everyone already *loved* Brock - he had such a winning way.

Sonora was nervous. She had put a lot of her own money into this venture and this was the company's first public exposure to the Santa Fe arts community. Everything depended on a good reception this evening. She needed to persuade Santa Fe that this was a valuable artistic asset. And she needed to persuade a lot of people to join her in making this company a success.

Oz came over to where Sonora was greeting the guests as they arrived. "Well, here we are – finally. It seems like decades since the company moved to Santa Fe, doesn't it?"

"And thank *you*. You've done a splendid job. I couldn't have done it without you," Sonora said, gratefully.

Connye came up. "My, what a beautiful studio. However did you find it?"

"Bit of luck, I suppose. We started with the company rehearsing in my living room. Couldn't find a space for love nor money. Then this came on the market."

"It's a gem."

There was a comfortable buzzing as the guests assembled and visited. Finally the lights flashed, indicating the performance was about to start and people should take their seats.

As it was not a true performance space, the lighting was simple. There were no curtains or off stage areas. The dancers were just *there*. The work had to stand on its own. The house lights dimmed, the music began, and the stage lights came up.

The concert started with a wonderful jazzy piece choreographed by Daniel. The costumes were simple but suggestive.

All was going well. The audience was electrified by the performances. Then, without warning the electricity went off. The lights were gone, the music stopped, and the entire studio was in complete darkness, except for some votive candles burning on the food and drink tables. The audience was at first surprised then started to be restless.

Someone ran to the front door, looked out, and announced that the electricity was off in the whole neighborhood.

Brock came over to Sonora. "It's going to be okay. I'll take care of it." He worked his way back to the front of the audience and announced. "One moment, folks. Just a momentary pause. You ain't seen nothin' yet."

He retreated, and soon the music was transferred to a boom box with batteries. The dancers broke glow sticks which provided some light and the dance began again. And it was pure magic. The concert continued to an even more rapt audience. Just before the concert ended the lights came back to loud cheers from the audience. The dancers concluded the last dance, and the audience members swarmed onto the dance floor to mingle with and congratulate the performers.

Oz came over and gave Sonora a big hug. "Wow. Marvelous. Just marvelous."

"Yes, they surely are. I think we might just make a go of this," Sonora beamed.

"You gotta be mighty proud."

"Oh yes."

"Now I gotta do *my* job." Oz scooted off to mingle with the guests and encourage generous donations.

The whole of the coffee circle swarmed Sonora with praise and congratulations.

"Thank you ladies, it's a happy moment, indeed."

Honey was all excited. "Can you introduce us to Brock? What a sweetheart."

"Yes. Yes," Sonora agreed.

"Oh, the whole company is adorable," Roberta grinned. "Will they be coming out again to visit with us?"

"Oh certainly, soon as they change."

Connye pulled Sonora aside. "I understand you had a meeting with Bella about helping you with your support group."

"Oh yes..." Sonora did not feel like being catty just then, and didn't elaborate.

"A little birdie told me she was a bit of a bitch."

Sonora smiled, "Well, let's just say she showed her true nature."

"So it's true she refused to help?"

"Exactly."

"Well, if you would consider me, I'd like to assist, and I bet a few other of the ladies would too. You've done just a marvelous thing bringing these talented people to Santa Fe."

Sonora looked at Connye with some disbelief. "Really? You'd like to help?"

"I would. However, I might not always be available as there is a development I can't disclose just yet that might mean I would not always be in residence. But I'm sure I could still be of some assistance."

"Oh? A development? And what might that be?"

"Not yet," Connye blushed and patted Sonora's arm. "But soon, I promise."

"Does it involve Jefferson?"

"It might," was all Connye would acknowledge.

Lionel was assisting Oz at the registration table where they were collecting names for the mailing list, donations, and volunteers. They were also fielding a number of inquiries about the school, and brochures were flying off the table.

Candice and Olivia were together, chatting. Candice in her official capacity was helping oversee the food table. Sonora regarded her and went over.

"Oh Sonora, I was just telling Candice how wonderful the performance was. And what a beautiful space. You must be very proud," Olivia praised.

"Yes, thank you. Very pleased. But really the work is only beginning. It's nice when friends and acquaintances love what you do, but there's that big, grey mass of the general public out there that need to be enticed as well."

"Well, word of mouth after this splendid evening will help, I'm sure."

Sonora turned to Candice and took her arm, then said to Olivia, "May I steal your adorable sister away for a few moments. Would you mind helping at the food table while we chat?"

"Delighted to."

Sonora led Candice away from the crowd. Candice was a little nervous. "Is there a problem?" Candice asked.

"No, not at all. I just wanted to tell you how very pleased I am with all the great help you and Oz have been. I could never have done any of this by myself."

Candice beamed. "Oh, I'm so glad. I was afraid you would be mad at me."

"Whatever for?" Sonora asked.

"Well, you know.... Oz and me."

"Well actually, I did want to discuss that with you."

"Are you really angry?" Candice asked hesitantly.

"My dear, I'm delighted."

"You are?" Candice reacted with surprise, "But I thought...?

"Can't tell you what a relief it is. I mean, Oz is a total sweetheart and all that, and he did come all the way to Santa Fe to court me. But, my dear, I am *much* too independent to be in *any* relationship. I realized it quite finally while I was in France."

"Can't tell you what a relief that is. I have been feeling so guilty thinking I'd stolen him from you."

Sonora came closer and almost whispered. "To be quite honest, the moment I met you at the coffee circle I had my eye on you for Oz. I knew he wouldn't let go of me unless I supplied him with an even prettier alternative – you."

"Oh my."

"In fact, I planned to set the two of you up, beginning with hiring you for the dance company. I just felt the chemistry would take over and the two of you would come together. And I was right, wasn't I?"

Oz came over, seeing the two ladies chatting intimately together. He was a little worried that Sonora might have it out for Candice and he wanted to protect her if he could. "Hey, ladies. What's going on? Anything I should know about?"

"Just lady talk," Sonora reassured him. "Nothing to worry your sweet face about." She patted his cheek.

"Everything's fine," Candice assured Oz as she took his arm.

"Okay," he said a little uncertainly. "Don't want any trouble between my two favorite ladies."

"Everything is *absolutely* fine," Sonora announced, flinging her arms out to the welcoming heavens.

Extra, Extra, Can't Read All About It

HEIRESS BELLA HARRINGTON – CRENSHAW FOUND MURDERED

Pinky was in shock. It was only last night he'd been over at Bella's going through her closet, as she was getting rid of some old dresses and she wondered if any might be suitable for his act. He'd found a couple that Lionel might be able to adapt, and while he was in her bedroom asked if he might try on some of her splendid jewelry. She hesitated for a moment, but finally agreed. After all, what would an FBI agent do? To her he was above reproach. She went to her office, opened the safe, and took out the jewelry box, carrying it back to the bedroom.

"Oh my, these are truly lovely," Pinky cooed as he reverently touched the diamond and sapphire necklace and bracelet he had put on and was now admiring in front of the mirror.

He held the bracelet up to catch the light from the lamp, and turned his head to let the light dance on the necklace. How they sparkled. Just like his act. Oh, if he weren't such a good boy who knows what naughtiness he might be tempted to commit.

Bella had taken him to dinner at one of her favorite restaurants. She was in an uncharacteristically pensive mood. Apparently she had squabbled with several of the local ladies, and was bemoaning the squalid social life in Santa Fe - so unlike the New York City and Washington scenes, she assured him. Despite her removal to Santa Fe and her recent redecoration, she was seriously questioning whether she wanted to remain in New Mexico. And she was considering downsizing. What did she need with all this much space and so much *stuff*. She'd instructed Angelica to enquire about the best auction houses to perhaps sell several of her minor contemporary artworks. She'd lived with them so many years she hardly noticed them anymore. And they didn't exactly go with her new, more stunning décor, she lamented. Then Pinky had escorted her home, as he was still concerned for her safety, and she was a little tipsy.

"Here take a look at this," Bella offered, handing Pinky her diamond diadem – clusters of platinum, gold, and silver leaves, encrusted with diamonds surrounding a central yellow diamond. "This was once part of the Romanoff treasure. Though it might be a copy. There is no clear provenance."

"Does it matter?" Pinky asked. "It's truly splendid. Doesn't it worry you, having jewelry of this quality in the house? I'd keep it in a safe deposit box if I were you."

"But I have my study safe. It would take a bull dozer to move it."

"Just the same…" Pinky became entranced as he placed the diadem on his head.

"And try these emeralds. Sea green. Quite the loveliest I've ever seen." Bella placed the necklace around his neck.

"Oh Bella…"

Later, as he was leaving, Pinky gushed, "Thank you, thank you for such a lovely evening," Pinky kissed Bella on both cheeks as he stood by the front door. He stopped for a moment to admire the new décor. "And doesn't your place look lovely now. Are you pleased with the do-over?

"It takes some getting used to. But yes, I'm happy with it. It's a bit like living inside a rubix cube at the moment – but it certainly is lively, don't you think?"

"I hope the furniture is comfy. Looks a bit like a lawyer's office at the moment. Needs your personal touch to give it some hominess. Perhaps dozens of flower arrangements. Now, I must go. Way past your bedtime, I'm sure."

Bella waved good-bye as he headed down the walk to his car. That was the last time he saw Bella alive.

◘   ◘   ◘

"Hey, splendid one." It was Jefferson.

"My darling, so happy to hear your voice," Connye replied.

"I've got a little surprise for you."

"Oh really? Do tell."

"I've found *the* most perfect house on the northeastern edge of the French Quarter. It's on a very quiet street – far from the Madi Gras hustle and bustle, and almost no tourists wander this far. But it's walking distance to our favorite restaurants, and there is even a little local grocery store down the block. It's two stories, with the front entrance leading into a secluded garden courtyard, and the front overlooks a church. Lots of open space and sunlight."

"Oh my, sounds delightful. For rent or for sale?"

"Either. Could you come out for a viewing?"

"But I haven't decided for sure if I want to do this."

"I know. But just come take a look. I think you'll really love it. High ceilings, wood floors, working fireplaces in every room, and even a completely remodeled kitchen."

"Jefferson, you are too wicked. How you tempt me."

"I certainly hope so. If I set the viewing for tomorrow at noon will that be enough time to get down here?"

"Oh yes, I suppose so. You really are a very naughty boy."

◘   ◘   ◘

Pinky's chief had called Pinky into his office. "We have a situation."

"Yes sir and what might that be?"

"It's not been announced to the press yet, but the medical examiner has just completed his examination on Bella Harrington-Crenshaw."

"And how is that a situation?" Pinky asked, wanting to get on with this.

"During the examination it was discovered that Mrs. Harrington-Crenshaw was a man."

Pinky sat in utter silence. This was, to say the least, a complete surprise - even for him. How had he not noticed? How had he not detected the certain signs? Looking back he could certainly see the evidence.

"You have nothing to say?" his chief asked.

"I'm processing."

"Well, as this seems to be somewhat up your alley, and since you worked so closely on her case previously, I want you to take lead position on the investigation. You have all the Santa Fe police reports on the murder. You decide who you want on your team and run with it."

"I prefer to work alone. I think I can accomplish more. But I might need some investigative resources."

"Whatever you decide. As long as I get results."

"Will this information about Bella be given to the press?"

"Can't really keep it back. It's public record, or it will be once it's released."

"How long could you keep it under wraps?"

"Few days, maybe. But not a lot more."

"Is it possible to keep a lid on this with the media till I can conclude my investigation?"

"If you get your butt in gear and get this solved pronto."

"I'll get right on it."

Pinky rose to leave. The chief stopped him. "Oh, and Pinky, try and be a credit to the service. Keep the dresses for the club, okay?"

Pinky smiled, "Ooo, you are such a gloom."

◘   ◘   ◘

"Sonora, I am so-o-o bored."

"Roberta, I can't believe it. You were so anxious to get back to your old life. Sleep in. Coffee at Portabellos. Start a new hobby. I can't believe you're saying this to me already."

"I know. I'm awful, aren't I?"

"What do you want? Go back to Pie as head chef?"

"Well no, actually I was thinking of something else?"

"And what might that be?" Sonora humored her.

"Well, after that terrible business with Bella, I keep thinking life is so short. I want to do something really constructive."

"That's admirable."

"And I was wondering if I might be able to assist you with your dance project. I know you need volunteers, and I'd love to help. And maybe you could introduce me to those yummy dancers."

Sonora laughed. "Of course, I can. And I would be delighted if you could help me with the company promotion. But you will stick with it won't you? At least for a little while."

"Oh Sonora, you know me all too well, don't you?" Yes, I promise to be available - for at least a little while."

Sonora chuckled as she hung up the phone. Lionel was due any minute. She wanted his input on the new promotional material for the dance company. And while it looked fine to her, she wanted an artist's eye to give it final approval. Henrietta set out the tea tray with some homemade scones with grapefruit marmalade.

"Oh Sonatina. Are you decent?" Lionel called from the entrance.

"Never," Sonora teased back.

"So relieved to hear it." Lionel came waltzing in. "Isn't it dreadful – poor Bella."

"We all mourn her loss – each in our own unique ways, of course."

Lionel eyed her. "Are you being naughty?"

"I decline further comment. Now, some tea?" Sonora poured.

"Oh Sonora, how absolutely splendid the dance performance was. Fell in love at least two or three times."

"There are only three men in the company so you certainly covered all the bases."

"Don't be rude."

"And how is the memoir coming? Do you have a release date yet?"

"Oh Sonora, they want tons of rewrites. I'm in a thither. I'm struggling. Don't know when it will get finished - or if it even will. I'm not really a writer, you know. If I could just sit down and tell my stories, I'd be fine. But all this formal structural business – and, of course, there's all that punctuation and spelling. It's driving me crazy. Wish me luck."

"Or you could work with an editor, as I so cogently suggested earlier, if you remember."

"Yes, I *am* working with an editor from the publishing house, and she is *so* demanding." Lionel pouted a little, but finished his scone to comfort himself.

"Now, dear boy, down to business. I need your expert advice," Sonora continued. "I have some print promotional materials I would like you to review. Your opinion would be invaluable before we go to press."

"Yes, of course, anything you ask."

◻   ◻   ◻

Connye and Jefferson stood on a quiet little street in the Quarter, gazing at the front of the lovely house across from the church. The filigree balcony was one of the best on the street – with boxes of bright flowers flowing over the side. They had just finished viewing the inside.

"So, what do you think?" Jefferson asked.

Connye was thoughtful. "It's really quite marvelous, isn't it?"

"I think so. Glad you like it too."

"I saw a coffee house down the block. Do you mind if we sit for a bit and discuss this?"

"Certainly."

They ambled thoughtfully down the block, glancing at the other houses, and appreciating the quiet of the street. They ordered coffee and sat at a table by the window with a good view of the neighborhood.

"It's a big step. And a big commitment," Connye opened.

"But it would mean we could be together much more than we can be now." He paused. "If that's what you want, of course. And I'd be able to see Sophie every week instead of every month."

Connye nodded, but didn't reply.

"And it's a good investment if we decide to buy," Jefferson continued.

"How long do we have before we need to decide," Connye finally asked.

"They said they could give us till the week's end." Jefferson looked over and took her hand. "I sense some hesitation. Is it because of the house or because of us?"

"Oh no, not us. It's just I'm so established in Santa Fe. My lovely home. My art. My activities. Not sure what living here would mean for all of that. And remember, I lived in New Orleans before. Not the best memories of those times with Kostas. I thought I'd left all of this behind me."

"Would another city suit you better?"

"But my business is headquartered is here. That's a plus. I could be more involved and wouldn't have to make constant trips for meetings."

"It's like I've said, I believe you can still be in Santa Fe *and* here. Really the best of both worlds, and we could be together much more."

"And it is a lovely house, isn't it?" Connye said, warming to the idea.

"It's settled for me. I'm decided. Now it's entirely up to you."

"Then I think we should buy. It's far too lovely a house to just rent. I'm sure I would fall madly in love with it. And the garden... Can't wait to put my hand to that. Wonder if there are any nature spirits and devas in New Orleans?" she pondered.

"Well there are certainly plenty of liquid spirits and tons of divas," Jefferson joked.

"It's going to be fun, isn't it?" Connye placed her hand on Jefferson's arm.

Jefferson pulled out his phone and called the listing agent.

◘   ◘   ◘

It was quite late at the FBI office. Most of the agents had gone home. But Pinky was still at his computer. He had been doing a lot of digging on Bella. He had access to files the general public did not, and had come across some very interesting information.

It had taken some intense research but he had found a case in the Wilmington district court. It seems a Delbert Harrington-Crenshaw was arrested and charged with lewd and lascivious behavior in a men's room in one of the city parks. While the charge had stuck, a considerable amount of money had been spent to cover up the incident.

Doing some further research on the Harrington-Crenshaw family history Pinky discovered that Delbert was Bella's brother. However, while there was a birth record for Delbert, there was none for Bella. Was Bella adopted? There were no records of such an adoption. Then he stumbled across a sealed court document which only the FBI could access. It appears Delbert had changed his name and become Bella? Did the scandal drive Delbert underground, assuming a new identity? Oh my, dear Bella was certainly becoming more and more intriguing. No wonder Bella had taken a liking to him. They were both sisters of the sparkling cloth.

But, of course, this did nothing to solve Bella's murder. Pinky sat back in his chair and pondered the situation. He was well aware of the animosity amongst members of the inner social circle, and he knew Lionel knew all these ladies. That is where he would begin his active investigation.

"Are you still under deep cover?" Lionel inquired, as he welcomed Pinky into his living room.

"Oh no, that cover was blown long ago with the capture of Kurchner. It was in all the papers and on TV," Pinky answered.

"Oh, a real live celebrity."

"Well yes, in the club - but hardly on the street."

"So have you come for me to repair another of your torn dresses?" Lionel huffed, just a little.

"No, not at all. Strictly FBI business."

"Oh really, how thrilling. Am I to be given the third degree?"

"Oh Lionel, really. No, but I do need to ask a few questions about some of your lady friends."

"I am not a stool pigeon," Lionel said, prepared to be a staunch martyr defending his ladies.

"Oh gracious. You are becoming silly and tiresome. Just need to ask a few simple questions is all."

"Oh, very well. Ask away." Lionel settled himself in his favorite chair ready to be grilled.

"First, the most obvious question. Do you know of anyone who might want to kill Bella?"

"Well – dozens. But *capable* of killing Bella – none."

"Can you be more specific? Who exactly would want her dead?"

"Oh Pinky, all my dear ladies have the roar of a lion and the claws of a kitten. Dear Bella was generally detested by most of the ladies. But there can be no question that any of them would have either the courage or the strength to strangle a lady of Bella's size and might."

"Hmm, good point."

Lionel continued, "What I'd suggest - it was more likely a disgruntled gardener or a jewel thief. I understand she had quite the jewelry collection."

"Oh she did. She even let me try them on. There's this one absolutely gorgeous diadem…. but I digress," Pinky added, correcting his enthusiasm.

"Could any of your lady friends have put out a hit on Bella? They might not be able to *do* the deed, but they might be able to have it *done*."

Lionel thought about that. "Well, several certainly have the funds to accomplish such an act, but the actual will – I truly doubt it. The cats love to show their claws but they really wouldn't want to ruin their manicures."

Pinky had to laugh at that. "And you can think of no one else who might be motivated and have the ability to carry out such a deed?"

"Oh Pinky, we live such simple and sheltered lives in our little village. Routine rules, and anything more exciting that a jaunt to the market puts everyone into a tizzy."

"Well thank you. Now I believe I must look elsewhere for the culprit."

"Oh, and by the way," Lionel added, "can you reserve me a table for Saturday next? My agent will be in town and I promised him a fun evening."

◘   ◘   ◘

Pinky still had Bella's house key and alarm code. He crossed the police tape and went up to the house. There were no longer any police guarding the crime scene. Rene and the chauffer were gone, and the house was dark and silent. Pinky could wander the house undisturbed - it helped him concentrate. There was an intuitive side to Pinky that could blossom if he was solitary.

The first thing he did was check on the jewelry. He knew there was no theft so, finding the dressing table cleared, he surmised the jewelry was either back in the safe or under police custody.

He wandered the house hoping to discover some striking detail that could give him a clue. The one thing that stuck in his mind, and nagged him, was that fact that Bella had been garroted by picture wire. How ironical the lady (or rather the man) with the stunning art collection should be murdered with his own art, as it were. Pinky always appreciated irony. But where did the wire come from? Did the killer bring it with him? Or was it an impromptu instrument taken from the art collection itself?

And how had the killer gotten in, since it was definitely not a break-in? Especially since the murder took place so soon after he had left Bella. He wandered the silent house, finally settling in the living room and looking around. Pinky stared at Bella's paintings and wondered which ones she had contemplated selling. Such masterpieces – certainly worth several fortunes – each. Then it dawned on him, and he raced out of the house to get to his computer. He needed to do some further research.

◘   ◘   ◘

He began with the alarm code. Who besides Bella and himself might have the code? Rene, certainly, but she had an airtight alibi and was not a suspect. And he quickly established the chauffer never had the code. Who else? Any maintenance people? He was able to quickly rule that out. Workmen doing the renovation installation? No probably not the workmen, but Angelica certainly did. But what possible motivation would she have to kill Bella? And she wasn't even *in* Santa Fe the night of the murder. The decorating project had been completed by then, and she had already returned to Washington.

But something about Angelica kept at nagging him. What was it? He thought back to his encounters with her, particularly at the luncheon. Yes, she was odd, and rather full of herself – a Principessa, come on. What was *that* all about?

He walked through his memory of that day. Was there anything out of place?   Then he remembered her taking photographs of all the masterpiece paintings after lunch. At the time he'd thought nothing of it – just a decorator planning out how the pictures might be hung in the new design. But then he remembered, it was not so much that she *was* taking the photographs, but rather, *how* she was taking them. These were not mere snapshots to identify each picture for later placement, but rather each painting was being meticulously lit and photographed for detail. Now, why would that be?

Pinky accessed the FBI main computer. He did a search on Angelica. Pretty typical immigration profile for when she entered the country many years ago. Basic bio and upgraded visa until she got her green card. No criminal record to speak of. Minor traffic citations.   But there was one interesting incident. Apparently she had been investigated about a forged painting that one of her clients purchased from her.   However, the investigation led to nothing, as the provenance for the painting was inconclusive, and the matter had eventually been dropped.

However, this was like a beacon to Pinky, and he immediately connected to the Interpol data base through the FBI. He did a search on Castelleri and the screen lit up with references. The family property had been taken over by the mafia some years ago, and ongoing connections, through her family, had continued with the mafia ever since. No proven misdeeds, but plenty of suspicious activity.

Pinky sat back in his chair and processed this new information.   Then he got on the phone and called the Albuquerque office.

"Chief," Pinky asked, "have we got any art experts in the department?"

"No, too specialized for our agents, but we have people we can contact. What's up?"

"I'm following a lead and I need someone to take a look at some of Bella's paintings for authentication purposes."

"Do we need to bring the paintings in?" the chief asked.

"Depends. Contact your experts and let me know if they can do the examination on site. If not then we will need to bring them in. But remember we are under the gun with the press. The sooner I can get this solved the sooner the press will be off your back."

"I'll get right back to you."

◻   ◻   ◻

"Hum, can you help me take this one down?" The art expert asked Pinky. He had been examining a series of Bella's paintings in her home.

"Certainly."

Pinky and the expert took the painting off the wall and laid it out carefully on a library table. The expert went to work with his swabs, his black light, and other paraphernalia that Pinky did not recognize. He also photographed each painting that he felt was suspicious.

Finally the expert turned to him. "There's no doubt, whatsoever. Every one of these supposed masterpieces are forgeries. In fact, it is clear they were painted very recently. Certainly within the past several months."

"Oh my God. Any idea where they might have been painted?"

"Oh yes, there is a thriving fine art duplication market in Mumbai, India. Decorators do it all the time. They have their clients select a masterpiece they would like to hang in their home, and then have an artist in India make an exact duplicate. It's a whole industry. There are streets and streets of small shops with young artists turning out copied masterpieces. I would almost guarantee that is where these are from."

"Thank you. You have been most helpful." Pinky smiled. "Might I have copies of the photos?"

"They are digital so you can download them right now if you have a laptop."

"I do."

◘   ◘   ◘

He had the why, now he just needed the how. It seemed likely that if Angelica had stolen the original masterpieces and replaced them with copies, then the next area of investigation would be where the originals were taken, and how were they disposed of. The black market for rare paintings was very tricky. Selling hot paintings of that quality and renown was not something an individual could easily accomplish by themselves. The thief would have to have excellent connections to the underworld. And what better connections than the Italian mafia.

Pinky calculated. It would have been just over a week ago that Angelica would have completed Bella's redecoration. Would she have had time to ship the paintings back east – then disguise, pack, and reship the paintings to Italy? Maybe, maybe not.

Pinky need to act quickly. Once the paintings were in the mafia's hands they would disappear into the underground and be almost impossible to trace.

He called his office.

"Chief, do I have the authority to deal directly with the Washington FBI headquarters and Interpol, or do I need to go through you?"

"Whatcha got?"

"I'm pretty sure I know why the murder was committed. I'm pretty sure I know who was behind it. And if I can impound the evidence, I'm pretty sure I can get at who actually committed the murder. But I need to act immediately. Time is of the essence."

"Yes, go ahead. If you have any problems have them contact me and I'll give clearance. You really getting close?"

"I believe I am."

"Good work, keep me posted."

"Of course."

Pinky immediately contacted the Washington office. He asked for the art fraud department. He was connected to an Agent Mouyat. Pinky explained the whole situation.

"What do you need from me?" Mouyat asked.

"Well, first, I believe we have enough evidence to bring Castelleri in for questioning. Secondly, you need to search her home and shop for any evidence of the paintings, then if they can't be found you need to see if she might have shipped them already. Check outgoing international freight companies, then contact Interpol and see if they can determine if the paintings might have been sent to Italy. I will send you an email with the information I have, including photos of the paintings. Keep me in constant touch. Can you do all that your end?"

"You bet. Sounds intriguing. Look forward to working on it.

◘   ◘   ◘

Pinky barely slept all night. He would doze for fifteen minutes then awaken, twisting around in his top sheet like he was wrestling an anaconda. His mind raced as he went over every detail of the case. He got up several times to check his email in case Agent Mouyat had sent him a message. He considered if there might be anything more he could do this end until he heard from Washington. But his thoughts just kept going around in circles.

Divas in Cahoots   Jon McDonald

But what kept bothering him was how the murderer (for it was clearly *not* Angelica) got into the house so soon after he left. And what was the motive for the murder? Angelica had already taken the paintings and had departed Santa Fe without detection. Had Bella then discovered the secret after Angelica left? But if she had she would certainly have informed Pinky when she saw him that last evening. Was Bella a threat to Angelica that needed to be eliminated?

Finally – at ten the next morning Pinky received a call from Agent Mouyat.

Mouyat started by saying, "Oh man, what a story... I'm emailing you a video right now of our interrogation of the Principessa. What a character. She pretty much spilled all the beans."

"So was she responsible for Bella's murder?" Pinky just had to know the bottom line.

"Well, actually – no."

Pinky was surprised. "No? Then were you able find out who did do it?"

"Okay, this is way too interesting to dole out in increments. Let me tell you exactly the way it played out."

"I await with baited breath."

"The first thing we did was interview Angelica at her showroom. She danced around the issues and pretended she knew nothing about any forgeries. But when we brought up the fact that Bella had been murdered, and she was a suspect, Miss Angelica folded like a house of cards. She spilled everything. And you were spot on about the forgeries being painted in India. But she absolutely assured us she knew nothing about who might have murdered Bella. She swore her only involvement was to forge Bella's paintings."

"Were you able to find the paintings?"

249

"We were, and here's where it gets really interesting. In an effort to save what skin she had left, Angelica directed us to the shipping company that was handling the paintings for shipment to Italy – just as you suspected. They had not been shipped yet, and were waiting to be loaded onto a plane for shipment later that same day. We were able to seize them just before they got to the cargo door."

"That's a relief."

"Oh yeah, but here's where it gets *really* interesting. We had our experts examine the paintings to verify they were what we were looking for. And guess what we found?"

"Oh, you are as bad as I am with your little games. What?"

"The original paintings stolen from Bella are forgeries too."

Pinky was totally confused. "What! No, no - you must be mistaken. Our art expert absolutely verified that the paintings here in Santa Fe are the forgeries painted in India."

"I know. But, nevertheless, the paintings Angelica stole from Bella are as fake as a bad toupee."

Pinky was stunned. "Did Angelica know that?"

"She does now. She didn't then."

"And you have no idea where Bella's original forgeries came from?" Pinky asked.

"Not at all. Maybe you can find out more your end."

"Then what about the murderer? Any leads there?"

"More than a lead," Mouyat responded, "We've actually got the guy."

"Oh my…. That was fast. How did that come about?"

"Homeland Security. We contacted them with the information we had, and they were able to do one of the sophisticated searches they have these days and identified a thug from the Italian mafia that had come through immigration recently and headed to Santa Fe, right around the time of the murder. We apprehended him in Baltimore at the wedding of one of his American cousins and got his full confession."

"Was that difficult?"

"Let's just say we have our ways."

"But why would the mafia want to kill Bella?"

"It seems she was in deep debt to them – going back many years - both the American and the Italian organizations. She still had some assets, but her family connection to Harrington Bank had been severed years ago. She had no income from them. And she had been borrowing money from the Mafia using her supposed masterpieces as collateral for years. When the thugs discovered Angelica had stolen them, and *they* were expected to fence the paintings that were *their* collateral in Europe, they decided their investment with Bella was in grave danger, and they sent their goon to steal her very valuable jewelry collection as repayment of the loans."

"But then why kill her?" Pinky asked.

"In his confession Salvo - that's the thug's name - described how he had gotten the key and alarm code from Angelica, telling her, falsely, he needed the certificates of provenance for the paintings - which Angelica had neglected to secure. He went to Santa Fe, and on the evening of the murder watched the house till he saw Bella leave. He used Angelica's key, deactivated the alarm, and went inside the house hoping to easily find the jewels, but he said they were locked away securely in a safe. He had no choice but to await her return. He then relocked the door and reactivated the alarm so she would not be suspicious on her return. He hid in the conservatory and planned to force her, upon her return and thinking she would be alone, to open the safe and take the jewels.

"However, you returned with Bella and he had to wait until you left. It was only then he felt safe enough to reveal himself to her. However, Salvo tripped over an obstacle in the dark conservatory as he headed towards her bedroom and fell against a glass table which shattered. That alerted Bella and she had time to push the panic alarm button in her bedroom before she raced to the kitchen and grabbed a knife. She confronted Salvo, saying the police were on their way; they struggled; he grabbed some picture wire lying on a counter top where a small painting was being repaired, and he was able to strangle her with it. However, he suffered a cut to his hand which we verified, and we are currently waiting for a DNA report to confirm it matches the blood found in Bella's kitchen.

"As the murderer fled, he reactivated the alarm and locked the front door so it wouldn't look like an intruder had broken in, and left New Mexico the next morning. And that's the whole story. Does it fit the circumstances as you know them?"

"But if he had come to take the jewels why didn't he snatch them before he left? It was my understanding the jewelry was still in her bedroom, and the safe was wide open with money and other valuables."

"Panic. Pure and simple. He knew the police were coming and needed to get out of there as quickly as possible. He wasn't the coolest cucumber in the fridge."

Pinky was speechless for a moment as he processed this amazing story. "I was there, I could have protected her – him," he finally answered.

"Him?" the agent asked.

"Yes, didn't I tell you? The medical examiner discovered Bella was a male.

"Really? Most bizarre. Well, your Miss Bella certainly is a most interesting case. Have I answered all your questions?"

"Mostly, thank you. But there are still a few unanswered ones. One of which comes to mind is, if Angelica gave Salvo the key and code, why didn't she tell you that when you questioned her? Seems to me she is culpable if she withheld that very crucial piece of information."

"I asked her that later, after we apprehended Salvo and got his story. Her answer was, she was terrified she might be implicated if she told us that."

"And indeed she will be."

"Yes, big mistake on her part, not telling us up front."

"Well agent Mouyat, thank you so very much for your excellent assistance. I will continue my investigation this end, and if I need any further help I'll get in touch."

"Okay, sending you all I have in a couple of emails. Great working with you, Pinky."

◘   ◘   ◘

Pinky notified his Chief, who was most gratified to be able to release the story to the press. And what a story it was. There would be headlines on this for days to come. And, of course, Pinky would once again be the hero in the spotlight.

But there were still one or two loose ends that kept nagging at Pinky, and he just had to investigate further even though the crime was solved. He needed to satisfy these questions for himself and because of his regard for Bella.

Why were Bella's paintings forgeries? And might the transition of Delbert to Bella have something to do with it? And how had Bella been able to so lavishly fund a new costume shop for the opera if she was so much in debt?

Pinky realized, from a cursory search that Delbert had been Bella for a substantial number of years. And Pinky suspected Delbert would have securely covered his tracks. Back when the transition took place there was no internet. Records were all on paper or microfilm, and with enough money almost anything could be covered up and all records expunged. And, indeed, that is exactly what Pinky found – a cold and trackless trail. His only option was to see if he could find any record - by painting name or by artist - of either the theft of, or the sale of, any of Delbert/Bella's paintings any time within the last 50 years. He used every means at his disposal from the general internet to the FBI mainframe, and was unable to come up with any listings. He was just going to have to let that question go unanswered for now.

And as for how Bella funded the opera, Pinky found a lead. Amongst Bella's papers there was an inventory of Bella's jewelry. He carefully checked that list against the list the Santa Fe Police had of the jewelry they held as evidence. There were one or two spectacular pieces not listed on the police inventory. However, Rene had sworn that *all* the jewelry Bella possessed was accounted for after the murder. There was nothing missing she attested, as she regularly had to put Bella's jewelry away after it was worn and she had intimate knowable of all the jewels. To further substantiate her claim Rene's house had been searched and nothing was found there. It appeared all of Bella's jewelry was accounted for after the murder. So it seemed unlikely that the murderer had taken any jewelry.

But Pinky had an idea and he did a little further search. He remembered seeing a listing in Bella's address book for Dupuis Fine Jewellry Auctioneers in Toronto. He gave them a call, identified himself, and inquired officially if Mrs. Harrington-Crenshaw had sold any jewelry using their services in the past two years. Indeed she had. Several very fine pieces had been auctioned, bringing in a considerable amount - more than enough to enable her to purchase her Santa Fe house *and* donate to the opera.

Poor Bella, Pinky realized, felt the need to keep up appearances even though she was greatly in debt. This endeared her even more to him.

◘   ◘   ◘

As predicted there was a hurricane of press attention on this most unusual case, and once again Pinky was in the eye of the storm.

After the latest round of press briefings the Chief called Pinky into his office.

"What can I say? You are the most unlikely agent I have ever had to become a mega press star. What the fuck am I gonna do with you now? I have had requests from Washington for you to move up to the main office. I've had requests from San Diego, Atlanta, Charleston – God knows where all. I guess it's going to be up to you to choose where you want to go next."

"Well, I'm sorta settled pretty well in Santa Fe. I got my wonderful act and all. Do I need to move on?"

"Yeah, ya do. You are too well known here, now. Would compromise your ability do constructive undercover work from now on in New Mexico. Need to be inconspicuous, ya know."

"What are my choices, then?"

"Here's what I've go so far. Look these offers over and let me know what you want to do." The Chief shuffled a stack of papers over to Pinky.

Pinky took them. "I'll let you know soon as I decide."

Pinky went back to his desk. Oh how this whole business rankled. How did all this crazy business get so blown out of proportion? It used to be his act was his main focus and his day job was secondary. Now it was all reversed.

He put the papers before him to look through his new assignment choices. It was then he noticed an envelope addressed to him someone had delivered to his desk. It was from Rudolph, Rangel and Stanley, a Washington DC law firm. He opened it. It contained a letter from the law firm and another sealed envelope with his name, handwritten, on the front. He opened that one first. It read:

My Dearest Pinky,

If you are reading this it is because I am no longer in the land of the living. I have been in great apprehension ever since that nasty business with Senator Spangler launched me into a hornet's nest of turmoil. And since I am dead, I am sure my true identity has been revealed to you by now. You see, we were much more alike than you imagined – we two Bellas. Poor Delbert, had to go undercover, I'm afraid. But more of that later.

But I must also make another little confession, or two. I have a bit of a checkered past, you see. Yes, my family founded the Harrington Bank. But I'm afraid we lost our financial interest in that long ago, and since then, not all of our income has been – how shall I put this? - strictly legitimate. I will not bore you with the details, except to warn you that when you come to examine my priceless impressionist paintings, they will not be quite so priceless after all. You see master Delbert got into a spot of financial and criminal trouble before he became Bella, and the poor dear just had to do something. And as a result, any number of very valuable paintings were sold on the black market and replaced with very well executed copies. None of the family ever found out – except by his dear "sister," of course. And as for the criminal activity – well, it consisted of a minor lapse of judgment in a men's room one hot summer's evening – regrettable, but never repeated - well, almost never. Now, listen to me – bringing out all the family's dirty laundry.

And that brings me up to today. I'm afraid I have gotten myself into a rather large amount of debt. And it is not conventional debt. I've been naughty and I've borrowed substantial sums from the Italian syndicate, using my precious paintings as collateral. However, as you now know, they are not valid collateral, so one day soon I'm afraid the piper must be paid. The good news is, the house is paid for, and the jewels are real – my only valid assets.

I tell you all of this because you will need to know. If there is more to know later, I'm sure you can ferret out the details with your fine investigative skills.

Dear Pinky, it has truly been an honor to know and play with you. You have brightened up an otherwise rather dull adventure here in Santa Fe. And I hope what I am about to do for you will truly help you in some little way to give you the freedom you so richly desire and deserve.

Your ever devoted,

Bella (Delbert) Harrington-Crenshaw

Well that was certainly a surprise, but it did clear up the origin of Bella's forgeries. He turned to the other letter, from the attorney. It read:

Dear Mr. Powell,

This is to inform you that you have been named as sole beneficiary in the will of Mrs. Bella Harrington-Crenshaw of Santa Fe, New Mexico.

Pinky let out a yelp that was heard even on the floor below. Reluctantly, the Chief came out of his office to see if an agent had been assaulted.

The letter continued:

However, I must also inform you that as a result of substantial debt, there must be a liquidation of Mrs. Harrington-Crehshaw's estate which consists of a dwelling, art work, and jewelry. We regret to say that it is unlikely any funds will be realized for the beneficiary after liabilities are satisfied, as it has come to our attention that her, so called, masterpieces are, in fact, worthless copies.

We will keep you informed, and should any balance be due you, we will send you a check upon close of probate. (But don't hold your breath)

Sincerely, for Rudolph, Rangel and Stanley,

Benjamin Rangel, Partner

"Oh shit." Pinky picked up the stack of papers from the Chief and began considering his next move. And would this require a new drag persona, or could he take Bella Le Balle with him this time? And would his continuance as Bella honor or dishonor his dear benefactress? This would require some further consideration.

◘   ◘   ◘

"Sonatina, is that you?" Lionel sang out at the unexpected knocking at his front door.

A deep voice answered, "No, it is your darling Bella Le Balle."

Lionel opened the door somewhat piqued. "Don't you *ever* call first?" Lionel ushered Pinky inside and led him to the living room. Lionel was holding a dish towel, "I was just doing some dishes, but can I get you anything?"

"Nothing, my dear Lionel." He stood with a wide grin, facing Lionel.

"Well, then, what is it? You look like you just swallowed the canary."

"I have a little surprise. And I've come to ask your permission about something really important."

"Very well, enlighten me."

"I need your permission for something."

"Oh, do cease beating around the bush. Out with it."

"Guess who is going to LA to be on the Ellen show?"

Lionel was truly stunned. "No... Tell me *all* about it." He sat down and indicated Pinky should sit too.

Pinky launched into his story. "Bella knew Ellen and sent her the DVD of my show – the one you so kindly facilitated. And here I was all ready to go off on a new FBI assignment to San Diego."

"No..."

"I was being 'promoted' and needed to go to a new city."

"Oh, how I'd miss you."

"I know, but what could a poor working girl do? Anyway, I had packed up my belongings at the FBI, prepared to leave for San Diego, notified my landlord, and then – out of the blue – I get this call from Ellen's people. Could I please come to LA for an interview – all expenses paid, of course."

"And?"

"I went. They taped the act and said they'd let me know. I didn't hear anything from them for ages and decided that they weren't interested, so I just let it go."

"Why didn't you tell about the audition?"

"I didn't want to be embarrassed if it didn't happen. Sorry."

"No, I do understand."

"But then I got this call yesterday. They want me to do the Ethel Merman part of my act on the show. I'm to leave tomorrow and will be on the show live Thursday."

"Oh Pinky, I am so proud. My little protégé all grown up now."

"And I need your permission to use your costumes."

"Well, of course. Absolutely. Oh Pinky...."

"I appreciate it. And thank you for *everything* you've done for me."

"So will you still be moving?"

"I don't know. While I'm in LA I'll see about getting an agent. And if that happens who knows where my career might take me. But I'll stay in Santa Fe for now. And, in any case, I've left the FBI *forever*. Enough of all of *that*."

Lionel dabbed at his eyes with the dish towel. "Law enforcement's loss – Glam's gain."

Pinky rose. "I won't keep you from your dishes, but I just wanted to let you know I'm off to LA tomorrow."

"Well, I hope you find every happiness - and a delightful new boyfriend as well now that you're a great big star."

Pinky stopped and looked at Lionel. "But my dear, I am straight. I thought you knew."

"No-o-o...." Lionel was momentarily stunned, but unsure. Was Pinky joking?

"I truly am. I have a little girl in Quebec who lives with her grandmamma, and a small boy with his mom in Tupelo." There was absolutely no expression on Pinky's face.

Lionel looked at Pinky a long moment. "You are *such* a liar."

Pinky was calm, he smiled, and with a twinkle in his eye, turned, and did a little backward kick, flinging his scarf around his neck, and reaching into his bag he flung a handful of fairy sparkle into the air as he left.

Lionel looked after him with a slow burn, "Bother - now I'll have to vacuum again."

◘   ◘   ◘

"With the jet I can get a call from any one of you by mid-morning and be in Santa Fe for tea. It's not much different than if I lived just out of town a ways." Connye was detailing her new adventure to the Portabellos coffee circle. "And I am still keeping my house and can attend *all* the most important functions, as well as keeping up all my own lavish entertaining."

"But then who is going to keep us all in line?" Sonora joked. "Without you we will just fall apart."

"I will delegate that delightful function to you, dear Sonora."

"Are we to expect wedding bells, then?" Honey asked.

"Unlikely. We quite like our little arrangement as it is. Maximum delights - minimum restrictions," Connye answered.

"But what is going to happen to all of us?" Roberta asked. "Connye, you are moving part time to New Orleans, Sonora wants to spend more time at her charming mill in France. And where Sonora goes, Lionel follows. Honey your kids are off to college. I've left Pie. The sky must be falling."

"Yes, dear ladies, things certainly are changing," Sonora added.

Honey spoke up, "And I've just heard through the agency that Portabellos has just been bought by Whole Foods and they are planning to close this store."

There was a sober silence as everyone took in *that* bit of news.

"But where will we meet?" Roberta wailed.

"My dears, we will just have to adapt – as we always do," Sonora added, once again, very sensibly.

About the Author

Jon McDonald lives in Santa Fe, New Mexico. He currently has four published works of fiction - a satire, *Divas Never Flinch*; a humorous vampire thriller, *Bloodlines – the Quest*; *The Seed – An Ironic Political Thriller:* and an eclectic collection of stories, *Ya Gotta Dance with the One who Brung Ya - sex, scandals and sweethearts*.

He won first prize and was published in the *Santa Fe New Mexican* holiday short story contest, 2009. He has also been published in *Raphael's Village, ImageOutWrite, Bay Laurel,* and *Jonathan*.

Author's website is: **www.jonmcdonaldauthor.com**

20744160R00142

Made in the USA
Charleston, SC
24 July 2013